STOLEN
MOTHERS

BOOKS BY STACY GREEN

STOLEN MOTHERS

STACY GREEN

bookouture

Published by Bookouture in 2024

An imprint of Storyfire Ltd.
Carmelite House
50 Victoria Embankment
London EC4Y 0DZ

www.bookouture.com

ISBN: 978-1-83525-533-9
eBook ISBN: 978-1-83525-532-2

PROLOGUE

MONDAY, 19 MAY 2014, 1:08 P.M.

Jefferson National Forest, Smyth County, Virginia

Nikki slammed her brakes, spewing dirt and gravel. Sugar
Grove Highway passed the Mt. Rogers Recreation Area, the
road winding along the Appalachian Trail. Homesteaders were
scattered throughout the wilderness south of Mt. Rogers. Nikki
double-checked her notes. "Mile Marker 7, another hundred
feet, turn right onto a non-maintained county road, cabin at
end."

She drove ahead slowly and then turned right onto what
barely passed as a trail. White chickweeds had nearly choked
out the yellow rattlesnake weed. Pine cones crunched beneath
the tires. Brilliant Virginia creeper stretched around the pine
and hickory trees, while the massive oaks drenched the area in
shade. A dilapidated mailbox announced she'd arrived. Nikki
parked a hundred yards away from the cabin and rolled her
window down. Eerie silence greeted her. Nikki checked to
make sure her weapon was loaded and then adjusted the
uncomfortable Kevlar vest. She didn't think it was necessary,

but she'd promised her husband she'd start wearing it in situations like these.

Weapon at her side, Nikki eased out of the vehicle, making sure to kill the engine and take the keys. Wild pink trillium flowers scattered the unkempt lawn before her. She held her breath, trying to avoid the native plants also known as stinking Benjamins for their foul, wet dog smell. A large patch had practically taken over the clearing in front of the cabin, the smelly flowers choking out the green grass.

Nikki's heart lodged in her windpipe as she crept through the empty, stinking cabin. It looked every bit of its hundred years, with a single room containing a kitchenette and a small living space. A dingy curtain covered the lone window that overlooked the clearing in front of the house, but the sun shined through the thin fabric. Nikki tried not to gag at the sight of animal feces strewn in the cabin. A small television with an antenna sat across from a well-used easy chair. A table and two kitchen chairs were the only other furniture in sight.

The local police believed that only dead souls remained in this cabin, but it looked like they were wrong. Gun ready, she crept toward the bedroom door. The man she'd chased here from D.C. had been spotted in a stolen vehicle more than two hours away. She knocked on the door only to find it unlocked and cracked open. Despite the abundance of animal feces and urine, the distinct smell emanating from the back room told Nikki something awful waited behind the door.

She listened for movement, on alert for any sign of life, but heard nothing. Sweat beading across her forehead, the odor intensified as she pushed the door open. The bedroom window had been boarded up, but a few streams of light still squeezed through the wood slats—enough to see the horror in the middle of the room.

Nikki backed away, fighting nausea. She barely made it out to the crooked front porch before vomiting up everything she'd eaten that day. Her shaking hands made Nikki nearly drop her cell phone. She scrolled through her previous calls until she found the Smyth County deputy's cell number.

His voicemail picked up. "This is Agent Hunt. I'm at the cabin—" The sound of heavy footsteps crashing through the woods stopped her short. Nikki turned her head in time to see a figure darting between the trees.

She didn't stop to think. Nikki shoved her phone in her jacket pocket without ending the call. She raced into the woods, her tunnel vision blocking out everything else. She barreled into the thick forest surrounding the cabin, her eyes on the black shadow darting through the trees.

The path wound through the dense woods. Nikki's legs burned at the steady incline. She couldn't remember the elevation, but she could see the path narrowing ahead of her. Her sides stung from running. She breathed hard, sucking in the damp spring air. A half-dead white pine tree appeared to be growing out of the side of the mountain. She didn't have time to marvel at Mother Nature. She'd lost sight of the man, who likely had an intimate knowledge of the area. Her thighs burned and her lungs felt raw, but she had to keep going.

Near the lone pine, the steadily inclining path turned sharply right. Nikki didn't bother to look at the ground; her focus was on the monster crashing through the forest.

Just as she passed the pine and turned the corner, her left ankle rolled. She stumbled, arms flailing for balance. Her hiking boots sunk into the crumbling earth, gravity pulling her to the steep side of the hill.

Suddenly the man loomed before her on the path, only his eyes visible. Nikki swore they twinkled when the ground collapsed beneath her. She tumbled down the slope, grabbing in vain for anything to stop her fall. Pain ricocheted through her right knee as Nikki hit the ground on her side with a thud, knocking the air out of her lungs. She fought to catch her breath. Head throbbing, she barely noticed the excruciating pain in her knee or the reek of the trillium that helped break her fall.

She clutched her abdomen, praying she wasn't going to lose this baby too.

Chunks of dirt rolled towards her. The man slid down the hill, his face still covered, his eyes angry. Nikki had lost her weapon in the fall.

He gripped a spear-tipped dagger with a brown handle. Despite the bits of rust on the blade, the gleaming steel looked deadly sharp. Nikki scooted backwards, but her legs barely had enough strength to move.

"Please." Her voice sounded like someone else's. "I'm pregnant."

ONE

16 OCTOBER 2024

Stillwater, Minnesota

Cass inhaled the last bit of her cigarette, watching the smoke unfurl into the night. She'd quit smoking when she'd found out about the pregnancy, but since she'd come back to work a few weeks ago after having the baby, she'd struggled not to sneak out and smoke.

Some nights she hated her husband.

Their oldest son was a junior, the youngest in eighth grade. Cass's tubes had been tied after her youngest son was born, but thirteen years later, she'd come up pregnant at forty. By the time Cass had realized she was pregnant and not just dealing with perimenopause, ending the pregnancy wasn't an option. She probably wouldn't have gone through with it anyway, but she also didn't want to start over at forty.

Finding out they were having a girl made it worse. Cass had grown up with brothers, and she'd always gotten along with men better than women. Ten years ago, finding out she was having a girl would have made her ecstatic.

Now she was just tired and bitter.

Her husband still hadn't forgiven her for suggesting they consider giving the baby up for adoption, and, deep down, Cass was glad she didn't.

Her baby girl was pretty awesome. And she was ashamed that she'd ever not wanted her.

Shane could have helped more with little Emma, but he never did. He just slept. No matter the time of day or how tired Cass might be, he chided her for not being excited to be with her baby, for asking him for any help. Apparently, that made her less of a woman.

Cold October air cut through the thin sweatshirt she'd worn tonight. Shane was supposed to put up Halloween decorations this week, but he'd yet to do so. He also didn't seem to understand that since baby Emma was a good sleeper and slept through much of the night, she spent more hours awake each day. Cass wanted to be a good mom, but she was so freaking tired that every moment of sleep lost affected her mood.

Before she'd left for her shift tonight, she'd broached the subject of hiring someone for a few hours in the morning in order to get a few more hours of sleep. Instead of listening, Shane had accused her of not caring about her baby.

Cass told him to drop dead and walked out the door. Shane had spent the last three hours blowing up her phone because she refused to take his call, so she'd put the thing in her locker and came outside to get her head straight. At least her older boys would look after Emma for her. She knew she needed to keep her own income, just in case.

Of course, she didn't dare smoke in her car, not even a little bit, because Shane would yell at her about that too.

Selfish shit.

She dropped her butt, grinding it into the dirt with her boot. Cass's thoughts raced with all the things she should have said before she left, imagining the shock on his face when she stood up to him.

Cass was so engrossed she didn't notice the man hiding in the trees that lined the fence between her work and the empty parking lot next door. She didn't hear his footsteps shuffling through the dead leaves on the ground, or his accelerated breathing as he crept up behind her.

Cass didn't know anything until she felt the pain of a sharp blade in her side. "Not one sound," a gentle voice whispered into her ear. "I know little Emma sleeps through the night. And I know Shane could sleep through a tornado. Come quietly, or I'll slice their throats, and then I'll kill Sam and Logan."

TWO

Nikki tried to hide her impatience as she inched through the elementary drop-off line, stuck behind a blue minivan with a stick figure family on the back window. She'd solved cases faster than the line moved. She glanced in the rearview mirror at her daughter. "You have all your warm stuff and your backpack?"

"Yep." Lacey jammed her left foot between the two front seats. "Have you ever seen sparkle boots like this, Mom?"

The happiness in Lacey's little voice made it impossible not to laugh. "No, I haven't. Those are something special." She'd taken Lacey to Justice over the weekend for new boots and winter clothes. Her petite third grader had grown more than an inch since last winter. The boots' sequins changed from pink to white whenever Lacey brushed her hand over them. "You're going to get lots of compliments on those."

"I know." Lacey giggled as she gathered the last of her things. "Who's picking me up today?"

Guilt rippled through Nikki. Lacey was easygoing and understood that Nikki's schedule was always changing, but part of her felt guilty that she couldn't promise to be there after school.

"Rory's putting in a foundation today—"

"He's kicking his own ass, too, 'cos he knows he's pushing it with the cold," Lacey interrupted. "If he doesn't have it in the first week of November, he might be screwed."

"Don't swear, even if you are repeating what Rory said." Nikki hid a smile. "Grandma Ruth is going to pick you up today. Uncle Mark is probably going to be at their house too. He's helping Grandpa with some stuff." The "stuff" in question was the elaborate dollhouse Rory and Mark had spent months designing and were now racing to finish by Christmas. Miniatures took a lot longer than either had been expecting, and there had been more than a few nights of all three Todd men being ready to put in the time over the intricate work. But Lacey loved beautiful houses like her mom, and now she liked learning about building and making the houses look pretty from her stepdad.

Lacey grinned. "That means all the hot chocolate I can drink. See you later, Mom."

Nikki barely managed to say goodbye as Lacey hopped out of the Jeep and hurried over to meet her friends, who pointed excitedly at the boots. Nikki followed the blue minivan out of the line, her mind already on work. She'd been invited to speak at a major conference next month, and today was the first time she'd actually be able to work on her presentation.

A Stillwater Police Department number flashed on the Jeep's touch screen. Nikki debated not answering, wanting another moment to watch Lacey chatting animatedly with her friends, but she knew the ringing wouldn't stop. "Agent Hunt."

"Hi, Agent Hunt, this is Lieutenant Chen." Chen had worked with Nikki's team when two young girls had been abducted during a summer celebration. Gray was starting to take over his black hair, likely brought on from the stress of that case. He'd considered leaving the police and going into private security, but Nikki and the Stillwater police chief had convinced him to try a leave of absence first. Thankfully, those few weeks off had helped Chen clear his head, and Nikki was glad that the city had kept a good cop.

"I hate to ask but Chief Ryan is at a conference. Sheriff Miller's at an appointment and won't be here for at least thirty minutes." Chen's rapid cadence made the hair on the back of Nikki's neck stand up. "We've got a murder victim here... It's... the worst thing I've ever seen. Sheriff told me to see if you were able to help out, at least until he arrives."

Chen had experienced some tough cases, including the one he'd worked with Nikki's team. He wouldn't have called Nikki unless he had a reason.

"Send me the address."

Nikki winced as she unlocked her driver's side seat belt. Her shoulder still ached from a push down the stairs more than a month ago. She'd dislocated her shoulder, but had saved the girl she'd been searching for, so Nikki chose to call that a win. She parked behind a line of emergency vehicles on Linden Street, a quiet residential area of Stillwater, but this morning had been anything but quiet. She glared out of her window. How did Channel 9 always manage to be first on the scene? She hated to know who they had on their payroll.

Several evergreen trees flanked the average, two-story home nestled on the corner of Linden and Harriet Streets. With Halloween only a week or so away, nearly every house on the street had been decorated. An elaborate Halloween display spanned the right side of one house. Swaying cheesecloth ghosts hung from a bare maple tree. Homemade gravestones spanned one yard, guarded by the two skeletons sitting on hay bales. Large pumpkins sat next to the skeletons, with smaller ones on the edge of the bales. Painted and carved pumpkins covered the rest of the hay bales, which had been arranged as part of the graveyard's border. Chen stood on the other side of the bales, talking to someone behind the decorative barrier. Nikki couldn't see the medical examiner, but she guessed Dr. Blanchard was probably crouched on the other side of the display.

Nikki zipped her jacket to block out the late October chill, making sure she had a pen and latex gloves. She grabbed her phone and notebook and exited the Jeep. Nikki ignored the shouting reporter and ducked under the yellow crime scene tape that stretched across the front yard. The arthritis in her right knee ached from the drop in temperature, but she refused to limp in front of the cameras. She crossed the wet grass, wishing she'd thought to put her waterproof shoes in the Jeep. The grass was just long and wet enough that her sneakers were soaked through to her socks by the time she reached Chen.

"Thanks for getting here so quickly, Nikki." Chen hooked his thumb over his shoulder. "She's behind the display."

Chen looked as shaken up as he'd sounded earlier. "Whoever did this is a sick son of a bitch."

"And a ballsy one," Nikki replied. "Even with the fog all night and this morning and the property set up, this is still a high-risk place to leave a body." A well-worn path no wider than a foot was visible between the evergreens lining the property and the neighbor's privacy fence. Gaps in property lines happened occasionally, especially in river towns as old as Stillwater. She could see the gap extending to the wooded area behind Linden Street. "Do you have an ID?"

"She lives three houses down," Chen said. "Kiania Watson. Missing for three weeks. She works as a social worker at Hennepin County Medical Center, went missing on her way home from work. She'd only been back from maternity leave for a week or so."

Nikki's heart broke for the infant who'd never know its mother. "Where was she last seen? At work?"

Chen nodded. "She clocked out and headed for her car, and then disappeared."

"Have you informed Minneapolis PD?" Nikki asked.

"I had an officer take the husband down to the police station so he doesn't have to deal with all of this." Chen gestured to the growing crowd of media and onlookers. "The husband tried to get to his wife. I never heard anyone make the sound he did when we told him." The muscle in his jaw flexed as he struggled to rein in his emotions. "Anyway, the detective on the case is meeting him there."

"Is he a suspect?" Spouses always had to be cleared first.

"As far as I know," Chen said. "But this looks like prolonged torture. I've seen husbands stab, shoot and beat. This is like nothing I've seen before."

Nikki wasn't ready to rule the husband out based on the injuries alone, but Chen had a point. "What about her baby? Does the husband have someone to help while he goes through all of this?"

"Ty said the baby, Willow, is with his mother," Chen said. "She's also on the way to the station."

"Who found her?" Nikki asked.

"The homeowner," Chen answered. "Thankfully he spotted her when he left for work." He pointed to the camera mounted on the house's porch. "It captures the entire Halloween display. It mysteriously broke last week, and he hadn't had time to fix it."

Nikki pulled on her gloves and booties, wishing they could have blocked the scene off from the reporters. The family had to be stressed enough without the chaos across the street. She stepped over the bales, feeling like she'd stepped under a blazing spotlight.

She knelt next to the victim. Her beautiful, dark black skin had taken on an ashy tone. No rings, but colorful beaded bracelets adorned both wrists. Red nylon ropes were still tied to her ankles and hands, still pinned beneath her body.

"Clove hitch knot." She pointed to the knots. "Same kind of knot BTK used."

"That's what I thought," Chen said. "Isn't this sort of bondage indicative of a serial killer?"

"Ropes are often a big part of the serial killer's fantasy, yes," Nikki said. "I've also seen domestic murders where ropes were used. Let's not jump to that conclusion just yet." Nikki had years of experience, but she also had strong instincts, and the rock that dropped into her stomach just then went against what she'd told Chen. Nikki counted at least a dozen superficial stab wounds.

Blanchard finished noting the injuries to the back of the woman's body and then gently rolled her over. Bruising marked her face, including the yellowed ones around her lifeless eyes.

Nikki lifted the paper sheet someone had put over the victim's bottom half. Her clothes were gone, and it was clear she'd been abused. She'd died an excruciatingly painful death.

"There's some sticky residue around her lips. Perhaps her mouth was glued shut." Blanchard pointed to the mass of ligature marks around her neck. "Some of these show signs of bruising."

"Is that how she was killed?" Nikki asked. "Strangled?"

Blanchard lifted the woman's eyelids. "I'd expect to see more petechia, along with a deeper pattern in the skin, because of the force required to do that. Her neck is clearly broken. No sign of blunt force trauma. I won't know exactly how her neck was broken until I look at her X-rays. The killer could have twisted it until it snapped, or it may have happened during transporting her here—"

Nikki heard a familiar voice among the din of reporters and onlookers. She glanced toward the line of vehicles parked along the street. The other news channel had arrived and set up at the very edge of the crime scene tape, blocking the Evidence Response Team's path.

"I don't care what channel you're with." Courtney's voice carried through the crowd. "I don't have to play nice like the cops, so I suggest you move before I have you removed."

The heavyset cameraman jumped like he'd been swatted, and Courtney strode toward them, carrying her bag. Despite working with Nikki's team for more than seven years, Courtney struggled with hiding her emotions at crime scenes. "Who in the hell leaves a body like this?" She hissed as she reached the hay bales. "Just to traumatize the neighborhood?"

"That's my assumption. Our victim lived a few doors down. Killer wanted her found," Chen answered.

Nikki ascended the porch steps, noting the cracks in the cement. Like most of the houses in this area of town, the home had been built in the late nineteenth century. Vinyl windows and siding gave everything a fresh appearance, but the foundation never lied.

The homeowners must have been watching out the window, pulling the cherry-red front door open before she could knock.

A stout black man introduced himself as Craig and motioned her to come inside. Nikki wiped her boots on the mat before stepping on the wood floors. She followed the man into the small but tidy living room.

"I still cannot believe this is happening." He walked to the adjoining kitchen doorway. "Perry! The police have more questions."

"I'm actually with the FBI, Agent Hunt," Nikki said.

"Oh my God, it's a serial killer, isn't it?" Craig looked terrified. "My daughter was in the house when that monster left Kiania—"

Nikki had noticed the cache of Barbie and Bratz dolls. "Your daughter didn't see anything, correct?"

Craig shook his head. "No, thank God."

"Small miracles, right?" Nikki flipped her notebook open, her pencil down to just a couple inches before she'd need to replace it. "How long have you been neighbors with the victim?"

"About eighteen months," he answered. "Kiania was the first one to welcome us."

"Do you know her and her husband very well?"

Craig shook his head. "Just from seeing them around the neighborhood. They seemed so happy. And the baby..."

"I'm sorry, Craig." Nikki waited until he gathered himself. "Can I ask, what's your normal morning routine? And where do you work?"

Craig took a deep breath and then slowly exhaled. "I'm an assistant principal at the middle school. I'm usually out of the house by seven a.m. so I can be at school in plenty of time for the teachers' and kids' arrivals. Today started just like any other," Craig continued. "My husband, Perry, works at a salon in Wayzata, so his day starts later. He usually takes our daughter, Elle, to school."

"Is Elle here now?" Nikki asked, hoping the little girl hadn't seen the victim's body.

"No, Perry took her out the back door and they walked to another neighbor's house. Elle's in the same class as Jodie Barry's son, Marcus, so she took them both to school. Thank God she didn't see what I did." He hugged his chest. "I was torn about sending her to school when we're dealing with a tragedy, but school is the safest place for Elle today."

"I think you did the right thing," Nikki assured him. "Seeing the police and technicians crawling all over her yard would have caused its own issues."

Another man appeared. Perry was at least two inches taller than his partner, with unruly blond curls and fear in his blue eyes. Craig made the introductions, as Perry sat down next to him on the sofa.

Nikki addressed them both. "Have you noticed anyone hanging around in the neighborhood who didn't belong?"

"No," Perry said. "Like we told Detective Brenner, it's a safe, quiet neighborhood."

"Brenner from Minneapolis?" Nikki had worked with the young detective a few years ago on a case involving fraternity brothers. Both men nodded. As lousy as the circumstances were, Nikki looked forward to catching up with Brenner. Nikki remembered that Brenner had been pregnant when they'd worked together. Nikki was happy to learn she'd decided to be a working mom. Good detectives willing to learn were hard to find.

"Can you walk me through this morning?" Nikki asked Craig. "Try to remember as many details as possible, not just about the victim but anything else you may have seen."

He shuddered but nodded. "I left the house at about five past seven. Our garage is detached, so I walked down the porch steps and followed the sidewalk over to the garage. That's when I saw her." Craig's voice caught. "At first, I hoped it was a mannequin. A Halloween decoration. I don't know how long I stood there trying to make sense of what I was seeing before I called the police. I was just shocked."

"That's understandable." She looked between the two men. "What time did you guys get home last night? I assume you parked in the garage and took the same route. You didn't notice anything out of place then?"

Craig and Perry shook their heads. "Craig's usually home by five thirty," Perry answered. "Craig picks Elle up from her after-school care. I work in a salon, so my hours vary," he continued. "I didn't get home until almost ten last night. And no, that poor girl wasn't there. I would have seen her."

"Elle and I had dinner and worked on her homework,"

Craig said. "Her science project is due in a few days. It's on the solar system."

"What about security cameras?" Nikki had noticed the Ring doorbell on the way inside.

Craig and Perry looked at each other. "The thing goes off every time someone walks by or drives by, and I get an alert." Perry's face turned red. "It's not actually on. It's more of a deterrent."

He wasn't the first person she'd heard say the same thing about Ring. "Well, the tree blocks that area of the yard," Nikki said. "Between it and the dark, it's unlikely the doorbell camera would have caught anything. Do you have any other cameras?"

"As I told the policeman, the camera on the front porch broke about a week ago. Other than that, just inside the garage, but I already checked," Craig said. "There's nothing on there."

Nikki checked her notes to make sure she'd written things down correctly. "Perry got home about ten, and the yard was clear. What time did you guys go to bed?"

"I went to bed about eleven thirty," Perry said. "Craig was already snoring. I checked the front door to make sure it was locked, but I honestly don't remember if I even looked out into the yard. It's a safe neighborhood," he added, red splotches on his cheeks.

"That's okay," Nikki said. "What about anyone outside of the neighborhood? You guys have a couple of elementary schools nearby, and the Cub Scouts are doing their yearly canned food drive. Has anyone outside of the neighborhood stopped by recently? Maybe a salesman? Or someone claiming to be a Cub Scout parent?" Nikki added. "We can't rule anyone out right now."

Both men considered the question before answering. "I'm not going to act like it's all been roses for us," Craig said. "I don't recall the Scouts knocking on our door. But we don't have any mortal enemies. At least not that we know of." He looked nervously at Perry.

"It's unlikely that's why the killer chose this location," Nikki assured them. "But we have to ask." She gave both men her card and said she'd be in touch if she had any further questions.

"I hate to ask this." Craig's deep voice trembled. "But when will we have our yard back? We don't want Elle to come home and see this."

"The FBI's Evidence Response Team works quickly," Nikki answered. The weather was okay clear today and Nikki knew the rain normally slowed things down. Courtney had brought Arim Shah, her second in command. Between the two of them, she expected them to be done with the front yard today. "The medical examiner is here, so she will be taking the body with her."

The couple breathed a sigh of relief. "How's Ty doing? Is someone helping with Willow?" Perry asked.

"Ty told Lieutenant Chen the baby was with his mother, and she's on her way to the police station."

"Nikki." Courtney's tone sent a chill down her spine. She turned to see her friend standing a few feet in the house, clutching a paper evidence bag in her shaking right hand. "I need to speak with you."

Nikki thanked the homeowners and promised to keep them informed as much as possible, but Chen would be their main contact. She strode down the hall, heartbeat thundering in her head. She'd never seen her friend look so unsettled.

"What is it?" Nikki asked.

"Blanchard said the horizontal marks and indents on her legs indicate she'd been kept on some sort of grate or mat."

Tension rippled between them. "That's not entirely unusual."

"There are marks on her neck. Infected and nearly a

quarter of an inch deep. Her right hand was bound into a fist with brown rope."

"Just her right hand? Was she holding something?"

"Pink trillium." Courtney had been Nikki's closest friend since they'd met. She alone knew what happened in the Appalachians ten years ago. She opened the evidence bag, the faint smell coming off the semi-fresh blooms, staining the air between them. The flower petals tucked inside made Nikki's legs weak, but she managed to keep her balance.

"You said brown rope?"

"Jute rope." Courtney's voice trembled. "Isn't that what Mariah's killer used on her?"

Her knee throbbed like it always did every time she thought about that day in Appalachia. "The road is Linden Street." She'd grown up in Washington County, so the street name's familiarity hadn't struck her as anything out of the ordinary. "Mariah's body was left in a dumpster behind Lindon's Whole-sale Meats near Anacostia. How could there be so many coincidences in one murder?"

"But it can't be him, right? They found him dead."

"That's what the Smyth County deputy told me." Nikki's throat felt like it had been punched. "But no one else would know about the flowers. It's not like they were in a report."

"That's what I thought," Courtney said. "Is it possible?"

"I don't know. Keep this between us right now," she told her friend. "Let me make a few calls before we go drawing conclusions."

Courtney raised her dark eyebrows. "Pink trilliums aren't native to Minnesota. He left them for you."

Nikki couldn't suppress the shudder down her spine.

THREE

Nikki spoke more to Courtney than the rest of the team. She was close to Liam, her second in command, as well, but Courtney was her closest friend. "He chose to leave her in such a public place to make sure I heard about it. He must have chosen Linden Street to connect to Mariah. That's why he didn't leave her outside of her own front door. Kiania's house is technically on Williamson." Courtney nodded.

Chen's forehead wrinkled in confusion. "What are you talking about?"

Nikki flinched; she didn't realize Chen could hear her.

"Not necessarily me," she recovered. "But whoever murdered this poor woman didn't want the police to miss her." She pointed east. "Plus, the street isn't an outlet or high traffic area. A neighborhood with only stop signs usually means no CCTV footage. He's smart. He's purposeful. A lot of the signs are telling me this is an experienced killer."

Chen spoke into his shoulder mic, ordering officers to make sure they asked for all security footage. He let them know they were looking for someone who probably staked the place out at least a few days before, if not earlier. Any CCTV footage in the vicinity could reveal an important clue.

Nikki knelt next to the victim. "The bruising around her neck suggests some sort of ligature bigger than a rope. More likely the size of a standard belt." Nikki could see Mariah's autopsy photos in her mind. The killer she was hunting all those years ago had used a jute rope, and left it around his victim's neck, using the clove hitch knot.

"You think there are more?" Chen looked worried.

"There are a lot of signature elements to this murder." She pointed to the intricate knots in the binding still around the woman's wrists and ankles. "As we discussed earlier, bondage is a hallmark of a signature killer." She tasted acid, but she needed to get to the next part.

"Doctor Blanchard, have you looked at her hands?" The soil and minerals beneath Mariah's fingernails had led Nikki to Virginia. If any organic material had been left under the victim's fingernails, they might be able to track this killer the same way, and further connect this death to hers.

Blanchard reached for the dead woman's balled right fist. With rigor passed, she gently opened the hand, and they all flinched. "Jesus, I hope he didn't do this while she was conscious."

Every single fingernail had been removed, all the way down to the root. Nikki was shocked. If this was the same killer, perhaps he had learned from his past mistakes and removed any traces of evidence from under the victim's fingernails.

"She must have scratched him." Courtney's eyes locked with Nikki's. "Or he learned from earlier crimes. If he's done this before."

Even if she and Courtney turned out to be wrong about Mariah's killer being responsible, Nikki was certain they weren't dealing with a first-time offender. Leaving a victim in such a public place was one thing, but with all the Halloween decorations out, and neighbors coming and going, he definitely risked being seen.

Nikki glanced up at Courtney but addressed the medical examiner. "These healing bruises around her throat... Do you think he strangled her to the point of losing consciousness and then revived her?"

"It's possible," Blanchard answered. "But I won't be able to tell you for sure until I have her on the table."

Nikki looked at Chen. "Do you think you can handle things for a few hours? I'm happy to help, but I have a meeting this morning I can't miss." She'd never make it in time for the morning briefing. She needed to call Smyth County, Virginia, and search the FBI database to make sure a mistake hadn't been made.

After her near-death that night in 2014, Nikki had implored her boss to throw every resource at finding Mariah's killer, and Elwood had assured her they were doing just that. But what if they'd been wrong? How many others had lost their lives in the last decade?

"Sheriff should be available by lunchtime," Chen confirmed. "Now that your people are here, I'm feeling a little less overwhelmed. I guess I panicked a little when I called you. Ever since we searched for the girls that summer, I'm not able to handle my emotions as well, and I didn't want to start losing it with no one else here to lead the investigation."

"No apologies needed," Nikki reassured him. "There's nothing wrong with struggling emotionally through these murders, especially after what you've been through. That's a sign of healing. I'd be more worried if you were in denial." She patted him on the shoulder and looked pointedly at Courtney. "Walk me to the Jeep?"

Courtney tapped her second in command on the shoulder. "Arim, I'll be right back."

Arim Shah worked with Courtney in the lab, and he was

the only person Courtney would trust to take over her crime scene, even for a short time.

They made their way past the reporters, eyes on the ground.

"What are you going to do?" Courtney asked as Nikki unlocked the Jeep's door.

Nikki's mind raced with blurry memories. "Call Smyth County, to start. The deputy who found me in the woods called me a few weeks later to let me know Mariah's murderer was dead." Her mentor Elwood had talked about having another agent follow up. Had he?

"This sounds like something out of a conspiracy novel." Courtney kept her voice low. "But the flowers..."

Nikki's stomach bottomed out. She didn't believe in coincidences. "I know. I'll call you once I know more. If you notice any other similarities, beyond the flowers, call me first."

Courtney nodded, apprehension in her eyes. "Be careful. If it's really him, he told you—"

"I will be," Nikki reassured her, hoping she sounded more confident than she felt.

She kept her head down as she climbed into the Jeep and started the engine. Bowie's "Rebel Rebel" played on the radio, his mellow voice a shock from the darkness she'd just witnessed.

She navigated the tight street, resisting the urge to squash the reporters. They were just trying to do their job, and the media could be a major asset in big investigations. But Nikki didn't have the patience for them this morning.

Despite the flowers, it couldn't be the same person who'd killed Mariah Gonzales in 2014, she reminded herself. The Smyth County sheriff had personally told Nikki the suspect had been found dead in a car, body badly decomposed. She'd had her doubts at first, but the man matched the description of Mariah's killer and the man Nikki had spoken to that fateful day on the mountain. Nikki's injuries had kept her out of the field for the next two months, but Elwood, Nikki's mentor and head of the FBI's Behavioral Analysis Unit during Nikki's time at Quantico, had assigned an agent to follow up with Smyth County and make sure they had the right man in the morgue.

By that time she was heavily pregnant with Lacey and preparing to return to Minnesota and what she and Tyler thought would be a more normal, safe life. The events that day in the woods had shaken her to her core, and she vowed not to put her baby in danger ever again.

After all she'd endured in her life, Nikki should have known it wouldn't be that easy.

FOUR

Jefferson National Forest, Smyth County, Virginia

Nikki stayed motionless as he stared down at her. Between the red bandana around his face and ball cap, she could only see his ice-blue eyes. His steel-toed boots were stained with crimson. Long sleeves and jeans prevented her from seeing more than the white skin around his eyes.

"You're not local." His gentle voice sent terror down her spine. How could he be this calm, even if he had her right where he wanted her?

He had to know she was law enforcement. Her plates were government issued. Nikki kicked herself for not taking the time to get a rental.

"I'm from Quantico." Nikki's credentials and other identification were in the small leather wallet she carried in her back pocket. He'd find out soon enough. Honesty was likely her best chance at survival. "Mariah's mother asked me to help solve her case."

"FBI? Without backup? Seems very careless of you, especially if you really are pregnant."

Nikki tried to ignore the guilty voice in the back of her head. He wasn't telling her anything she hadn't already thought of, but the Smyth County deputy had been confident the old Mercury Grand Marquis the man had stolen from the dead homesteader had been seen heading south. She told him to check her credentials. "I'm not armed." Her gun had fallen God knows where, and she didn't dare take her eyes off the man to search for it. "I'm getting my badge out of my pocket."

Nikki leaned forward, holding her wallet, searching his face for more details. He took the wallet from her outstretched hands. Nikki's FBI badge and security key were inside, along with the ultrasound photo she'd tucked into it before leaving Quantico that morning.

"I recognize your name." If he was intimidated, the man didn't show it. "You just caught a serial killer you've chased for several years." He knelt in front of her and waved the ultrasound photo in her face. "Still needed more glory, didn't you?"

"No." Nikki managed to keep her voice steady. "Mariah and I went to the same OBGYN. Her mother asked for my help. That's the only reason I'm here." For some reason, she kept talking. "I had a miscarriage during that case. It nearly killed my husband. Please don't take that from him again." She waited a beat. "He's also an agent."

Deep wrinkles appeared at the corner of his eyes. "Listen, I'm not naïve enough to kill a federal agent, much less a pregnant one. Kind of makes it hard for me to slip away into the night, you know?"

Nikki nodded.

He shifted closer, tossing her wallet into her lap and eyeing her leg. "You're lucky that's not a compound fracture." He looked around the musty smelling earth until he retrieved her cell phone. "Consider yourself lucky, Agent Hunt." He smashed her iPhone into a hickory tree until only pieces remained. "Smyth County know you came out here?"

"Yes." The trees blurred as vertigo rushed over Nikki. Pain ricocheted through her head. "So does my boss at Quantico."

"Then they'll find you eventually."

Nikki stilled, afraid to do anything that would change his mind. Right now, the only person she cared about was the tiny one growing inside her.

He crouched in front of Nikki, close enough she could see the flecks of brown in his eyes. He smelled like cinnamon gum and sweat. "You're lucky I don't like pregnant women." He brushed an unruly curl off her face. "But don't worry. I'll find you one day and we can finish this."

She tensed as he reached past her and ripped a big, tangled mass of the pink trillium flowers out of the ground. "I'll take these to remember you by."

He stood, blood trickling down his right arm. He must have cut his arm coming down the mountain. "Hopefully the deputies find you before the bears and mountain lions get hungry." He touched the flower to her cheek. "I'll see you again someday, Agent Hunt."

FIVE

Nikki usually preferred coffee from local places, but she opted for the drive through at Caribou near the FBI campus. Armed with her usual amount of caffeine and sugar, she showed her ID at the front gate. The five-story building in Brooklyn Center, a working-class suburb of Minneapolis, contained multiple divisions, including an entire floor devoted to the laboratory services.

She struggled to keep her mind away from the past on the drive, but the memories from the day in Appalachia ten years ago demanded her focus. Hours had passed in the woods, the light fading into a dark night. Every time a twig snapped or leaves had crunched, Nikki had made herself as small and still as possible, praying whatever animal made the noises wasn't hungry.

At some point, she'd dragged herself to the nearest tree, hoping its support would keep her awake. She couldn't remember what time the deputy had shaken her awake, and the ride to the hospital and following day remained relatively blurry in her mind. She'd had a grade two concussion along with a torn right meniscus from twisting her leg falling down the mountain.

Between the concussion and pain, Nikki really didn't remember much about the first few days after she'd been rescued. She'd still been struggling with morning sickness, and it was the last thing she needed to add to her already aching body.

Thankfully, she'd kept the deputy's cell phone number from back then. She knew where she could find it in her files.

Nikki parked in her spot next to her boss's black BMW, cursing his inability to park in the middle of a spot. Garcia had only been the new ASAC for a few months. He was a competent agent but excelled at dealing with red tape and the stress that came with heading an entire office. Nikki had been at Quantico at the same time as Garcia. He'd been brash and flashy back then, but the FBI had squeezed most of that out of him over the years, save for the expensive SUV. Nikki didn't hold that against him, but since Garcia knew her spot was next to his, he took advantage, parking closer to the line separating the spots.

Like all government buildings, the lobby had a gray, sterile look despite its shiny floors and cherry administration desk.

She nodded to the security guards in the lobby without breaking stride. Nikki held her key card to the gray pad next to the elevator. The Bureau took security seriously, and only the right key card could access certain floors and areas of the lab.

Nikki closed the elevator doors before anyone could join her and hit the silver button for the fifth floor. Violent Crime occupied the entire floor. Field agents outside of Nikki's unit handled "regular" violent crimes, including murders. Shootings in the Twin Cities area had increased significantly in the last few years; many were drug related. They worked the cases Nikki had described to Sheriff Miller as snatch and grab crimes.

Nikki's exclusive unit dealt with the other kind of murders. She hated to call them "worse" because all murders were huge losses to the victims' families. Her unit took on the complicated, multi-layered cases throughout Minnesota, Wisconsin, and other Midwestern states. Her team's ability to travel also set them apart from the other agents, but they didn't have a personal jet or all the other bells and whistles shown on television shows. They had a budget, and it didn't include flying first class.

She stepped off the elevator and grimaced at the stink of burnt popcorn. The gray partition was six feet tall, ensuring some privacy for the agents. She kept her head down as she walked past the Violent Crime cubicles. Their break room was located near the end of the corridor, and Nikki had to pass it in order to get to their side of the floor.

"Agent Hunt!"

Nikki didn't recognize the female voice. She considered pretending she hadn't heard, but it wasn't unusual for an agent to ask for her opinion on a case. She still had a job to do.

She pivoted to the break room door, surprised to see a petite Asian woman in a lab coat. Nikki glanced at the embroidered name. "Melissa? I'm not sure we've met before."

"We haven't; I'm new. I'm working in the DNA laboratory."

The fourth floor housed all laboratory services. The labs were all interconnected through a series of locked doors. Only certain individuals had access to all of the labs.

"Doctor Hart hasn't been in yet this morning," Melissa said. "I've got a result I'd like her opinion on." She bounced on her heels. "It's such an honor to work with her. I'm sure you know how amazing she is, but in our world, she's a legend."

Courtney had earned her degree at Hofstra University in Long Island, New York. Hofstra consistently ranked high in forensic sciences, noted for its robust program. Over the years, she'd become one of the most sought-after forensic examiners in the country. Nikki first met her at a forensics conference, where Courtney gave a presentation on familial DNA and using genealogy to identify victims. Her research had been pivotal in the technology that had eventually identified the Golden State Killer.

Nikki smiled. "She's a legend in my world too."

"Do you know when she'll be in?"

Nikki and Courtney's friendship was well known within the unit, but Courtney worked very hard to prioritize things by the case's necessity, not her friends. Since Courtney had only recently hired Melissa, Nikki was surprised she'd shared it with her.

"I'm sorry to be so forward." Melissa's gentle voice sounded sheepish. "I was looking for her and another tech said you would know, so when you walked by, I just blurted it out. I'm sorry if I crossed some kind of line."

"You didn't," Nikki assured her. "She's at a crime scene that's pretty complicated, so she may not be in until later. Arim is with her as well," she added, referring to Courtney's second in charge. Arim Shah had been the assistant director of the Evidence Response Team for the last year, often going out to scenes when Courtney couldn't.

"Oh, Arim." Melissa flipped her black hair over her shoulder. She could tell by the pink in Melissa's cheeks that she had noticed Arim's good looks.

Nikki smiled. "I'll let Doctor Hart know you're looking for her if I speak with her."

"Okay, thanks." Melissa tossed her coffee cup into the trash. "I'm headed back to the lab. It's so great to meet you. You're a legend."

Nikki doubted that, but she thanked Melissa and continued down the hall to her small unit. Kendall and Jim had only been with the team for a couple of years. The polar opposites somehow worked well together. Jim was ten years Kendall's senior, his prior law enforcement experience giving him patience that Kendall was still learning.

Jim often regaled the team with stories about his three

rambunctious sons, but Kendall had no interest in children. She'd also been a pageant queen throughout high school, but Kendall made it a point not to wear makeup or wear her contacts because she wanted to be taken seriously and not ogled for her beauty. She kept her blonde hair in a twist or bun and made sure not to wear skirts that showed off her legs.

Nikki debated encouraging Kendall not to hide her beauty because no male in her office would get by with treating her like a sexual object, but in reality, they were just a small team in a big building. Nikki considered herself an attractive woman, but Kendall reminded her of Claudia Schiffer. She certainly could have been a model if she'd chosen to, but Kendall had other plans. She was intelligent and a keen observer.

Thankfully, Jim adored his wife and half feared, half admired his partner. Nikki was confident the two would eventually work as well together as she and Liam. They had the right kind of chemistry that law enforcement partners needed.

Nikki's gaze slid to Liam's desk, noting the large box that had contained a massive cinnamon roll before he wolfed it down. Liam Wilson had been Nikki's first choice as agent when she'd agreed to the Minnesota assignment. He'd saved her life more than once, and she couldn't think of a single case she could have solved without his help. He could also put away more food in one sitting than anyone Nikki knew.

She debated running straight to her small office across from the bullpen, but the sight of Liam's red hair changed her mind. He looked up as she approached. Nikki didn't have to say anything. He could read her as well as anyone.

They didn't speak until she'd closed the office door.

"What's wrong?" Liam asked.

Nikki slipped her jacket off and hung it on the coat rack next to the door and cursed. She'd left the coffee in the Jeep. "Want some coffee?" Nikki put her bag on the metal bookshelf that ran the length of the office. Its three shelves overflowed with various crime manuals and studies, some as recent as the past year while others dated back to the BAU's early days.

Framed diplomas from the University of Minnesota and Florida State University hung on the wall above the bookcase. She'd earned her graduate degree in FSU's prestigious criminal justice program. She'd met her former boss and mentor during a guest lecture he'd given during her second year of graduate school.

Elwood had been in grad school at Florida State when Bundy murdered the women from the Chi Omega sorority. Since he worked part-time as school security, Elwood had been one of the first responders at the sorority house. That experience had inspired him to switch to Criminology, one of the school's specialties. He'd already heard about the Behavioral Analysis Unit, so by the time Elwood had earned his postgraduate degree in 1981 and applied for the FBI Academy, he'd been assigned to the Green River task force and worked the case with profiler Douglas until Gary Ridgway, nicknamed the Green River Killer, was finally caught in 2001.

By the time Nikki started the criminology program at FSU, Elwood had become one of FSU's most distinguished alumni, popping in when his schedule allowed to give the occasional lecture. Nikki managed to get up the nerve to speak to him after a lecture during her final year of graduate school. Later, he'd admitted he knew who she was and had intended to speak to her about considering the FBI before she approached him. He believed that her parents' murder and subsequent experiences would help her relate not just to victims and their families, but to criminals as well. So she could catch them.

Various other certifications surrounded the diplomas in Nikki's office. She hated the idea of broadcasting her achievements but hanging her degrees had turned out to be the best way not to lose them in a pile of junk at home. Since she'd moved back to Minnesota, a string of high-profile and sometimes bizarre crimes made her more recognizable than most FBI agents, and her skills as a profiler had been covered in numerous national publications.

Nikki didn't need to keep records of those. They remained imprinted on her brain.

She walked to the tall filing cabinet in the corner. It contained all of her solved cases in Minnesota, but more importantly, Nikki's single-cup coffee brewer sat on top, along with a half-dozen assorted mugs with sarcastic sayings that Nikki liked to collect.

"No thanks." Liam patted his stomach. "I think I ate that cinnamon roll too fast."

"Shocking." Nikki selected a pod from Peace Coffee. The fast-growing local company had launched biodegradable pods in the past year. Even better, their coffee actually tasted good.

Nikki punched in the lock code for the second drawer while her coffee brewed. She found Mariah Gonzales's file and searched through the small batch of information, finally finding what she'd been looking for in the back of the file.

Nikki handed Liam the photocopied paper. "Read this first."

APPALACHIAN HOUSE OF HORRORS

Human remains and evidence of sadistic abuse found in rural Smyth County cabin. An FBI agent discovered the scene yesterday, when she arrived at the cabin to interview eighty-year-old Zebulan Wahlert, the property owner. According to the FBI, Wahlert's vehicle had been spotted in Arlington, Virginia, driven by a suspect in the murder of eighteen-year-old Mariah Gonzales.

Drug issues sent Gonzales to the streets, but her pregnancy changed her life. She'd recently given birth to a daughter, and both were living with Mariah's mother in Arlington. Mariah also attended classes at Northern University of Virginia's Annandale Campus and was last seen getting into a tan, older model Mercury Grand Marquis after night class. A witness described the man as white, with brown hair, wearing heavy work boots and a dark coat.

Gonzales was discovered two weeks ago in a dumpster in one of D.C.'s most dangerous neighborhoods. Her body showed signs of torture and sexual sadism. Washington D.C. Metro Police believed Mariah had gone back to the streets and been killed by a john, but her mother insisted that her daughter would never abandon her seven-week-old infant.

Anita Gonzales, a data analyst for the FBI, reached out to profiler Nikki Hunt to help find out what happened to her daughter. Hunt is no stranger to tragedy, having discovered her parents murdered when she was sixteen.

Hunt spoke with two different women working as prostitutes who had known Mariah Gonzales and still worked in the area where her body had been found. Both women described a man and vehicle similar to the one Mariah had been seen with the night she disappeared. Hunt tracked the owner of the vehicle to Smyth County.

Inside, the scene was far worse. Many of the details are too graphic to print, but the small bedroom had been turned into a sexual torture room, with bloodstains throughout the room. Agent Hunt and Smyth County Sheriff Barry Holtz said they believed the room could contain the blood of more than one victim. The remains of Zebulan Wahlert were also found in the second bedroom. Cause of death is still pending autopsy.

During her investigation of the property, a man matching the suspect's description arrived at the cabin and immediately fled. Agent Hunt followed, but the unfamiliar, rocky terrain caused her to fall, suffering a minor concussion and a leg injury.

The suspect is described as an average-sized white male,

with no identifying marks. He's believed to be armed and dangerous, and anyone with information should call the number below.

"I don't think I've heard you talk about this," Liam said.

"I haven't." Nikki dumped artificial creamer into the cup and sat down behind her desk. She slid the rest of Mariah's file across to him.

Liam looked through the original police report. "A dumpster diver in the Stadium-Armory area found her body. Was that a busy area, or—?"

Nikki knew why Liam was asking this question. Was the body left there to be found? It was an important question in any serial killer case. She directed him to Google Maps. "The Armory is actually an arena, where they have concerts and sporting events. RFK Stadium is here, on the other side of the street."

"But wasn't it long closed by that time?" Liam asked.

"Yes, sitting empty and wasting away. I heard the mayor is trying to revitalize it," Nikki answered. "The Anacostia River is just west of the stadium."

"And it's really dangerous."

"I don't know the current stats, but it's historically important, and locals had started gentrifying the area when I moved back here, but at the time, yes. The entire area on both sides of the river wasn't great."

"So the killer was buying time dumping the body in an area no one would find it." Liam looked at the date on the article. "This happened during the Cherry Blossom Festival?"

D.C.'s Cherry Blossom Festival usually ran from the third week in March to the third week in April. The world-renowned celebration of spring offered a variety of amazing food, culture and entertainment, culminating with the April races.

"On the busiest day. The 10-mile run takes place at the

Tidal Basin, but the festival stretches through the National Mall and parks. It runs for a month and always taxes the police," Nikki told him. "On Sunday, April sixth, the Armory had no events. Most nearby businesses were closed. Police focus was on the race route." It was more evidence to suggest that the killer didn't want Mariah's body found quickly.

"Did they pull security footage?"

Nikki nodded. "No cameras facing the dumpster. Police looked at the CCTV in the area in the hopes of spotting something, but never did. No one suspicious coming or going."

"So this is a smart killer? Or someone who knows the area well."

Nikki nodded. "D.C. police refused to consider any option other than Mariah being killed by someone she knew, likely because of her working on the street. Look at her injuries."

"Jesus," Liam whispered as he studied the photos of Mariah's injuries. "A sexual sadist, for sure." Liam tossed the papers onto the table. "Now tell me what actually happened. How did you get involved in the first place?"

"This was just a few months after we caught the Ivy League Killer," Nikki said.

SIX

FBI, Quantico, Virginia

Nikki found ASAC Elwood in the evil minds research museum, located deep within Quantico. The locked unit's purpose revolved around research and the better understanding of the criminal mind through their own possessions. The artifacts had been taken from the offenders' most personal possessions that had been removed during the investigation or provided by family members who wanted to wash the stain of a murderer out of their family.

Elwood had taken residence at a long table, with several files from Suffolk County, New York. She recognized the one he currently studied, his reading glasses resting on the bridge of his nose. Just four years ago, a woman named Shannan Gilbert had made a frantic 911, insisting she was being chased in the area of Ocean Parkway, near the remote towns of Gilgo Beach and Oak Beach. Shannan had stayed on the phone for twenty-three minutes, insisting that "they" were going to kill her. The call had eventually dropped, and Shannan was never seen or heard from again. A search for Shannan's body eventually unearthed the remains of four women on Gilgo Beach, Long Island. Shannan hadn't been one of them, but as the search continued, six more sets of remains, including a toddler, were discovered buried in the sandy, cold beach. Shannan Gilbert's body was found a year later, with law enforcement still divided on whether or not she'd been a victim of the same killer.

"Are we actually going to be in the game?" Nikki asked Elwood as she walked towards him. Suffolk County Police Chief James Burke had ended cooperation with the FBI, drawing fire from law enforcement across the country. The police had started investigating Burke for beating a suspect in custody, and he'd lost his job. Nikki knew Elwood had fielded several calls from Suffolk County investigators since Burke's removal.

"I think so," Elwood said. "Not officially, but I think it's going to happen soon. Investigators now agree that all ten victims were killed by the same person. The new chief of police asked me if I'd work on a profile." He gestured to the mass of information spread across the table. "Starting at the beginning, of course."

Only senior agents within the BAU and vetted researchers were allowed inside the museum. Nikki's capture of the Ivy League Killer just weeks ago had earned her promotion to Supervisory Special Agent. "Do you have a couple of minutes to go over a case I'm working?" she asked Elwood.

He looked up from his notes, his blue eyes critical. "Do you mean the Mariah Gonzales murder? The one the D.C. police didn't invite us to help with?"

"That's the one." She handed him the file. "Her mother works as an analyst for the FBI, and she asked me to take a look. Once the Annandale police discovered Mariah is a sex worker, they lost interest. Apparently her friends reported a man who had been acting strangely around her. He just paid Mariah to talk sometimes, which is odd in their line of work."

"And Mariah texted her mother four days after she disappeared?" Elwood asked.

Nikki nodded. "Mariah's phone had been off up until that point, and it shut down right after the text sent. In the text, she claimed that she needed time away from the 'incessant' stress the baby caused. Her mother, Anita, told police that the text and vocabulary did not sound like her daughter at all. Anita also insists that Mariah was clean and had been excelling as a mother. The baby was happy and had been a pretty good sleeper. Mariah never indicated she was unhappy. Anita insisted she wouldn't have left."

"Her body was found three weeks after she disappeared, during the Cherry Blossom Festival." Elwood read the file out loud. His graying eyebrows raised. "In a dumpster shared between Bell Capitol Apartments and a halfway house on the morning of the 10-mile run. Which district is that?"

"107," Nikki answered, referring to the police districts. "That's the area around RFK Stadium and the Armory, east of the Tidal Basin and race route, but not so far away that the police wouldn't be stretched thin because of the race and the festival."

She sat down across from Elwood. "Her body was about halfway down the dumpster. A homeless man searching for food discovered her. The dumpster was emptied on Friday afternoon. Mariah was lying near the bottom, which means she was likely left early Saturday morning. Police did pull security videos, but the camera on the dumpster's side had been disabled a week before and with all city resources strained thanks to the Cherry Blossom Festival, it was never fixed. The D.C. police told Anita Gonzales that Mariah had likely run off with the john, and he got rid of her when he no longer needed her." She didn't bother to hide her disgust. The police may be stretched thin, but that had nothing to do with basic human empathy.

"Her mother asked me to look at the case."

Elwood studied her. "We have many analysts. Why did she ask you? Because of the press coverage from catching the Ivy League Killer?"

Nikki debated lying to Elwood, but she'd never been very good at lying, and Elwood read body language better than anyone Nikki had ever met. He'd call her bluff before she even finished a sentence. "Mariah goes to the same OBGYN as I do. We met several months ago... early in Mariah's pregnancy."

Elwood knew Nikki's personal history, and he also knew why she'd taken yesterday morning off. "How did the appointment go?"

Nikki smiled and showed him the ultrasound photo she had been given. "See those three little lines? That means it's a girl!" She fought against the emotion building in her throat.

"This good of a photo at sixteen weeks?" Elwood was astonished. "My kids looked like blobs up until they were born. Have you picked out any names?"

"We've got a long list for boys, and about four names for girls, none of which I like," Nikki said.

"Well, maybe you and Tyler can figure it out over the long weekend. I still can't believe you took a vacation day."

Nikki made a face. "Neither can I." She cleared her throat. "A friend of mine who works in Vice for D.C. Metro went back to Mariah's old work route and talked to some of the girls who knew her when she worked the streets. Turns out, two of the women were able to describe the john's vehicle in some detail—a tan, late model Mercury Grand Marquis. Our tech guys went through hours of footage from the area and found a car that matches it. It's registered to Zebulan Wahlert, from Marion, Virginia. It's down in Smyth County."

"That's Appalachian territory," Elwood said. "Rough terrain through there."

"Wahlert is also eighty years old. The women told Vice this man was somewhere in his thirties," Nikki said. "He doesn't have a registered phone number. I'd like to go to Smyth County this weekend and see what I can find out."

"The D.C. police won't like that." Elwood leaned back in his chair.

"I don't care," Nikki said. "And unless I discover something linked directly to Mariah, they'll never know."

"I understand you feel a kinship with this girl and her mother," Elwood began.

"It's not just that. Look at the crime scene photos. I don't think this was just a john beating a prostitute to death."

Elwood flipped to the back of the thick folder, his expression grim as he studied the graphic images. "How many stab wounds?"

"At least forty, with all but three being superficial wounds."

"Done to torture her," Elwood said.

"That's what I think," Nikki said. "The medical examiner believes she died less than a day before her body was discovered. And the stab wounds aren't what killed her, although they would have." Nikki directed him to the photo of Mariah on the autopsy table, her petite body riddled with bruises varying in color and dozens of superficial but likely very painful stab wounds. "See the wound on her neck?"

"It was infected?" Elwood surmised.

Nikki nodded. "Bacterial infection that had spread through her bloodstream. The Metro PD. refused our initial offer for help, but they did send some samples taken from Mariah's body to the lab at the D.C. office. They found traces of the minerals dolomite, pyrite and fluorite on her body, primarily in her fingernails. Kind of unusual to have on her if she'd remained in the metro area, right?"

Elwood nodded. "But my guess is they're all found in Smyth County, Virginia?"

"Yep," she answered. "A lot of the mines in the Jefferson National Forest have closed, but those minerals have been found in heavier concentrations in the area between McMullin and Sugar Grove. They're all in Smyth County. I'd like to drive down there today and check things out. I'll make contact with the county sheriff as soon as I get into town, explain everything."

"I thought you and Tyler were spending the weekend together." Elwood didn't bother to hide his concern. "How does he feel about all of this?"

"He was pulled into a major fraud case this morning and will be working all weekend." Nikki anticipated her boss's next question. "I think we could be looking at a serial killer, given the sadistic violence Mariah was subjected to. Her killer is turned on by her suffering, and he kept her alive to prolong it."

"What are you basing that on?" Elwood asked.

"Autopsy report. Mariah was missing for over three weeks before her body was found, and she'd only been dead around twenty-four hours. Have you ever seen a victim in that situation only lose a few pounds?" She didn't wait for him to answer. "Stomach contents showed that in the last twenty-four hours, she'd consumed two protein drinks, as well as significant doses of caffeine and creatine."

"I can't believe you can buy caffeine in a powder form," he said. "Creatine? Doesn't that have to do with the kidneys?"

"It's one of the tests they use to assess kidney damage," Nikki said. "It helps with energy during workouts."

Elwood leaned forward, eyes flashing. "He wanted to keep her strong, prolong her captivity?"

"I think so," Nikki admitted. "And I'm certain he'll do it again if we don't stop him."

SEVEN

"So you ended up going to that cabin alone?" Liam asked.

Nikki shook off the chills she always felt every time she thought about that conversation with Elwood. "The sheriff's office was my first stop," she said. "Smyth County has several small towns that date back to the state's mining heyday, but it's a small-town kind of area. They had little information on Wahlert. Apparently, he lived out there like some sort of recluse."

"Driving the same car?" Garcia asked.

"No, some kind of SUV," she answered. "That's how I managed to convince the sheriff to put out an APB on the car since it had probably been stolen. The sheriff seemed satisfied, but I decided to drive out to Wahlert's."

"And he was dead too?"

Nikki nodded. "Face up on the bed, and he'd only been there a few days. But it was already warm out, so the coroner had to confirm that."

"Who had access to the cabin?" Liam asked. "Did you talk to the other family members?"

"I assume Smyth County handled that after I was injured," Nikki said.

"Doesn't sound like they did their job properly," Liam said, and Nikki nodded her agreement. "If we're talking about the same killer. Why did Mariah's mom ask you specifically?" Liam asked the question she'd been dreading. Sweat dampened the roots of her dark, wavy hair. She hadn't told this part of the story in many years. Even though Nikki had long since come to terms with the miscarriage, she still remembered the way her heart had plummeted when the doctor told her.

"Courtney is the only living person who knows the entire story." Nikki struggled to contain her emotions. "Tyler was the second."

Liam nodded. "I'm honored you trust me."

"I met Mariah at an OBGYN appointment." Nikki choked back the knot in her throat. "My first pregnancy ended in a miscarriage."

"I'm sorry."

"We heard the heartbeat at six weeks, but I started spotting a couple of weeks later," she continued. "Mariah and her mother were in the lobby, waiting to see the doctor."

Nikki didn't usually eavesdrop on others' conversations, but on that day, she listened to a young, pregnant girl arguing with her mother about changing her life. "I was the only other patient in the lobby. I heard them bickering. Mariah had been working on the streets, using drugs, when she got pregnant. That eventually brought her home to her mother, who convinced her to stay and get her life together in time for the baby. She was in her last trimester.

"The doctor confirmed I'd lost the baby." Nikki could still see the pity in the woman's eyes. "I didn't understand what happened. The doctor explained that early miscarriages like this usually means the pregnancy wasn't going to be viable. Then she told me that my stressful job could have played a part, and if I truly wanted to be a mother, I might want to rethink being a field agent."

"You went through our government health care system, didn't you?" Liam asked.

Nikki nodded. "I don't think a doctor in the private sector would have spoken the way she did. Now I see she wasn't judging me. She was just blunt. But I was devastated and felt like she was telling me that it was my fault. I ran out crying.

"Mariah and her mother were arguing in the parking lot. Tyler and I had done everything right and were punished, while this young girl who'd been working on the streets and had drug issues got to have her baby. Mariah started cussing at her mother, and something in me just snapped."

Nikki hated the memory of her confronting Mariah like an entitled jerk. She'd taken her loss and anger out on an easy scapegoat.

She knew Liam wouldn't ask for details. "I caught myself when I saw the mother's civilian badge. She's an IT analyst for the Bureau, or she was then. Ironically, there were two other OBGYNs closer to where we lived in Alexandria than the one I'd ultimately chosen."

"What made you decide to go to one so far away from your house?" Liam asked.

"At the time, I'd just been promoted to Supervisory Agent over two male agents who were just as qualified. I earned the promotion, but since Elwood had recruited me, the other two agents grumbled about preferential treatment. I didn't want anyone finding out about the pregnancy before I was ready and using it against me," Nikki said. "I'd seen it happen to other female recruits and agents."

"Gross," Liam said. "Just like Kendall needing to downplay her beauty to be taken seriously. What freaking century are we in?"

"Don't get me started on that issue," she warned him. "You know what happens when I get going about it."

"Yeah, you and Caitlin start drinking and someone has to come get you before you end up in jail." Liam rolled his eyes.

Caitlin Newport, a local reporter and documentary maker, had once been Nikki's enemy. Since she and Liam started dating, Nikki got to know Caitlin. Both women had strong personalities, and combining deep discussions like women's rights with alcohol usually led to someone telling them they were being too loud, as it had a few weeks ago when she and Rory had gone out with Liam and Caitlin. They'd been discussing a court case while the guys played pool and things had gotten a little heated.

"People shouldn't eavesdrop on us," Nikki countered. "Anyway, I was so ashamed of how I treated Mariah that I wanted to track her mother, but all I knew was that she worked at the Bureau. At the time, I didn't even know Anita's first name."

"You were injured?" Liam glanced at the photocopies. "I see the local paper snapped a photo of your rescue. What happened?"

Nikki told him how the mountain had given out from underneath her. "Somehow, I didn't lose Lacey." She took a deep breath. "I lost my gun in the fall. When he slid down the mountain, I was certain he would kill me."

Nikki glanced at the 5x7 framed photograph taken of Rory, Lacey and herself this past summer, her daughter proudly displaying her missing front tooth. A smaller photo of Lacey with her late father, Tyler, sat on the other side of the desk next to one of the few good photos Nikki had of her parents. "I told him I was pregnant."

"Is that why he let you live?"

Nikki could still smell the moldy forest if she thought hard enough. "He said he didn't like pregnant women. But he also knew I was an agent and help would be coming." She told Liam about the killer's quiet, confident demeanor. "Mariah Gonzales was not his first victim. I thought she was his last until this morning."

She explained what they'd found this morning in Stillwater. "Kiania Watson disappeared from a Minneapolis parking garage after working second shift. Her body was left on her neighbor's lawn this morning, just yards away from her seven-week-old baby's room. Courtney found the flowers secured in the victim's hand with the same kind of rope he used to bind Mariah Gonzales. There were other similarities, but I need to look at Mariah's autopsy photos to really compare. The flowers though..."

"They aren't native to the area?" Liam asked.

"Nope," she answered. "A Smyth County deputy tracked me down in the woods. He's actually part Cherokee and comes from a family of trackers, but that's another story. I had some pretty bad injuries, including a grade two concussion that kept me out of commission for a while."

She still remembered the phone call just a few weeks before Lacey's birth. The detective in charge of Mariah's case told her they'd found the decomposed body of the killer, the man Nikki had chased in the woods. Since she'd given them all the information she'd gathered after Mariah's mother asked for her help, Nikki had foolishly assumed they'd gotten it right. "Elwood had assigned another agent to follow the case. He told me the agent confirmed it was the right person."

Nikki woke up her computer and logged into the criminal database. "I left a message for the Smyth County deputy, but I'd like to track down the agent who replaced me. I remember hearing the suspect had something of Mariah's in his possession." During the call, she'd fought the bad feeling creeping through her and decided to believe the police and focus on her incoming new arrival. She'd questioned that decision off and on over the years, but no more than she had today.

"Doesn't necessarily mean he's the right guy, though," Liam said.

"Exactly." The head injury had made her forget details.

Liam looked up from the report. "Was it ever an FBI case? Officially, I mean."

Nikki honestly wasn't sure. She'd stuffed the trauma of that day as far down as possible and focused on her baby. She logged into the Bureau's private database and searched for the D.C. Bureau's criminal records from 2014. "I remember that the killer had no history of violent crime. His specialties were petty theft and misdemeanor, simple robbery. Lust murders like the one who killed Mariah escalate.

"According to the minimal news coverage I can find, the guy grew up in Anacostia. He worked at a factory a few minutes from the college Mariah attended. He had the night off when Mariah disappeared, and his body was found with her bracelet and pair of socks.

"There's nothing in the Bureau solved cases database, either." She glanced at Liam. "The Smyth County news did a better job covering the story than the D.C. papers." She searched through the paper's digital archives until she found what she was looking for. The article named Smyth County Deputy Jason Horner, the man who'd rescued Nikki from the woods, along with the D.C. investigator who received credit for finding the decomposed body of Johnny Trent. "No mention of the FBI agent at all."

That wasn't unusual. The D.C. cops and FBI had a long-standing rivalry, and her choice to keep them out of the loop when she went to Virginia hadn't made things any better. Nikki and Elwood had gotten into a shouting match with the chief of police and lead investigator over their mistakes and lack of empathy for Mariah. Her killer should have been caught by them. They should have cared more about her instead of labeling her as a prostitute, as though that somehow made a woman less human.

"Agent's probably retired," Nikki said. "But I'd like to speak to them."

"Me too. Did you see the guy's face?" Liam asked.

"Just his eyes and bridge of his nose." She stilled, a snippet of memory coming back. "Icy-blue eyes, light eyebrows, fair skin." Nikki wanted to bang her head against the computer screen. She knew she gave all of these details to the police, but she didn't remember if Johnny had those same features.

Liam tipped his chair back, balancing on its back legs. "What was the guy's name? The one the D.C. found?"

"Johnny Trent." Nikki's fingers trembled as she searched the violent crime database for a photo of Trent. Her fingers stilled. Brown eyes and a darker skin tone. She turned her monitor around so that Liam could see it. "Can someone's eyes dull over time? Could they have looked blue in the bright sun up on that mountain? Could he have tanned?" She shook her head. Her pulse raced even faster than her thoughts. The hours and days after her rescue had blurred together. "I was in and out of it the first couple of days," she said. "But I've never forgotten his eyes. I don't think this is him. Why didn't I check?"

"Because you'd been through enough. You should have been able to trust another agent," Liam reassured her. "You're sure it's not the same guy?"

But Nikki knew in her gut that the killer was still out there.

EIGHT

Minutes later, Nikki and Liam were sitting in the hard, straight-backed chairs in front of Garcia's desk. He'd replaced the cushioned, semi-comfortable chairs issued by the Bureau with two miserable chairs that Garcia said made people stay alert and focused.

He was a few years older than Nikki and they'd met during her first year at Quantico. Garcia had shed most of the arrogance he'd had back then.

Nikki still missed Hernandez, the man who'd convinced her to return to Minnesota. She hadn't known what to expect when Garcia took over. He'd made it clear that protecting the Bureau's reputation was his main priority and briefing him twice a week on her cases had been an adjustment. She'd expected him to second-guess everything even though he didn't have nearly the field experience Nikki did, but most of the time, he agreed with her assessments. As long as she played by the rulebook, Garcia promised he'd have her back.

"Sorry I missed the meeting this morning," Nikki told her boss. "Stillwater PD called me to a scene since the sheriff was busy."

Garcia might not have the investigative field experience that she did, but he had a keen eye for the minor details. He sat up straight. "Given how frazzled you are, I'm guessing this is a bad one."

Part of Nikki hated for Garcia to see her so vulnerable, but her pride had no place in this situation. "Do you mind if we try calling Sheriff Miller? He hadn't arrived when I left, and I think we should fill him in as well."

Garcia gestured for her to call.

Miller answered right before the call went to voicemail. "Hey, Nikki. Thanks for coming this morning. This poor woman. I assume Chen told you everything we know at this point?"

"He did," Nikki said. "Listen, I'm putting the phone on speaker. Garcia and Liam are here, and I don't want to have to tell the story over and over."

"What story?" Miller's gruff tone surprised her. "Does it have to do with this murder? Because if it doesn't, I don't have time right now. Her family is waiting at Stillwater PD."

"It does." Nikki skipped over her miscarriage and meeting Mariah. "In early 2014, I tracked a killer to a remote cabin in Appalachia," Nikki said. "I chased him and fell. He left me there, and a few weeks later, I heard he'd been found dead in North Carolina. Police found items belonging to the victim, Mariah Gonzales, in the Virginia homesteader's car. As far as I know, both the state police and the FBI agent overseeing the case believed they had their man."

"Who was the agent?" Garcia palmed an onyx stone in his right hand.

"I don't know." Nikki handed him the driver's license photo of Johnny Trent, the man who'd allegedly murdered Mariah. "But that is absolutely not the man I chased in the woods that day."

Garcia stopped turning the stone in his palm. "Are you saying police identified the wrong man?"

Nikki nodded. "I should have looked him up when Deputy Horner first told me they'd caught the guy, but I'd just gotten out of the hospital, and my late ex-husband, Tyler, didn't want me discussing the case at all. I was pregnant with Lacey and lucky to be alive. I wanted to put it behind me."

"What does this have to do with our victim?" Miller demanded.

"I think North Carolina may have made a mistake and we're looking at the same killer's work." Nikki gave her boss a copy of Mariah's autopsy report. "At the time, I had no doubt Mariah wasn't his first victim. He was too calm, too patient. And I think Kiania Watson is another of his." Nikki described the tragic scene from earlier this morning. "This is a signature murder, not a domestic."

Garcia's eyebrows drew together as he looked at the autopsy report. "What are the similarities?"

Nikki described the knots, stab wounds, injury pattern and bondage.

"Agent, I understand your concern," Garcia said. "But it seems like you may be reaching on this."

"I agree," Miller said.

"I haven't told you everything," she said. "When I fell, I landed in a patch of pink trillium flowers. They grow wild in Virginia, and they have a distinct smell."

"Stinking Benjamins," Garcia said. "Like a wet dog. I think some grew around the campus at Quantico."

Nikki couldn't remember. "That's right. I was pregnant with Lacey and begged Mariah's killer not to hurt me." She struggled to keep her voice steady. "He knew I was an FBI agent, but that's not why he didn't kill me. He said he didn't kill pregnant women, but that I'd see him again someday, pulling that exact flower from the ground as he spoke. Courtney found dried, pink trillium petals inside our victim's hand bound with the same type of rope he used on Mariah Gonzales in 2014."

"You're basing this off of flowers?" Miller asked.

"The flowers aren't native to Minnesota. They're a message, for me. And there's more."

"What else?" Garcia asked.

"Why leave Kiania three doors down from her own home? She lives on Williamson and she was left on Linden Street. Mariah's body was dumped at a place called Lindon's Whole-sale Meats. Plus, both women were recently postpartum—"

"Nicole, I can't do this right now," Miller cut her off. "Right now, I have to focus on the facts. Detective Brenner's with the family, and Chen and I are up to our ears canvassing the neighborhood—when we're not fighting off reporters, that is. Can we discuss this when you have something other than a wild theory?"

Liam shifted in the chair next to her, irritated at Miller's tone.

"Of course." Nikki felt heat creeping up her neck and cheeks, her stomach flipping just like it used to do when she was in the FBI Academy and still making dumb mistakes. "I'll check in with you later." She ended the call.

Garcia leaned back in his chair. "You really think Johnny Trent isn't the same guy?"

"I know he isn't."

She met Garcia's dark eyes, shocked to see the sympathy shining through. "I know being taken off the case must have been hard for you. Are you sure you're remembering everything perfectly? Any agent who hears this all happened while you were pregnant is going to say you're misremembering the details."

Nikki knew Garcia was right. She knew he didn't think she'd make a mistake, but she needed to be sure if she was going to convince every alpha male in the building and get Mariah's case reopened.

"I remember his eyes, his face. Now that I've looked at Johnny Trent's face for the first time, I'm certain he's not the man I chased in those woods."

Nikki unlocked her phone and opened the photo she'd taken of the pink flowers in Kiania's hands. She thought of the poor mother and her baby. "These only grow in warmer climates, and they're pretty common in parts of Appalachia, including the area the cabin the killer used was in. I landed in a bed of these." She handed her superior her phone with the photo cued up. "Even if the Stillwater police hadn't called me, I would have heard about this case."

Garcia considered that for a moment. "If this were anyone else, I'd probably be a lot more cynical, but you don't jump to conclusions or lose your composure easily." He glanced at Nikki's fingers. "You're shaking."

She clenched the chair arms. Garcia shook his head. "Nikki, we had our issues in the FBI Academy, but you know how much I support women in law enforcement, and I'm not going to condemn you for having emotions. I also don't want you to get into this so deeply that you take risks like you've done in prior cases that were personal. And you'd only be human if you did." He looked at Liam. "What do you think?"

"I've never seen her this rattled, not even when the Frost killer came for Lacey," Liam said. "I think we should look for other cases throughout the country while we wait for forensics. Our case load right now"—he reached up and knocked on Garcia's wooden desk—"is light, and Kendall and Jim already have their assignments. Why don't Nikki and I go over Mariah's case and try to find out if there have been similar crimes?"

"Fine," Garcia said. "Let's reconvene when you're done."

Liam stood, and Nikki followed suit, unable to hide her surprise at Garcia's open mind. "Thank you."

"My only request is that you keep me in the loop through all of this, because I don't want us repeating past mistakes, especially in this political climate," Garcia said.

"Understood." Nikki followed Liam out of Garcia's office.

Liam leaned against the wall, waiting for her, his red hair aflame against the eggshell paint. "That went better than I expected."

"Don't get too excited. If we don't find evidence of other murders, he's liable to tell me to leave it alone."

NINE

Nikki started with ViCAP. The FBI's Violent Criminal Apprehension Program was spearheaded by Robert Ressler, one of the first profilers and credited with coining the term serial killer. Created in 1985, ViCAP was used by law enforcement to track violent crime across the country, providing a vital link between agencies. If ViCAP had been around in the 70s, Bundy may not have gone under the radar for as long as he had.

Armed with fresh coffee, Nikki and Liam settled in her office. Nikki found Mariah's autopsy report in the system. Her stomach churned as she read the graphic details to Liam. Mariah had been tortured, her body riddled with healing bruises. She'd had internal bleeding from the violent attacks, and the coroner believed she'd been strangled to the point of losing consciousness only to be brought back around for more torture.

"She had a crisscross pattern on the backs of her legs and butt," Nikki explained. "The coroner believed the marks came from being forced to stay in the same cramped place for extended periods of time. We never figured out what caused the marks. Nothing in the cabin matched."

She'd forgotten about the markings on Kiania this morning. Blanchard said the horizontal marks and indents on her legs indicated she'd been kept on some sort of grate or mat. She should have mentioned that to Garcia and Miller. It was another link.

"Mariah had more than forty superficial wounds and burns," Nikki said. "The cause of death was ultimately a broken hyoid, but one of the wounds on her neck had become so badly infected she likely would have died from it if he hadn't killed her."

"He bound her?" Liam confirmed.

"Both her wrists and ankles still had standard nylon rope," Nikki answered. "He used a clove hitch knot." She looked up at her partner. "It's tied by passing the running end of the rope around the object and back over itself to form an X. The running end goes around the object in question again, and both ends are pulled tight, secured under the intersection of the prior turn."

"BTK's favorite," Liam said. "Same thing today?"

Nikki showed him the photos she'd taken of the ropes still around the victim's ankles and wrists. "Yes. I'm not a knot forensic expert, but most people, even serial killers, aren't thinking that clearly when they're killing someone. When they're in that perfect fantasy moment, they resort to base instincts. Right-handed people kill with their right hand. They also bind people with their dominant hand."

"How can you tell if the person who made the knot is right or left-handed?" Liam asked.

"In theory, it's based on what direction the rope is drawn through the loops, as well as the direction the rope was twisted in. In the heat of the moment, they revert to what they know, just like the rest of us."

Knot forensics was a very specialized field with a handful of experts scattered around the world. "The International Guild of

Knot Tyers has a handful of individuals qualified to examine the knots. We can send them photos of both victims and knots. At the very least, they will be able to tell if both knots were made by a right- or left-handed person."

"Most knots in murder cases aren't sophisticated." Liam examined the photo. "But these look pretty intricate to me, suggesting experience."

"Mariah was Hispanic, and today's victim is black." Since profiling became popular, the next generation of profilers learned that the victims didn't always have to resemble each other. Nikki would argue that Bundy choosing similar women was part of his own ritual-driven psychosis. He might have started out fantasizing about a brown-haired female with hair parted down the middle, and the fantasy became so strong that's what he had to have. In her opinion, the choice of victim for serial killers came down to opportunity and means far more often than fitting a specific physical type.

"How exactly did you initially track him to some little county in southern Virginia?"

"The car. Plus the minerals." Smyth County, like much of Virginia, had a rich mining history. "The physical scientists at Quantico matched minerals found under Mariah's fingernails with the specific area where the cabin was."

"This morning's victim had her fingernails removed?" Liam clarified. "In 2014, did you tell the man how you found him?"

"The minerals?" Nikki wished she could remember all the details from that miserable day. "It's very possible. It could have been in the news as well."

Liam considered that for a moment. "If this really is the same killer, my bet is he learned his lesson and started removing the fingernails. What about trophies?"

"A lock of Mariah's hair was cut," Nikki said. "She wore a couple of cheap, beaded bracelets. One was found in the car with Johnny Trent's body in North Carolina. As far as I know, the other disappeared."

Liam crossed his arms, stretching out his long legs. "One to plant on Trent, one for his personal trophies. You said the way he disposed of Mariah's body showed he had prior experience?"

Nikki unlocked her phone and searched for last year's Cherry Blossom 5K route. She showed Liam the image. "He left her in a dumpster near the route, at Lindon's Wholesale Meats. Their dumpster was always emptied on Friday night and Sunday afternoons. Mariah's body was discovered near the bottom of the dumpster Saturday morning by a dumpster diver. That's the only reason her body was even discovered before it went to the landfill."

"He must have scouted the area, learned the garbage routes," Liam said.

"Exactly. He was banking on timing and the festival to hide his crime. Pretty calculating and patient for a first-time murderer."

They spent the next few hours combing through unsolved murders throughout the eastern half of the country, focusing on the commonalities between the two victims. Using the flowers and fingernail removal, Nikki and Liam managed to cull the list to a handful of murders since 2014.

"Pink trillium." Nikki finally found the first possible match. Her heartbeat thundered against her temple. "Detroit, 2015." She wanted to throw her computer across the room. "Kara Smith, white female, thirty-two. Real estate agent who disappeared while she was attempting to flip abandoned houses. Found a month later, same bondage and injury pattern. Pink petals found in her hands."

Liam found the most recent victim prior to today.

"North Dakota, eighteen months ago," Liam said grimly. "Female in her mid-twenties, found on Standing Rock Reservation. Flower petals near the body."

The largest Sioux reservation in the country in southeastern North Dakota meant the Bureau of Indian Affairs likely offered resources and aid to local agencies within the community. Since the BIA fell under the jurisdiction of the Department of Justice, just as the FBI did, they should be able to access most of the information without jumping through a bunch of needless hoops.

"I'll call the Bureau of Indian Affairs agent out there and see what I can find out." Liam sat up straighter. "The Detroit victim had an eight-week-old baby. The North Dakota woman's baby was nine weeks. I thought it might be a coincidence since so much time passed between the two murders, but this looks like a pattern."

The room seemed to spin around Nikki. Two more victims. Had he been sending her signs for years? Suddenly she felt responsible for not noticing, for not stopping him. For letting these poor women die. She steeled herself. She'd assumed he hadn't killed her because she was an FBI agent, but had she been wrong? "He's definitely focusing on post-partum women."

"Maybe he has a skewed moral compass about someone carrying another life," Liam suggested.

Nikki tried to catch her racing thoughts. "He's been doing this for ten years—maybe longer. How many innocent women have died?"

"You can't think about that right now," Liam told her. "If postpartum women are his victim of choice, then he's killing new mothers. Maybe he had a newborn who died and he blamed the mother. What has he been doing all this time?"

Nikki opened a map of Detroit on her browser. "The 2015 victim was found near the Canadian border, and last year's in North Dakota. Standing Rock isn't that far from the major inter-states connecting the United States and Canada."

"Canada's got its own version of ViCAP," Liam said. "All

that open country sounds like the perfect playground for him to hide."

TEN

1984

Smyth County, Virginia, Appalachia

Fifi trod down the worn, winding path that cut through her grandfather's property. She clutched a bucket in her right hand and swatted flies with her right, careful to dodge the puddles of stagnant water from another round of summer rain. Papaw would whip her butt if she got her new shoes dirty.

Well, not new exactly. As the youngest child, Fifi's wardrobe consisted of hand me downs from her brothers and sister. Papaw only bought her new clothes and shoes for church. She'd heard him tell her brothers that keeping her as shiny as a penny for church and raising her as a lady would go a long way towards acceptance.

One had practically rolled on the floor laughing. "They won't accept her. She's half-black, but even worse, born because Mama was—"

Their older brother had smacked the younger one. "Don't talk bad about Mama."

Fifi didn't remember her mother. She'd overdosed before Fifi's first birthday. All she had of Mama were a handful of pictures, all taken before her life fell apart. Her sister looked a lot like Mama, right down to the golden hair. People always went on about how she was the spitting image of Mama. No one said that about Fifi, but she'd seen pictures of Mama when she was ten years old, and Fifi did look like her, even if her skin was darker than her mother's.

Her sister's shrill voice rang in her head. Fifi was supposed to be helping her sister with chores, but the clear afternoon sky was too pretty not to enjoy. Fifi would hear about it later, but one of the boys would eventually say "Shut up." Papaw would wink at her and then start talking about running around barefoot on the family farm when he was her age.

Fifi hopped over a wide rut full of water and pushed her way through the waist-high ferns and yellow ragwort until she reached the big pond. She'd been craving catfish, and no one else could catch a big one but Fifi.

She kicked off her tennis shoes and socks. Fifi dipped a toe in the water, knowing it would be warm. The biggest catfish lived in the mud, and they had to be wrangled out of their hiding spots.

"What are you doing?"

Fifi dropped the bucket, the fillet knife almost rolling into the water. She grabbed it just in time. A rough hand grabbed her arm, pulling her to her feet. "Answer me."

Fifi shaded her eyes and looked up at her oldest brother. "I want catfish."

"Does Sis know you're out here?" Nathaniel crossed his muscular arms over his chest.

"She'll figure it out." Their sister tolerated Fifi at best. If she wasn't scolding her for something she did, she yelled at her about something Fifi had said.

"You know you aren't supposed to come out here alone," Nathaniel admonished.

Fifi studied her brother for a few moments. "Did you catch a skunk?"

Somebody snorted behind her. Fifi turned to see her brother's friend emerging from the ferns, a stinky joint between his lips. He was tall and wiry, and, according to Papaw, a troublemaker.

Fifi clapped her hand over her mouth. "He's not supposed to do that." She told her brother, "Neither are you."

Nathaniel smirked. "We won't tell your secret if you don't tell ours." He glanced at his friend. "Right?"

"Right." Jerod had been Nathaniel's friend for as long as she could remember. He was always nice to her. "Sure. I'm not a tattletale, anyway." She brushed past him and picked up the bucket.

"You aren't supposed to go in the water without anyone here," Nathaniel shouted.

She turned around. "You're here, dummy."

"Hey, Fi." Jerod and Nathaniel shed their shoes and rolled up their jeans before following her into the muddy water. Jerod caught up with her first. "I heard about what happened."

Her skin felt hot from the inside. "I don't want to talk about it."

"What happened?" Nathaniel hadn't lived at home for a while. "I just got home. What's going on?"

Jerod pushed his hair out of his face. "That miserable, red-headed Clegg kid threw a rock at her yesterday. Everett gave the kid a black eye."

Fifi touched the goose egg beneath her corkscrew curls. "I didn't even do anything, but he said I walked too close to their car."

Nathaniel's nostrils flared like they always did when he got angry. "Those inbred morons aren't worth the time and energy."

"Everett got in trouble," Fifi said. "Even though I fell right down in the dirt. Papaw whipped him."

Anger flashed in Nathaniel's eyes. "I'm sure he did." He took a deep breath before he said anything else. "But violence isn't the answer, right?"

Fifi watched Jerod smoke the joint. "He didn't care about that. Papaw said we couldn't expect people to change their values just because Mama did." Fifi hated how differently Papaw treated her when other people were around. She was allowed to have an opinion and fun at home, but not in public. She was to make herself small and unnoticeable. Papaw said that was the best way to make people leave her alone.

"After all," he'd said. "You didn't choose to be half-black."

Jerod patted her head. "Our little secret, right?"

"Right."

Nikki decided to check in with Garcia before she left the building. Her mind was racing with everything they'd found. Two more victims, which made four in total. And they'd only been looking for a few hours. She was scared at what else they might find. She knocked on Garcia's closed door, willing icy-blue eyes out of her mind.

"Come in."

Nikki was surprised to see Garcia sitting at his large desk in just his dress shirt and tie. Garcia always wore his suit jacket. He'd opened the top button of his shirt and loosened his tie, his feet propped on his desk. Nikki half-expected to see a decanter of whisky in his office.

"We may have found additional victims."

Garcia looked out of his window while Nikki told him everything they'd learned today. "Unbelievable," he finally said.

"I know," Nikki agreed.

Garcia's feet smacked the floor as he sat up. He looked at her sympathetically. "You know you can't feel guilty, Nicole. Hindsight's twenty/twenty. For what it's worth, I think you made the right decision. Any other woman in your position would have done the same. That's what mothers do—protect their babies, at all costs."

Nikki swallowed the lump of emotion in her throat. "Thanks for not judging me. I didn't expect that."

"Have I been that much of monster so far?" A smile played at the corners of his mouth.

"Not at all." Nikki returned the smile. "I admit, when I heard you were going to take Hernandez's position, I wasn't happy. We didn't see eye to eye much back at the FBI Academy."

"We were different people," Garcia said. "Kids, really. And like most of the other students, I resented you for Elwood bringing you into the closed program. Seems so stupid now." He leaned forward, compassion in his eyes. "Think of all the families you've brought justice to, Nikki. You can't be Superwoman no matter how hard you try."

"But I'm expected to try," she reminded him. "Women in law enforcement—and just about any other male-dominated field—have to be nearly perfect in order to be seen, even today. Having a kid does add to the pressure, but women without kids are simultaneously lauded for work performance and heavily criticized for choosing not to have a child."

"You're held to a higher standard," Garcia agreed. "It's not fair. But if it's any consolation, you've exceeded every standard set."

Nikki thanked him for the surprising support. "You don't have children, do you, sir?"

"Nope." He shrugged. "I'm too selfish to split my time between career and family."

"Nothing wrong with that." Nikki turned to leave. "Takes a lot to admit though, I'm sure." She flushed, suddenly feeling exposed. Garcia's positive attitude always surprised her. He hadn't been known as the nice guy at the FBI Academy.

"Go home and enjoy your family, Nikki," Garcia said.

Before she left for the day, Nikki stopped on the fourth floor. Nikki waited for Courtney to open the doors to the biometrics lab. The labs were interconnected, with the exception of ballistics, which operated in a separate building, and, like the rest of the building, you needed a key card to open the door. Only a handful of people could access every room on the floor, and technicians' key cards helped make sure rules had been followed and no evidence compromised.

The antiseptic smell in the lab made Nikki's eyes water. Courtney oversaw both biometrics labs, which included any biological evidence that needed to be tested.

Courtney barely glanced up from her work. "Did you and Liam find any other victims beyond the two you already emailed me about?"

Nikki shook her head. "That doesn't mean there aren't any. Lots of open country in the northern part of the country. Plus Canada. Liam's waiting for access to their system," she added.

"Good plan considering the lack of physical evidence," Courtney said.

"I've been thinking about that," Nikki said. "Can you have Arim look for specific minerals on her body?"

"I can, but I assume the fingernails indicate he's learned from that particular mistake. We're not going to find his new base that way again."

"Might help us narrow down a geographic area, at least."

Courtney looked unconvinced. "I'll tell Arim, but don't get your hopes up. If he's the same guy... doesn't that mean he's likely perfected his process?"

"Everyone makes mistakes." Melissa's cheery voice startled them both. Nikki hadn't realized she'd entered the lab. "Even the smartest serial killers. Look at Bundy."

Nikki resisted the urge to tell her that Bundy was no genius but had succeeded with his charm, guile and the overall naivety about serial murderers. "They do," she agreed. "We just need to be ready to take advantage when they do so."

"This is about the woman in the front yard in Stillwater, right?" A hint of awe colored Melissa's tone.

"She can't talk about active cases," Courtney answered. "I thought you were leaving for the day?"

Melissa smiled. "I forgot my badge. Kind of hard to get on the elevator without it, right? I'll see you tomorrow, Doctor Hart. Good night, Agent Hunt."

"She's sweet and smart," Courtney said once Melissa had left. "But way too cheery. I almost look forward to her becoming jaded."

"No biological evidence from this morning at all?" Nikki asked.

"No biological evidence," Courtney answered. "We did get a couple of fibers out from in between her toes, along with soil from her toenails."

Nikki thought about what she'd said. "Barefoot, her feet digging into something?"

"Maybe," Courtney said. "Arim is going to test everything for particulates. He should be able to figure out what the killer used to clean her off—which is another reason I wouldn't hold out hope for specific minerals. No fingerprints or shoeprints, no hair or anything we could test for biological markers."

"Maybe I'm wrong," Nikki said.

"Maybe." Courtney started cleaning one of the microscopes. "Have you thought about calling Anita?"

The thought made Nikki's legs weak.

Mariah's friends said the man who had been driving Zebulan's car had been friendly with her, that he and Mariah talked for hours at a time. Now she was reviewing the case again, and knew that Johnny Trent wasn't Mariah's killer, it made Nikki wonder if Mariah had a close relationship with the man who took her life. Had she trusted him? Her friends had said he was the only customer she'd treat like anything other than a trick. And then Nikki had a horrible realization. "He could be the father of Mariah's daughter."

"What?" Courtney replied, shocked.

"If he was the focus of all of her time at work in the year before her disappearance. Perhaps they were in a relationship."

"But didn't you say that Mariah's friends claimed they never had sex?"

"She might have kept that from them..." Nikki countered. It was a horrifying idea. But it fit. It could have been the start of his focus on postpartum women. Mariah could be the reason he became a killer. Did he know he was a father? Did he question her fidelity? Nikki's mind was all over the place.

"Well if I discover DNA on Kiania's body, we could certainly compare it to Mariah's daughter's DNA and find out."

Nikki doubted Courtney would find anything. He'd honed his skills too long to make that kind of mistake. And she wasn't sure if she wanted to know. Or ask Anita questions that might make her theory clear to the woman. She didn't want to upset her.

Courtney glanced at Nikki. "Are you worried about him going after Lacey?"

Nikki's stomach turned at the idea. "He's had plenty of opportunity to target my family. But I'll keep away from Rory and Lacey for a few days just in case. I'm heading home now to enjoy time with them while I can."

ELEVEN

Nikki had started to hate driving at night. She had good vision, but she'd noticed the stoplights sometimes looked a little streaky. Courtney said she had an astigmatism and should go to the eye doctor, but Nikki refused. She was not ready for middle-aged glasses.

Growing up, both Nikki and Rory's homes on McKusick Road west of Stillwater had been decidedly rural. Now, the city stretched west, hoovering up farmland left and right.

She took the long way, bypassing the now abandoned farm-house where she'd lived until her parents' murders. When Nikki first moved back to Stillwater, the house had been rented, but the tenants had since left and now the property, along with the sixty acres of old cornfields, had gone up for sale. Once it was purchased and turned into another subdivision, Rory's house—the house he and Mark had grown up in—would be the next to receive pressure to sell. His family property was double the size of her parents', and a local farmer currently rented the majority of the acreage to plant his corn.

The clouds shifted, allowing the moon to shine through.

Most of the remaining cornfields had been harvested, their empty stalks ghostly in the murky night.

Rory's property was adjacent to Nikki's former place, and she and his older brother, Mark, had run in the same social circles as teenagers. Rory was a few years younger, but Mark usually let him tag along.

Nikki turned into the driveway, her new tires crunching the gravel. The maple trees in the front yard had lost the last of their stunning red foliage, and the yard was covered in dried, red leaves. Nikki loved the wild look of fall. Her late ex-husband had been fastidious about raking the leaves, but Nikki had grown up in the country, where the fallen leaves were left scattered across the ground. It wasn't fall without leaves blowing in your face.

Rory had put new, slate gray siding on the split-level house this summer, as well as a new front patio. Nikki, Lacey, and Rory's mother, Ruth, had planted fall bulbs and shrubs along the stone. The nearby butterfly tree they'd planted for Lacey's late father two summers ago had grown like a weed this year, according to Ruth. Rory had already prepared the plants and rest of the yard for winter, and Nikki missed seeing the pretty bush surrounded by monarch butterflies.

She parked her Jeep in the garage and then headed out to the large metal building where Rory stored equipment, along with the boat and snowmobile. Light streamed out from the open door. Lacey's giggle lightened Nikki's heart for a few moments.

Her daughter stood on a stepstool next to Rory's big, white work truck, wearing one of Rory's old work shirts. The baggy shirt hung to her knees, just brushing the top of the muck boots Rory had bought her so she could help him with stuff without worrying about her shoes getting ruined. "Is she changing the oil?"

Rory leaned against the front of the truck. "It's never too early to learn how to take care of your vehicle, babe."

Lacey had been so focused on her task she must not have seen Nikki arrive. She turned and grinned. Surprisingly, she'd gotten most of the oil into the truck instead of on her shirt. "Hi, Mom! How was your day?"

"Long." Nikki walked over and kissed the top of Lacey's head, breathing in the sweet scent of her hair. "But seeing you guys makes it better."

Rory's older brother, Mark, stood next to him in front of the truck. "I just want to say I'm the responsible one. I thought of the T-shirt."

Rory rolled his eyes, and Nikki laughed. "Did you guys eat yet?"

"Uncle Mark brought Joseph's." Lacey rubbed her belly. "I think I ate my weight in pasta."

"There's a plate for you in the microwave," Rory told Nikki. "Ready to heat up."

Nikki's stomach growled, reminding her she hadn't eaten since lunch. "Lace, you want to come in and clean up while I eat?"

Lacey made a face. "I kinda wanna finish my job."

Nikki almost laughed at her serious face. "Okay." She looked at her husband. "Walk me to the house."

Rory followed her out of the barn. He slid a strong arm around her shoulders. "Bad day?"

Out of nowhere the dam broke. Nikki buried her face in his neck and sobbed.

"Jesus." Rory wrapped both arms around her. "You want to talk about it?"

Nikki wiped the tears off her cheeks. "Yes, but you guys finish up. I'll get some food in me and then we'll talk."

Nearly an hour later, with Lacey bathed and settled in front of the television to watch *A Bug's Life* for the nine hundredth time, Nikki, Mark and Rory sat down at the kitchen table.

"I'm guessing this is about the woman on the news." Mark looked at his brother. "The body was left with Halloween decorations on someone's yard. I told you earlier I bet Nikki would have to deal with that one."

"I think the killer I almost caught before I left Quantico is responsible," Nikki said.

The brothers stared at her for a moment before Rory broke the silence. "Can you repeat that?"

Nikki gave them the abbreviated version of 2014. "The agent assigned to follow up believed the North Carolina police had the right man. I should have followed up myself."

"No way," Mark said. "If another agent can't do their job, that's not on you. Sounds like you're the only one who gave a damn about that poor girl."

Nikki's throat ached. "I don't regret letting him go." She looked into the living room to make sure Lacey's attention was still on the television show. "I don't think I could have forgiven myself if I'd miscarried again. I was allowed back in the field for a couple of months before maternity leave, but I was afraid. I should have done my due diligence, but I was afraid the stress would be too much for me."

Rory took her hand. "Stop. You can't change your decisions now. Are you guys sure?"

"I am. So is Courtney. Miller isn't so convinced." She rubbed her temples. "I'm glad he's questioning it, honestly. We need to look at every single angle. And if it's not the man from Appalachia, he's still a serial killer. No one does what he did their first time. We can't let him get away."

"Don't worry about Lacey," Rory said. "You know Mom and Dad love having her. And I can try to leave early a couple of nights—"

"You can't do that," Nikki cut him off. "I don't think he would do anything to her"—she lowered her voice—"but I can't take that risk. Mark, how is your schedule this week? I hate to ask, but I don't want to put your parents in the position of having to protect her if something did happen. It won't," she reassured them—and herself.

During his incarceration, Mark had learned to weld and since his exoneration, he'd apprenticed further and started working for Rory. He'd also started volunteering at a nonprofit that helped ex-cons find jobs.

"I can pick her up," Mark said. "And take her to school if you need me to. The security system we put in at Mom and Dad's is top-notch, but I'll stay in the main house if she spends the night."

A multimillion-dollar settlement for his wrongful imprisonment had allowed him to buy his parents a new house in a gated community. He lived in the guest house, close enough to help his parents out.

After she'd tucked Lacey into bed and watched her little girl sleep for a few minutes, Nikki went into the guest room across the hall. Rory had turned it into an office for Nikki so she could have a private place to work on her most gruesome cases without worrying about Lacey accidentally seeing them.

They'd taken her father's heavy, mahogany desk out of storage and set it under the window so she could see the bird feeders, as though she ever worked in the room any time it wasn't dark outside.

She opened her notebook and started reading the profile she and Liam had worked up this morning but found herself going to this morning's crime scene photos and comparing them to Mariah's from 2014, hoping to see something that changed her mind about the direction this case was heading.

A Minneapolis number flashed on her phone screen. "This is Agent Hunt."

"Agent Hunt, it's Detective Brenner, from Minneapolis PD. I heard you were at the scene today. Do you have a minute?"

"Of course," Nikki said. "I was just thinking about Kiania. Do you have any leads?"

"No," Brenner answered. "The neighbors have alibis; there's no evidence the killer went into the house."

"Nothing from CCTV?"

"Not so far," Brenner said. "When Kiania first disappeared, her husband was the prime suspect. They'd been arguing; he wasn't forthcoming about a couple of things at first. I wasn't ready to cross him off my list. Until today."

"You don't think he's capable of doing that to his wife?" Nikki asked.

"No," Brenner said flatly. "And I also don't think this looks like a domestic homicide."

Nikki didn't want to lead Brenner to any conclusions. "What about Chen and Miller?"

"Miller said it's my case." Brenner didn't hide her irritation. "And Stillwater PD's. He said it's not Washington County's problem until something happens outside Stillwater city limits."

Nikki took a few seconds to digest what she'd said. Miller didn't usually use jurisdiction to avoid a case. "Did Chen defer to you as primary?"

"Yeah," Brenner said. "There's a lot of things that bother me about this case, but Kiania's body being left three houses down from her own makes no sense to me. Ty had to go back to work or lose his job. He switched to nights so his mother could help out with Willow."

"Where does he work?" Nikki understood businesses had to run, and Kiania had been missing for over three weeks. Unless they had disposable income, Ty hadn't had a choice.

"He works for a distributor, either in the warehouse or on a route," Brenner answered. "Fortunately, his immediate superiors aren't as heartless as the company itself. They've had him working in the warehouse, so he doesn't have to deal with the public. That's why his alibi for last night's strong. But leaving her body at a neighbor's just makes no sense to me."

"I think it was more about the location." Nikki kept the possible connection to Mariah to herself and explained her theory about the killer's decision to leave her at that exact house. "He can essentially sneak in from the back unnoticed because of the natural privacy the property has."

"That makes sense," Brenner said. "The ropes and brutality look like signature elements. The brutality tells me he's a sadistic bastard. Would you have time to meet me at the parking garage in the morning so I can show you where she was last seen?"

"Text me the location and time, and I'll be there," Nikki said. "I can do it in the morning before I go into the office if you're able."

As Nikki ended the call, her thoughts went to Miller and his attitude. The sheriff had to have something else on his plate. Nikki scrolled through her contacts until she found Miller's cell.

"It's late, Nikki." Miller rarely bothered with "hello," letting caller ID do that work. "What do you need?"

"I just spoke with Detective Brenner," Nikki answered. "She said the husband has an alibi for last night."

"Yep. Like I told her, it's her and Chen's case."

"Brenner asked me to help."

"Good," Miller said. "I don't have the resources right now. Did you tell her your theory about the serial killer coming back from the dead?"

"No reason to." Miller's flat attitude disturbed her. "Off topic, are you all right?" Nikki asked. "You seemed really on edge today."

"Because I don't agree with your serial killer theory?"

"Because you've been rude every time I spoke with you," Nikki snapped back.

"Look, I told Brenner she'd probably hear from you. Just don't go bugging the family with this serial killer stuff. Let Brenner handle them. They don't need to go through any more unnecessary pain."

"Excuse me?" Who was the person on the other side of the phone? She'd worked with Kent Miller on some dark cases over the last few years, and while they disagreed at times, he'd never outright dismissed her. He respected everyone as long as they treated him the same.

The only thing the sheriff refused to tolerate was racism, from anybody, toward any culture. He was the county's first black sheriff, but the Twin Cities area, and, to a lesser extent, Washington County, was a true cultural melting pot: large groups of Kenyan and Somali immigrants, along with the Hmong people of East Asia, as well as a large community of Mexican and Indian families. George Floyd's murder had ratcheted up the racial tension in the entire area, but Miller wouldn't tolerate it from law enforcement or citizens.

"Can we pause this discussion for a second," Nikki said. "Are you all right? Is something going on?"

"Just overworked and underpaid." Miller's attempt at sounding cheerful failed. "Just because you can't convince me this is the right thing doesn't mean something's wrong with me."

"Do you really think her murder looks domestic, Kent?" Nikki asked. "I've never seen that kind of damage on a body that wasn't a signature killer."

"Do you really think you're the only one capable of finding a killer?" he countered. "What makes you think they got it wrong? I guess everyone but you is just too dumb to see the rouse."

Nikki counted to ten before she spoke. During her first week at the FBI Academy, Nikki felt like a fish out of water.

Despite progress being made over the last decades, the ratio of
male to female agents still skewed heavily toward the men.
Anthony Hopkins's Hannibal Lecter in *The Silence of the
Lambs* had spawned a new fascination with serial killers and
the men and women who spent their lives chasing them down.
More and more potential agents wanted to work with the
Behavioral Analysis Unit. Elwood had become so overwhelmed
with applicants that he'd stopped accepting them for several
months. During that time, he'd recruited Nikki from the criminology program at Florida State University.

Elwood had warned her to expect some rankled classmates
but promised to try to keep his recruiting her quiet.

That had lasted less than two weeks. During that time, the
other students at the FBI Academy had largely ignored her
presence, but when the news spread that Nikki had been
brought in by the boss, the jealousy started. Her youth didn't
help, either. Everyone else accepted into that year's program
had been well into their thirties with law enforcement careers.

They say hell hath no fury like a scorned woman, but high-
achieving white men eclipsed by a woman are a far worse
bunch. Every time Nikki tried to answer a question during a
lecture, one of the men would talk over her, even if she'd been
called on. They actively worked to make her look physically
weak during various trainings, but their treatment only made
Nikki work harder.

The final straw happened not at class, but in the dorm, in
one of the coed study areas. Nikki and another female classmate
had been discussing the terrifying appeal of interviewing serial
killers.

One of her biggest tormentors butted in to their conversation. Chad had the cockiness of the star athlete and the condi-
tioning of one who'd gone to seed. "Please. Women don't have
the ability to sit there and listen to the worst horror imaginable
and still control their emotions. You can't show your disgust,

and women can't hide their emotional baggage." He smirked at
Nikki.

"You don't think I have emotional baggage?" she'd asked in a
deadly calm voice.

"No," he said. "I think you probably have some kind of
legacy at Florida State or pull in the academy for Elwood to take
an interest in you. You know how many guys way more qualified than you are being shut out of the program?"

"Not my problem," Nikki said.

"Don't worry," Owen, the oaf who hung on Chad's every
word, chimed in. "She's never even seen a crime scene. Let's see
if you can even handle that before we start considering serial
killer interviews."

Both men had laughed.

During much of her time at the University of Minnesota
and later at Florida State, Nikki didn't tell anyone about her
parents. A few people had recognized her name, but Elwood
had been the only person who knew the whole story before
Nikki even told it to him. After escaping Stillwater, the last
thing she wanted to be was the poor girl who lost her parents all
over again.

"When I was sixteen"—Nikki looked Owen directly in his
uneven eyes—"I discovered my parents murdered at home. My
mother was in the bedroom, raped, in a pool of her own blood
that dripped on the floor. My father had been taken down in my
own room."

The entire dorm had gone silent. "Bullshit," Chad finally
said.

"Walsh murders, Stillwater, MN, 1993. Look it up." She
stood to leave. "Try to think before you run your mouth next
time, Chad."

She'd vowed that day to never be intimidated or disre-
spected by a male counterpart again.

Nikki ended the call with Sheriff Miller before she said something she'd regret.

Before she went to bed, she stopped to check in on Lacey. Her daughter sprawled across the bed, her usual bevy of stuffed animals and dolls in bed with her. Lacey seemed more grown up by the day, but curled in her bed, her cheeks flushed, she still looked like the beautiful rainbow baby Nikki had brought home from the hospital.

She'd made the right decision in the woods that day.

TWELVE

Since Mark had offered to get Lacey to school, Nikki managed to leave the house by six a.m., hoping to avoid the worst of rush hour traffic. She'd made good time until taking the I-35 toward downtown Minneapolis. Traffic inched along for what seemed like hours before Nikki took the exit for HCMC and the stadium.

The Mississippi River cut through the heart of Minneapolis, with the University of Minnesota on the east side and the hospital and stadiums on the west. Kiania had last been seen in the parking garage on 7th Street, which served the Hyatt and Hennepin County Medical Center, along with other businesses in the area.

Nikki grabbed a parking ticket and then stuffed her sunglasses into the cup holder. Between the low ceilings and the tight space between each row, parking garages always ignited her claustrophobia. Nikki followed the line of traffic, resisting the urge to blow her horn at the silver-haired jerk in the GMC Silverado ahead of her as he backed into two parking spots, straddling the yellow line. The entitlement never ceased to amaze Nikki.

Kiania had parked on the roof, and the early morning meant only a handful of people had parked up here. A slim, blonde woman exited a blue sedan parked next to the stairwell exit and waved at Nikki. Brenner directed Nikki to a spot three down from her own.

"Good morning, Agent Hunt." Brenner offered her hand. "Sorry we're meeting again under these circumstances."

"Me too." Nikki hopped out of the Jeep, zipping her jacket all the way up against the brisk northeast wind. "How's your little boy?"

Brenner had been in the very early stages of her first pregnancy when they'd first worked together. She'd been nervous about the job, having just made detective. Nikki was glad to see she'd decided to stay with MPD.

"He's a holy terror, just like my little brother when he was little," Brenner answered. "Barely two, and he climbed up on the dining room table to reach the chandelier at my parents' house a few weeks ago."

Nikki laughed. "That sounds about right. Smart little guy too."

"My fiancé calls it resourceful." Brenner rolled her eyes and then pointed behind Nikki. "That must be Sergeant Chen. You've worked with him before?"

"Two missing little girls in Stillwater summer before last," Nikki said. "He went through it, but he's a good cop and easy to work with." As long as he hadn't caught whatever Miller had up his ass.

Chen parked his Stillwater police car a few spaces down from where they stood. He waved as he exited the vehicle. "Thanks for meeting with me, Detective Brenner. I'm anxious to see the area Kiania disappeared from." He nodded at Nikki. "I'm always glad Agent Hunt's around."

"Makes sense." Brenner walked to the next spot. "This is where Kiania parked on the night she disappeared. She had the day off, but she was called in to cover a shift. Thanks to the game, Kiania parked in this garage that day instead of her normal one."

Nikki hooked her thumb over her shoulder. "I assume that's the one between 6th and Portland? That's the employee parking for hospital staff, right? Don't they ticket people who park there during game days?"

Brenner nodded. "You know how it is down here on game days. People are inconsiderate as hell, and they don't care about getting a ticket as long as the car's still there after the game."

"Had she parked here before?"

"Her husband said this rooftop was Kiania's second choice, because it was rarely full during her shift, and she felt safer. We found her car here. Both driver's side tires were slashed." Brenner gestured to the camera mounted a few feet from where they stood. "That camera recorded Kiania arriving that day, but it was shattered when we came to look for her car."

"Husband was initially a suspect?" Chen asked.

"He was," Brenner said. "But he's got an alibi for last night. He does have a history of misdemeanor drug use, and Kiania had accused him of hitting her a couple of years ago, but she recanted. Her family thinks he's the devil and have insisted he did something to her."

"What do they think now?" Chen asked.

"They're grieving," Brenner answered. "Her brother doesn't agree, but they still think Ty took her. He just had help." She worried her lower lip. "Explaining what we know about homicides like this only upset them, so I didn't push it yesterday."

"You haven't had any leads?" Chen asked.

"The only lead we have came from a couple of transients," Brenner told her. "Both men are familiar to the uniforms in the area and aren't known for causing trouble. Jerry and Vernon—the witnesses—are kind of the de facto leaders of the community down here and saw the interaction between Kiania and Ty when he brought food for her outside the medical center the night she went missing. They argued and Kiania eventually threw up her hands and walked back inside without eating the food. Ty gave the food to Jerry and Vernon.

Chen wanted to look at the security videos with a fresh set of eyes, so he headed into the parking garage's security hub.

Normally, Nikki didn't call a possible suspect to ask for an interview. She'd learned through experience that the best way to throw someone off their game was to show up at home or work, unannounced. Surprise often made it more difficult to control their micro expressions, which made spotting a liar easier. After talking with Brenner about Kiania Watson's husband, Ty, Nikki broke her rule and asked the detective to call and see if she could stop by.

Ty Watson said he wasn't up for it at first. Thanks to an intense media presence, he and his daughter hadn't been home since Kiania's body was found. Local news only seemed interested in pointing the finger at Ty.

Brenner managed to convince him the FBI wasn't interested in railroading him but investigating a series of murders and Kiania may have been a victim of an experienced predator.

"Agent Hunt just wants to learn more about Kiania," Brenner said. "Understanding the victim's mindset and general life is a big part of finding their killer."

Ty had finally agreed, and Nikki put the address into the GPS. It alerted Nikki to exit the interstate at the same time a Smyth County, Virginia, number showed up on her touch screen.

"Deputy Horner, thanks for returning my call." Horner had been the deputy who'd tracked Nikki's path through the woods in 2014 and ultimately rescued her.

"Sorry I didn't get back to you yesterday," he responded. "I wanted to do some digging before I called. I wasn't aware that anyone had ever been arrested or blamed for Mariah Gonzales's murder."

"I appreciate it," Nikki answered. "A man named Johnny Trent was found dead in North Carolina, at a little park in a tiny county with barely any police or medical personnel."

"McDowell County," Horner clarified. "The windows were rolled up, and the vehicle was parked in an area with no shade."

Which guaranteed fast decomposition, making physical identification difficult. "No fingerprints?"

"Body was too far gone, at least for McDowell County's coroner. They don't have a lot of resources."

"Was the car hidden?" If her hunch turned out to be right, the killer had done his legwork, making sure to leave the car in a county that wouldn't be able to properly investigate.

"Nope," Horner answered. "Parked at a lake where people were known to fish pretty much daily."

"So guaranteed that it would be found, in a county with limited resources?"

"Right," Horner said. "I made some calls and found out that the body initially couldn't be identified because of decomp. They identified the body as that of the killer because the car belonged to Zebulan Wahlert, along with a bracelet and socks found inside that matched one Mariah had been wearing when she was taken. Later the man was identified as Johnny Trent." Horner sighed.

"How did he die?" Nikki understood the local police's limited capabilities, but what happened to the state and federal resources? How had so many people dropped the ball on this one?

"Well, the body was pretty decomposed," Horner said. "After I got your message, I called the county coroner out there. The local police deferred to the FBI agent who'd been sent to follow up while you were injured. He said not to waste the resources on the autopsy because they were backlogged and he was confident they had the right guy."

"Did they give you the agent's name?" Nikki wanted to know what agent could have been so careless as to not even speak with Horner and the others at the Smyth County Sheriff's Office. No one reporting to Elwood would have done something so careless. If she managed to connect more victims to Mariah's killer, she'd track down the agent who'd done the bare minimum and force him to share part of the guilt she now carried.

"I wrote it down," Horner answered. "Henry Garcia."

Nikki almost rear-ended the Mercedes stopped at the light in front of her. "Henry Garcia?" There could easily be more than one Henry Garcia at the Bureau. The Bureau was a massive entity, and Garcia's name wasn't an unusual one.

"Quantico. He told the North Carolina authorities he'd been sent by SSA Elwood."

Nikki's throat dried out. Garcia had to have recognized Mariah's name. His careless mistake had cost more women their lives, not Nikki's decision to choose her baby over the killer. No wonder he'd been so kind. Surely he knew it was only a matter of time before Nikki found out he'd been the one sent by Elwood.

"I was surprised you didn't say anything about that rock."

Horner's question stopped Nikki cold. "What rock?" She searched her foggy memory of that day, but most of the hours spent alone in the woods were just blurred images.

"When I got there, you were propped against the tree. You told me the killer must have cut himself on the rock when he slid down the mountain. You don't remember dragging yourself over there and securing the rock?"

"No." As she spoke, a memory flashed through her head, but Nikki couldn't manage to grasp it.

"You had it on the ground below your legs, protecting it

from the wind," Horner told her. "You asked me to put it in an evidence bag and get it to SSA Elwood."

"Did you?"

"I personally handed it to him when he came to see you at the hospital. You thought they could get a DNA sample off it. Elwood was afraid it was too porous, but he said he'd take it to the lab and have them check."

Nikki thanked Horner for his help. She didn't remember her conversation with Elwood, but if he'd said he would take it to the lab, then that's what he'd done. She prayed the rock hadn't been thrown out years ago.

Nikki needed to talk to Courtney as soon as possible. But Kiania's family had to come first. She'd pull Liam in when she confronted Garcia, because right now, Nikki wasn't sure she could keep from throttling the man.

THIRTEEN

Nikki tried to calm down as she drove. *Everyone makes mistakes. You've made mistakes, Nikki.*

"Yeah, but not like this." She spoke to the empty Jeep. "How many lives did his arrogance and laziness cost?"

What about Tyler?

"What about all the children left without mothers?" Her face burned with anger. Garcia must have recognized Mariah's name, and he surely would have remembered traveling for such a gruesome case. It didn't change what had happened to Kiania, but they'd at least have some kind of direction.

Or maybe they wouldn't. That wasn't Nikki's issue.

He should have told them yesterday, but he'd flat-out lied. How could they trust him?

She had to stop thinking about it for now. Ty Watson had agreed to speak with her despite his misgivings. She might not get another chance.

The GPS announced the Woodbury city limits at least a block before the welcome sign.

More than 75,000 people called the suburb of Woodbury home. The town descended from one of the congressional townships in Minnesota, after the United States government had forced the Native Americans onto reservations, and was named after Levi Woodbury, the first Supreme Court Justice to attend law school. Nikki turned left onto Tamica Watson's street. According to Brenner, Ty's mother had raised him alone, working as a teacher's aide while she earned her teaching degree. Her condo in the City Walk community of Woodbury was only a five-minute drive from the middle school where she worked.

Liam stood next to his parked Prius, the sun glinting off his red hair. She took a few seconds to regain her composure after what Deputy Horner had just told her. Telling Liam about Garcia would make them both angry and distracted while they were speaking to Kiania's husband. The news could wait.

Liam had spent his morning trying to contact the law enforcement agencies involved in the murders of the women in North Dakota and northern Michigan. "What did you find out?"

"Not much. Detroit police are sending me everything they have on Kara Smith, including the autopsy report."

"What about the North Dakota victim?"

"Only that her name is Audrey Ritter. I left a message for the county sheriff," Liam said. "What about you?"

"Kiania wasn't supposed to work that day," Nikki said. "A couple of homeless men saw Ty arguing with his wife. They're well known in the homeless community and spend a lot of time around HCMC. I want to know what else they may have seen. Brenner's having Minneapolis police track them down."

A heavier-set black woman with an impressive set of burgundy braids walked outside onto the porch. "If you're the press, this is a private neighborhood."

Nikki held up her badge. "I'm sorry to make him relive everything, but Detective Brenner called earlier and arranged for me to speak with Ty. Is he available?" She kept her tone light as they approached the woman. "I just want to hear about Kiania and the last week or two of her life. Are you Ms. Watson?"

Her face softened. "Call me Tamica. You aren't talking to him without me, and I'm recording it. My son would never harm Kiania."

"I believe you." Nikki wasn't always that candid with a potential suspect, but she didn't think Ty had murdered his wife.

"Come on, then."

They followed her into the townhouse. Tamica led them past the stairs and into the kitchen. A tall, lanky light-skinned man sat at the kitchen table, his eyes rimmed with red. "Ty, honey. The FBI agents are here."

He looked at them and nodded.

Tamica told them to sit down. Nikki introduced herself and Liam, but before they could ask Ty any questions, Tamica jumped in. "Kiania's family thinks a couple of past mistakes mean Ty could have done this to her. Absolutely not."

"I understand." She knew Tamica Watson had raised three kids as a single mother. Ty was the youngest, and his siblings' careers overshadowed his. His sister was a paralegal and his brother a sous chef at a popular St. Paul restaurant. Ty worked as a delivery driver most of the time, but he'd worked in warehouses as well. Brenner had warned Nikki that Ty had a chip on his shoulder.

"First let me say I'm very sorry for your loss," Nikki said. "Let's get the drug issue out of the way. I know you were busted as a juvenile for selling weed. I don't care."

Tamica and Ty looked surprised. "You don't? Everyone else seems to."

"I'm not going into details," Nikki said gently, "but this will still be hard to hear. Kiania's death was very violent. She was held captive for an undetermined amount of time before she was killed."

Ty dropped his head into his hands and sobbed. "Tell that to Kiania's family. They never liked me. Now they want me arrested for murder."

"Kiania's family is well off," Tamica said. "They didn't like his juvenile record or his blue-collar job. Kiania hadn't spoken to them in weeks because of their attitude towards him, right?"

Ty nodded.

"Is that the only reason they don't like you?" Nikki asked. "Did you give them a real reason too?"

"No, I didn't." Ty looked embarrassed. "We met at a club. I didn't think it was going to go anywhere, so I lied and told her I owned the delivery service instead of working for it. I told her the truth before we got married, but that somehow made me a permanent liar in her parents' eyes."

"Can you tell us about the last time you saw her?" Liam asked. "She wasn't supposed to work that day, right?"

"Yeah," Ty said. "We had a fight that day about her going into work on a Sunday. She was on call, but I'd already taken an extra shift. The hospital could have called someone else. Kiania always felt like she was the only one who could do her job, so she went to the hospital anyway, and I had to track down my mom to watch Willow so I could go to work."

Brenner had already emailed Ty's original statement to Nikki, along with subsequent follow-ups. His story had remained consistent. "Did you see her after she left for work?"

"I went on her lunch hour. Or supper, I guess," he said. "I do a lot of deliveries down there. She asked me to bring her something to eat."

"How long were you at the hospital?" Nikki already knew the parking garage footage showed Ty Watson arriving around 11 p.m. and not leaving for another fifty minutes.

"Not long," he said. "We started arguing again. She went

back inside and I turned my phone off. It wasn't till she didn't come home for hours that I realized something was wrong."

"Of course the police dragged their feet," Tamica said. "Adults go missing on purpose all the time, and it didn't seem to matter that Kiania would never leave that baby."

"Why did you spend so long in the parking garage, Ty?" Nikki asked. "Your vehicle was in the parking garage for nearly fifty-seven minutes that night, yet you only spoke to her briefly."

Ty's jaw clenched. His mother rolled her eyes and patted his arm. "Honey, just tell her. She's here for the truth."

"I was mad as hell," Ty said. "Kiania knows how to push my buttons. I knew I had to calm down before I drove." He looked away again.

"What did you do to calm down?" Liam asked.

"I vaped some OG Kush," he said flatly. "I know it's wrong. I didn't tell the police initially because I didn't want to lose my job. I haven't smoked since I was seventeen. At least, I hadn't. I took a couple of hits and fell asleep." He ran his hand over his closely cropped hair. "Like I said, no tolerance."

"Did Kiania mention anyone following her? Or someone in the parking garage that made her nervous?"

"Everyone in the parking garage made her nervous," Ty said. "She worked nights. The homeless come and go. Most are harmless, but there had been a few assaults. Not physical, like mugging."

"Did she have any issues with the homeless community in the garages?"

"She never told me about any, but I know there were a few she'd talk to in passing. They didn't make her nervous. Made me nervous, but she didn't listen."

"How long had she been back to work after maternity leave?" Liam asked.

"Few weeks." Ty's voice caught. "Willow is never going to know her mama."

Postpartum women seemed to be part of his signature. Nikki wondered if he'd found a way to hang around OBGYN offices without being noticed. She tried to think of a way to phrase the question without leading Ty and Tamica.

"Let's think about the places Kiania went in those last days," Nikki said.

"She went to work and came home," Ty said. "Going back to work was really hard for her, but she loves her job, too. Or did."

"How long after her six-week check-up did she go back to work?" Nikki tried to reference the OB's office without giving any more information. "I assume she followed up with her OB at that time?"

Ty nodded. "I took her to the six-week check-up. We brought the baby. The doctor's got a wall of photos of the kids he's delivered. We brought him one."

Nikki confirmed Kiania's OBGYN's location, along with the name of her doctor. "Is that in a big medical building? Are they in a suite?"

Ty nodded. "You know, I'd forgotten about it until now, but Kiania pointed out a grounds worker that had always given her the creeps. He was doing something outside when we left, so we had to walk right by him."

"Did she tell you why he gave her the creeps?" Nikki kept her poker face, hoping her strategy was about to pay off.

"She just thought he looked at women weird."

"Do you remember anything about this guy?" Liam asked. "Height, skin color, tattoos?"

"He was medium height and pale as hell," Ty answered. "I remember his shaved head—the sun glinted off it. He looked overheated."

"You remember what he was wearing?" Nikki asked. How could she phrase her question without leading Tamica and Ty? "What made you think he was a grounds guy?"

"He looked like a janitor, but Kiania had only ever seen him outside messing with the landscaping."

"Kiania worked for Hennepin County Healthcare," Nikki reminded Liam when they left. "Her obstetrician is located downtown in the HCMC Specialty Clinic. Have Kendall call and find out who they use for janitorial services. She needs to get a subpoena for the employee records, but make sure she asks about a medium height, bald employee who would have worked at the specialty clinic."

"I can do that," Liam said.

"No, I need you to come with me when I ask Garcia why the hell he didn't tell me that he was the agent who finished the case for me with the North Carolina police."

Liam stared at her. "You're kidding."

"I didn't want to tell you until we were done here." Nikki started her Jeep. "Deputy Horner from Smyth County called me on the way here. Garcia was the agent sent from Quantico."

Nikki quickly explained what Horner had told her. "He feels bad because he didn't follow up, but the sheriff told him to let the feds worry about it."

"Does Garcia know that you know?"

Nikki shook her head. "I waited for you. I need someone to keep me from killing him."

Liam took the news about as well as she had. He didn't have the guilt of countless more women's lives cut short weighing on his shoulders and could be somewhat more objective, but Garcia prided himself on keeping the office on task and out of the news. The hypocrisy hadn't been lost on either one of them.

"We might have a shot at getting the 2014 killer's DNA, if the evidence still exists."

FOURTEEN

Nikki and Liam walked into the FBI building together from their designated parking spots on the eight-acre campus. The drive in from Woodbury had given them both time to calm down.

"I did some research every time I got stuck at stoplights," Nikki said. "We need to call in at the lab and talk to Courtney first."

"If she had anything she would have called," Liam told her. "She'll be irritated."

"It's not about that." They both scanned their IDs to enter the employee entrance. "I want to know if she can test the rock that I found—if it still even exists." She walked to the elevator. "There's been a lot of advancements in testing since 2014. The M-Vac, originally created for food safety after the 2008 Ebola epidemic, extracts pathogens and does a much better job of sanitizing. Not long after, biological scientists realized it could be a useful tool for DNA extraction and created their own version of it. It helped solve a twenty-year-old crime by getting DNA from a rock, ironically."

"Do we have one?"

"I'm not sure," Nikki admitted. "They're pretty expensive. But as the main lab for the state, we should have one."

Nikki and Liam exited the elevator onto the fourth floor. They headed down the long corridor until they reached the DNA lab. Nikki pressed the button. "Court, it's us."

The door slid open, and they entered the sterile lab. Nikki always felt out of place among the scientists. Science aside, Nikki couldn't imagine being trapped in a fishbowl for eight hours a day. "Any luck getting biological evidence from Kiania's shirt?"

Courtney looked apologetic. "Nada."

Liam smiled at Melissa, his tall frame dwarfing her. "Agent Wilson."

Melissa nodded. "I'd offer you my hand, but gloves. Melissa Young, DNA lab technician."

Nikki couldn't wait any longer. "We might have Mariah's killer's DNA."

Courtney yanked off her magnifying glasses. "How?"

"He left blood on a rock when he came down the mountain. I guess I secured it and kept telling Deputy Horner to make sure it went to Elwood for DNA testing."

"Is it still there?" Courtney's eyes lit up. "I don't remember you ever mentioning it."

"I'm not sure," Nikki said. "I wanted to make sure the M-Vac was feasible before I called and asked Elwood to go in and look for it." She didn't want to ask her retired mentor to make the long drive from Georgetown to Quantico if testing wasn't possible.

"The first time an M-Vac was used on a rock was in early 2015. Less than a year after Mariah's murder." Courtney seemed to read her mind. "Don't start blaming yourself because you didn't remember the rock. You had a grade two concussion."

"That's what I keep telling myself," Nikki answered. "Do

you have an M-Vac? If you don't, we need to find an agency that has one."

Courtney's eyes danced. "I convinced Hernandez to spring for one before he left. I've been waiting for a chance to use it."

Melissa hovered at her elbow. "I didn't know we had this."

"Because we don't." Courtney's smile was friendly, but her tone was firm. "I have one. I'm the only one cleared to use it."

"How exactly does it work?" Liam asked.

"It's basically a wet vacuum," Courtney answered. "It's great for surfaces where swabbing and other normal methods can't get the job done." She looked at Nikki. "If the rock is still in evidence, I'll go to Quantico myself."

Courtney's high clearance should allow her to be accompanied by the ASAC to avoid issues with chain of custody. "As long as the ASAC signs off on you taking it and you come right back here, we should be good."

Nikki and Liam walked down the hall to Garcia's open office door. During the drive here, she'd thought about nothing else than what she wanted to say to him and how to do it without losing her job. Garcia sat at his desk, staring out of the window, oblivious to their presence. How could he sit there, knowing he should have spoken up yesterday? Did he think Nikki wouldn't find out?

She raised her fist to knock on the open door, but Garcia swiveled to face them. Instead of his usual semi-arrogant natural expression, Garcia looked like a beaten man. "I'm sorry, Nicole. I swear to God, I thought it was him."

She hadn't been prepared for this. Liam nudged her elbow, and they entered the office, taking the two chairs in front of his desk.

"Why?" Nikki kept her question simple. Garcia wasn't

perfect, but he also wasn't an incompetent agent. She wanted to hear his reasoning.

"The body was in terrible shape, first off," Garcia said. "His build and height matched the description, he was in the car owned by the dead homesteader, and had Mariah's bracelet, among other things."

"There were so many more details about the killer." She stared at Garcia. "I was face to face with him. I had eye color, skin tone."

"I missed that in the report," Garcia answered. "I'm not sure I read it thoroughly, to be honest."

"How could you not read it?" Liam demanded.

Garcia sat up straighter. "There's a reason I was sent here to keep you guys from allowing personal stuff to screw up your cases. I did it ten years ago, and I've done everything in my power to learn how not to do that. The hope was that I'd impart some of that wisdom on you."

"False hope," Nikki said. "We're human. It's impossible not to be emotionally involved."

"That's not exactly what I mean," Garcia said. "I was in the middle of a messy divorce. My wife became pregnant by another man." Pink rose in his cheeks. "I can't have children. So I knew she cheated. She said it was my fault, that I was never home, and she wasn't wrong. We were high school sweethearts." Garcia cleared his throat, his voice strained. "I didn't handle it very well. I dropped the ball in Mariah's case, and I'm more sorry than I can explain."

Nikki's anger faded away. Garcia was a proud man, and this couldn't be easy for him. As much as she wanted to sit in judgment, he hadn't done anything that she and Liam hadn't over the past couple of years.

"I know." The only way to fix it was to find the killer now. "We might have a chance at DNA."

"From yesterday's victim? I thought he took her fingernails and cleaned her."

"He did." Nikki explained about the rock. "I don't remember much of this, but Horner said that Elwood took it as evidence, with my statement that I'd seen the man leave blood on the rock. I'm going to call Elwood tonight."

"Can we get DNA?" Garcia asked. "Rocks are usually too porous."

"Courtney thinks she's got a good shot. The M-Vac was originally designed to test food safety, but it's modified to collect DNA from extremely difficult substances, including a rock. If the rock's still in evidence, she can go to Quantico and collect it, and our chain of command will be secure. I know you have to get it approved for the budget—"

"If Elwood has the rock and Courtney thinks she can get biological evidence from it, I'll pay for her flight and expenses out of my own pocket."

"We'll keep searching the databases for additional victims," Liam said.

"I'm afraid to know." Ever since visiting Ty, Nikki couldn't stop thinking about his anguish over Willow never knowing her mother. Losing her own mother at sixteen had been awful, but she'd had those years with her. How many other babies never got that chance?

There won't be any more. I will stop him this time.

FIFTEEN

"Thanks for picking up the pizza." Nikki washed her plate in the sink as Rory wrapped the leftover pieces in tin foil. "I'm not sure if I ate anything else today." Nikki hadn't gotten home until after Rory had dropped Lacey off at his parents' for the night. "She didn't ask any more questions?"

"She just wanted to make sure you got your rest." Rory broke down the cardboard box and put it into the recycling bin. "Is it just me, or does it feel like she's jumped to middle school instead of just the fourth grade?"

"I'm just grateful she still calls me 'mommy' sometimes." The kitchen was quiet without Lacey, but her trail of things was a constant reminder she'd be back soon. Lacey had always been good at entertaining herself, often carrying a cadre of toys and stuffed animals that wound up all over the house. This school year, Nikki had noticed fewer toys left out and more big girl things, like nail polish or clothes without sequins and butter-flies. "When I was her age, we still played with dolls and Barbies. I never heard of some of the adult stuff she picks up at school."

Nikki hated how old she sounded. "Now, a lot of girls her

age make fun of the ones who still want to be little kids."
Today's technology made it easy for kids to grow up way too
fast.

Nikki rinsed their plates and put them in the dishwasher.
Rory had remodeled much of his childhood home by the time
Nikki met him, but he'd surprised her with a kitchen update
after Lacey had gone back to school in September. Rory ran a
successful construction business, and he'd been able to put in
new tile, cabinets and countertops at his cost. When he'd started
ripping out cabinets, Nikki worried he'd end up like a lot of
other contractors too overwhelmed to work on their own places.
Mark and their dad had pitched in, and the project had been
done in under a week. She loved the sleek Dekton stone and
cherry cabinets. She was still getting used to the slide-out
shelves.

"Do I dare ask about your day?"

Nikki shrugged. "I'd like to hear more about the new foundation you laid today."

He laughed. "I bet." Rory massaged her shoulders. "I know
you can't say much, but you had that look in your eyes when
you got home."

Nikki leaned against his chest. "What look?"

"I'm not sure how to describe it," Rory answered. "It's a
cross between exhaustion and rage."

"That's not far off." Nikki turned around and leaned against
the counter. "Do I look like that a lot?"

"Only on the worst cases." His green eyes searched hers.
"Usually after a bad day. What'd you find out?"

Nikki's emotional side wanted to cry but opening that box
would lead to discussions she wasn't ready to have. "The
deputy who found me in the woods in Appalachia called
today." Nikki told Rory about the rock. "Even if we can't use it
in court, it's a starting point. Unfortunately, that wasn't the only
new information the deputy had. My boss was the agent who

agreed Johnny Trent had killed Mariah and recommended closing the case."

"Shouldn't Garcia have mentioned that by now?" Rory asked. "How long did you scream at him?"

"I didn't," Nikki answered. "It's not like I haven't made mistakes. He didn't try to make excuses. As much as I wanted to be mad, I couldn't be."

"I hope Courtney's idea works," Rory said. "Is the deputy bringing the rock to you?"

Nikki explained Elwood's possession of the rock. "It's possible Quantico purged the rock out of evidence a long time ago. I'm hoping Elwood managed to keep it secure somehow."

"The news is still saying the husband probably did it," Rory told her.

Nikki rolled her eyes. "They're wrong." Like Brenner and Chen, Nikki and Liam were confident Ty Watson had nothing to do with his wife's murder. "The sheriff's the only one I haven't had an actual conversation with since Kiania's body was found, but I don't think Kent would disagree the husband isn't our killer."

Rory grabbed two bottles of beer from the fridge and handed her one. Nikki twisted off the top and took a long pull.

"You don't sound very happy with Miller," Rory said.

"I'm not mad," she countered. "He's not acting like himself, but I'm sure he's got his reasons."

Rory's eyes lit up. "Shit, I forgot to tell you. Mom and Dad went to lunch downtown a few days ago and saw Miller and his wife. They were going to say hi, but Mom said it looked like the Millers were having a pretty intense conversation. His wife walked out before he paid the bill."

Miller and his wife had been together since college, and both of their girls went to Stillwater High School. Nikki hoped Kent and his wife weren't having problems. "It's probably work-related." Miller spent much of his time as sheriff dealing with bureaucratic issues. He'd been appointed as interim sheriff five years ago and re-elected the next election cycle, so he not only had to answer to the public but the mayor, city council and who knew who else.

"He spends so much time putting out fires," Nikki said. "So does Garcia, and Hernandez, too. That's why I know I never want to be an ASAC like Garcia."

"It might be better hours," Rory said. "But you'd go stir-crazy not being in the field."

"It was hard for Elwood." Nikki checked her watch. "Speaking of, I'm going to call him about the rock." She stood on tiptoes to kiss Rory. "Thanks for listening, even if I couldn't tell you everything."

Nikki closed the door to her home office and scrolled through her contacts until she found Elwood. He'd retired several years ago, but he still lived near Quantico and often lectured at the FBI Academy.

Virginia was an hour ahead of Minnesota, but Nikki wasn't worried about Elwood being up after ten p.m. Decades of terrible things had made him a night owl that sometimes crossed over into an insomniac. She thought about just calling, but for some reason, Nikki wanted to see her mentor's face.

It didn't escape her that Elwood was around the age her father would have been if he hadn't been murdered. They'd talked more than once about that fact. Elwood never had children because he knew he was too committed to his job, too focused. He had tunnel vision. Fortunately, well into his career at the Bureau, Elwood had found a like-minded partner in his wife, Maisie. She'd worked as a trauma nurse at George Washington Hospital in D.C. and had seen her share of awful, so she understood Elwood's tendency to brood.

She hit the green icon for FaceTime and waited.

"Nicole, it's good to see your face." Elwood's kind blue eyes peered into the camera. His dark hair had gone fully gray, and she noticed a few more wrinkles on his face. He narrowed his eyes. "What's wrong?"

Nikki wasn't surprised by his reaction to her calling, or his quick response. She knew how much he still cared for her, and that Nikki would only call if it was important.

"Everything's fine," she reassured him. "I mean, I'm fine, Lacey's fine. Rory's fine, too."

Elwood raised an eyebrow and waited.

"Mariah Gonzales," Nikki said. "Do you remember her?"

"Of course," Elwood answered. "That case nearly killed you." Concern flashed through his eyes. "If I recall, he was found deceased in North Carolina somewhere. I had an agent go down there and confirm it."

"Garcia screwed up." Nikki told him what she'd learned from Jason Horner in Smyth County. "As soon as I saw Johnny Trent's photo, I knew it wasn't him. I should have followed up myself."

Elwood's white eyebrows knitted together. "What's brought this up now?"

"He told me he'd see me again someday," she reminded him. "I think that day has come."

Elwood listened in silence as Nikki went over the last two days' events and what little information they'd managed to learn. "We're trying to contact the North Dakota detective on that unsolved case. But I know I'm right."

She waited for Elwood to disagree, to tell her she'd misread things.

"My God," Elwood said.

"Jason Horner, the Smyth County deputy, is the one who found me."

"I remember," Elwood said. "I thought we were going to

have trouble finding you in the dark, but Horner's Cherokee heritage as a tracker took him right to you."

"I remember a fair amount from that day, but I'd forgotten him rescuing me. And I forgot about the rock with the killer's blood. Horner said I begged him to give it to you so it could be taken into evidence for testing, even though it was porous."

Elwood's eyes lit up with recognition. "We didn't have the equipment to get a good enough DNA sample from the rock, but the technology was just becoming available."

"Courtney, our Evidence Response lead and DNA specialist, thinks she could use an M-Vac to get a sample," Nikki said. "Is the rock in evidence at Quantico?" She held her breath, praying he'd say yes.

"Not exactly," he told her. "It's in the storage unit where I keep all the information from previous cases. I kept it in my office—in a sealed evidence bag, with chain of command clear—until we could either get the technology or the man was caught. I thought the latter had been the case."

Her hopes stalled. "We won't be able to use it in court. But we still need some kind of starting point. If it's there and we send Courtney out there, would you give it to her? She'll take care of the paperwork and all the chain of evidence stuff."

"Just tell me when she'll be here, and I'll meet her at the storage unit," Elwood answered. "But forget about the DNA for a minute. What's the profile?"

"White male, fair skin," she said. "Kiania Watson took her safety seriously, but he was able to catch her off guard. She wasn't supposed to be at work the night he took her. He stalks them, learns their routine."

Nikki described the very public area where Kiania's body had been found. "He wanted me to find her."

"Where were the flowers found on her body?"

"Secured inside her right hand with jute rope—the same type of rope used to bind Mariah in 2014."

"What other commonalities do these victims have?" Elwood asked.

"Postpartum," Nikki said. "I have a theory that Mariah might have known him. That her child, little Mira, is his biologically. I've been playing with the idea in my mind. What if he always questioned if he was really the father because of her... profession? What if that was the start of his obsession with postpartum women?"

Elwood considered the information. "The most important figure in a child's life until the age of six or seven is the mother," he said. "Nature versus nurture will always be an argument, but we know that kids deprived of love have emotional issues, including lack of empathy. Serious abuse, even mental, can create—in rare cases—a killer. What about geographical information?"

Nikki explained her theory that he might have grown up in Appalachia. "He moved too confidently through the mountains and rough terrain. Didn't even break a sweat. Perhaps he was from the area? Is that how he knew the cabin?"

"We know lust murders live in fantasy, usually violent porn," Elwood said. "Asphyxiation is up close and personal, but the violence of shaking her enough to snap a hyoid bone suggests hatred for women. Was Mariah's broken?"

"Our medical examiner is reviewing her autopsy information," Nikki said. "I have a vague memory of talking about Mariah's broken neck, but the concussion screwed my head up a lot more than I realized."

"You're right, she had a broken neck. What about the CCTV footage from the street where the last victim was found?"

"It's being studied, but there's no good shot of the yard. We're looking for a vehicle that comes back night after night, but it's a residential street. We have to rule out those vehicles first," she told Elwood. "He's got a means of travel large enough to incapacitate and hide a victim, and his movements at night suggest he could be a late shift worker. Like I said, Kiania took her security seriously. Video surveillance showed her getting on the elevator for the parking garage at 2:47 a.m. She already had a can of pepper spray in one hand and her car keys in the other. He either surprised her or had inserted himself in her life enough that she felt safe if he did approach her."

"You haven't mentioned what the sheriff thinks," Elwood said. "You two have a good working relationship. Have you gone through this with him?"

"Not exactly," Nikki told him. "He thinks Kiania's husband is a strong suspect, and if he didn't have an alibi, I might agree. Her husband's got a petty theft record and a misdemeanor drug bust almost seven years ago. Nothing violent."

"Have you spoken with him?"

"I have, and I believe him." Nikki worried the inside of her cheek. "But I know I can't be objective with this. What do you think?"

Elwood smiled at her. "I think you have the best instincts of anyone I've taught over the years. What's your gut say?"

"We need to find more victims, more connections. We need to look back into the original case. Into the car, Zebulan Wahlert and Johnny Trent," she said. "We're looking for similar murders in Canada as well, but their system is different so it's a bit of a slog."

"Why Canada?"

Nikki told him about the 2015 Detroit victim and the girl last year in North Dakota. "If those two victims were killed by the same person who killed Mariah, what better way to disappear? The 2015 victim lived about ten minutes away from the border. The victim in North Dakota was found farther south." She rubbed her temples. "How many other women has he killed? The number could be triple digits for all we know. Mariah wasn't his first, I'm sure of that. I can't allow another woman to die," Nikki said. "We have no way of knowing if he's got another victim already or is looking for her as we speak."

Elwood's expression had turned deadly serious. "You're forgetting about one potential victim, Nicole. Yourself. If you're right and this is the same man, he's had a decade to fantasize about catching you and doing what he wants. You need to take that seriously."

Nikki promised him that she would be careful. "I'll call you tomorrow when we know Courtney's timeline."

Nikki brushed her teeth before crawling into bed with Rory. He muted the ESPN highlights and put his arm out, drawing her to his chest. "How did it go?"

"He's got it in storage." Nikki felt weak with relief. At least they had a shot at getting a DNA profile. "Hopefully we can get Courtney on a plane in the next twenty-four hours." Nikki had emailed Liam, Garcia and Courtney before she'd come to bed. She'd also updated Brenner and Chen. But she couldn't bring herself to call Miller. "He basically told Minneapolis and Still-water police that Kiania wasn't his problem because she was found in city limits."

"But isn't that true?" Rory asked.

"Yeah, but Miller never refuses to help." Nikki justified her decision not to update the sheriff tonight—she'd tell him when he returned her calls. "Especially in unusual cases. He knows Kiania's husband didn't do this, and he's a good enough cop to know this is a signature. The MO doesn't have to be the same between victims. He knows that."

"What do you mean? I thought the signature was what the killer did to the victims. Isn't that also MO?"

"It's not that simple," Nikki told him. "Let's say you have two armed robbery cases where captives were forced to undress. One posed them in sexual positions and took photos. The other made the hostages undress so they would be too stressed to make a positive ID later. The first one is a signature because he didn't need to do it to rob the bank. It could cause him to get caught, but he had to do certain things in order to feel satisfied with the crime." Law enforcement pioneers had learned that a signature is unique to the individuals.

"So you can't figure out the signature until there are multiple murders?" Rory asked.

"Exactly. A killer's signature could evolve over time, but at its core, a signature is the ritual the killer has to go through in order to achieve satisfaction. Childhood fantasies riddled with violence and control usually morph into something worse. Not all of the monsters we fear are lurking under our beds become murderers, but there are ones who do."

SIXTEEN

Nikki dreamed about the dark, humid woods in Appalachia. She'd run and run, but every time she thought she was going to break through the tangle of trees and vines in the oppressive woods, Nikki was suddenly right back where she'd started. She'd slept in fits, falling back into the nightmare until she noticed the dawn peeking through the blinds.

She slipped out of bed. A long shower and hot breakfast managed to make her feel human enough to get ready for work. Instead of spending the forty-five-minute ride to the Bureau office in Brooklyn Park obsessing over the case, Nikki blasted her classic rock playlist. She needed to drown out the darkness for a while and at least try to enjoy the scenery. Most of the fall colors had faded, and a fine mist kept the windshield wipers on low, but at least she was present and not lost in the past.

Nikki managed to keep from losing her cool in traffic all the way to work. She sat in the Jeep for a few minutes, just breathing. She could not let this case eat her alive.

If she did, the murders would continue.

. . .

Hands full with coffee for herself and Courtney, Nikki knocked her elbow on the DNA lab window. Most of the lab was still dark, but Courtney's office light was on. She popped her head around the corner and waved. Moments later, she joined Nikki in the hall. "Which one's mine?"

"Americano with an extra shot and no flavor." Nikki handed the cup to Courtney. "Earliest flight into D.C. is tomorrow at ten thirty a.m. I'll pick you up by seven thirty."

"Did you put me in the exit row?" Courtney asked as they walked onto the elevator.

Nikki pressed the button marked "5." "Yep. And Garcia's reimbursing me."

Courtney snickered. "God, he must feel guilty."

"He does," Nikki agreed. "I wanted to be mad as hell, but it was obvious his feelings were genuine."

"How'd Elwood take it?" Courtney asked.

"He feels bad," Nikki said. "Not that it's anyone's fault but the D.C. police, who didn't investigate Mariah's case properly in the first place. And mine," she admitted. "I should have followed up."

"You did, and the case was closed," Courtney said. "You had no reason to question the North Carolina police or the FBI agent sent in your place. And you had a new baby." She nodded at Kendall and Jim as they entered the Violent Crime bullpen. "God, that woman is stunning without makeup," she whispered to Nikki.

"I know," Nikki said. "She's smart, too."

Courtney nudged Liam's desk with her toe. "Once you're done stuffing that breakfast burrito in your mouth, meeting in Garcia's office."

He grunted, grabbed his notebook and pen and followed them to Garcia's corner office.

His door was already open. Garcia sat at his desk, looking like he hadn't shaved. He directed Liam to grab a third chair. Once all three had settled, Nikki told Garcia the news.

"Elwood did keep the rock in a secure evidence bag." Nikki had been dreading the next part. She hoped Garcia would still let Courtney retrieve the rock. "But there's a catch. Elwood tagged the rock, but once the case was solved, he removed it from evidence. It's in his storage unit."

Garcia rolled his eyes to the ceiling. "Why? That completely destroys chain of command."

"Because he trusted your opinion," Nikki reminded him.

He looked at her for a beat, anger briefly sparking in his eyes. "Right. He might have tagged it as evidence, but without officially entering it as evidence, we can't use it in court."

"No, but it could still give us a suspect," Nikki said. "We have to start somewhere, and this is still our best chance at solid information at this point."

"If he's in CODIS," Garcia said. "He didn't leave any physical evidence on her body. We don't have anything to compare the sample to if Courtney's able to extract it. We can't pin him for Kiania's murder. Or Mariah's."

Nikki sighed. "We might be able to tie him to Mariah. We have reason to believe he might be the father of Mariah's child, Mira. I'm intending to visit her and get a DNA sample for comparison. It could give us a motive."

Garcia looked appalled. Nikki knew he was thinking of poor Mariah.

Nikki looked at Courtney. "Anita still lives in the area. I just hope she's got something of her granddaughter's so we don't have to ask the poor girl for a swab. Anita might want to keep this detail from Mira."

"She worked for the Bureau, right?" Garcia asked, unlocking his computer. "Any idea where?"

"She was an analyst at the Annandale Bureau when Mariah was killed."

Garcia entered the information. "Still employed, close to thirty years. She's the head analyst in her department now."

"All I need is a hair follicle," Courtney said. "What about the physical evidence from Mariah's murder? She had rope on her wrists still, right?"

"On her ankles," Nikki said. "Why?"

"The M-Vac works on a lot of items you might not think of. We can test the nylon restraints left on Kiania, but I wouldn't count on much from them. We haven't found a shred of DNA anywhere else on her body, so he likely wore gloves. The M-Vac has been successfully used on nylon knots. Is there any chance the D.C. police would still have Mariah's? That would give us another possible source of DNA."

"I don't know," Nikki said. "The case never went to court, but it was closed. If they got rid of it, it probably would have been destroyed."

"Why don't you call the D.C. Metro precinct who handled the murder and see if they've got the evidence?" Garcia asked.

Courtney choked back a laugh. "Nikki and the police on the case didn't end up on good terms. If her name's mentioned, they won't help."

"That seems extremely unprofessional." Garcia looked at Nikki. "Is she right?"

Nikki wasn't proud of the way she'd handled things in 2014. And she couldn't blame it all on pregnancy hormones. "Probably."

"Call Nash," Liam said. "He's in D.C. now, working in counterintelligence. He could track the evidence down for you."

Agent Justin Nash and Nikki's history dated back to the academy and hadn't always been cordial. They'd reconnected a few years ago when Nikki investigated a kidnapping.

"That's our best chance in terms of using any evidence from

Mariah at trial," Courtney said. "Hopefully he's able to work some magic by the time I get to D.C."

"Fingers crossed," Nikki answered. "Blanchard should have preliminary autopsy results for Kiania Watson today," Nikki reminded the group. "I'm going to have her review Mariah's autopsy, too."

Garcia raised a dark eyebrow. "You'll have to get a copy from the D.C. medical examiner, and that's going to take some time."

"I have a copy of the initial report," Nikki said. "Complete with pictures. I was never able to throw it away." She'd always believed her guilt at the way she treated Mariah kept her from tossing the file, but now she understood that somewhere in the back of her mind, Nikki had known Mariah's murder hadn't been solved.

"How certain are you about the postpartum theory?" Garcia asked.

"I don't think it's a theory, I think it's part of his signature. He told me he didn't mess with pregnant women, and every victim we know of was postpartum. That's not like having a preference for brown hair parted down the middle," she said.

"No," Garcia admitted. "How's it tie into his signature?"

"The signature is essentially the ritual he goes through to ultimately find release, often when the victim isn't present," she explained. "That usually starts with choosing the victim. There's a pathological connection to a postpartum victim, I'm certain. I just don't know what it is yet."

"We know he wanted your attention with Kiania," Liam said. "I'm worried about what he'll do to keep it, especially with the media still talking about Ty Watson somehow being involved."

"So am I." Garcia looked at Nikki. "If we have this information and don't release it, and another woman is taken, the Bureau isn't going to look good."

"You mean you won't." Nikki couldn't stop the words from coming out. Liam nudged her foot.

"No, I won't," Garcia admitted. "But ultimately, the reflection is on the Bureau and this office doesn't need any more bad publicity. Media is already reporting you're working the case. That alone is enough to put us under a microscope. I'm going to draft a statement warning that one theory we are pursuing is a killer targeting postpartum women."

"That could cause panic," Courtney said.

"Not to mention let him know we're closer than he thinks," Liam added.

Nikki told the group about her brief conversation with Miller the night before. "He's not going to be happy about the serial killer theory getting out."

"I don't care," Garcia said. "He told Brenner this was her case, and she's asked for your help."

"I know, but Kent's a good guy," Nikki said. "I don't want to burn bridges with the Washington County sheriff."

"I'll take the heat with Miller," Garcia said. "And I will make it clear in the statement that this is just a theory, and there is no reason to panic. The Assistant Special Agent in Charge feels it's in the public's best interest to let women know we are investigating this, and until we can eliminate the possibility, we urge them to remain alert to their surroundings."

Liam looked at her. "Nikki, are you truly okay with this? Putting something out like this is a hell of a gamble. People are going to be angry, especially if we turn out to be wrong."

"That's on me," Garcia assured him. "I'd rather risk having to admit a mistake than have more blood on my hands."

"It's a massive one," Nikki agreed, her eyes on Garcia. Despite its self-interest, she understood Garcia's feelings. "But I think it's worth it. This tells him I've seen the messages he's been leaving me. The flowers. Perhaps that will stop him taking another life. Or consider a trade."

"Trade?" Liam and Courtney both asked the question.

"I'm not saying I will swap places with a victim," Nikki assured them. "I'm saying putting the information out there gives us the option to let him think I'm willing to negotiate. And we might be able to save the next victim. But Liam's right about Miller."

"That's fine," Garcia said. "He and Chen can work their leads and we'll work ours. That's just good investigative work."

SEVENTEEN

Nikki had first met Justin Nash as a young recruit at Quantico. Nash was only a year ahead of her, but since his grandfather had been one of the FBI's first black agents, he carried clout the other recruits didn't. During their time at the academy, she and Nash had gone out a few times and had fun, but it was never anything serious. Nash had gone on to work at the Maryland field office before eventually ending up in the Midwest. A few years ago, he'd contacted Nikki for help on a case that turned out to be bigger and darker than anyone had suspected.

She tried his cell phone first.

"Nikki Hunt, how are you?" Nash answered.

"Pretty good," she said. "I heard you're back in D.C.?"

"Yeah," Nash said. "Joyce was offered a job out here, and I was lucky the Bureau let me transfer."

"How's she doing?"

"Great," Nash said. "We both love the pace of D.C., and there's endless things to do, you know. How are things there?"

After a few minutes of catching up, Nikki told him why she'd called.

"I can't believe Henry Garcia made that kind of error," Nash said. "He's meticulous about details. That's why he's a good ASAC."

"His wife had left him," Nikki said. "I don't exactly have room to lecture about letting personal life affect work."

"I'm sure he's much happier being out of the closet, anyway."

Nikki stared at her dark computer screen. So that was why his marriage had ended. She didn't want to pry, but this did explain why he didn't want to elaborate on what happened.

"The only reason I know is because a good friend of mine works at Garcia's last Bureau office," Nash said, clearly understanding Nikki's silence was shock.

"He's only been here a few months," Nikki said. "We haven't really talked about our personal lives. He certainly isn't obligated to tell me." Nikki wondered if Garcia had decided to feel out the office first or if he was keeping his personal life private to set an example.

"Don't say anything," Nash said.

"I won't," Nikki assured him. "It's not my place to ask. But my original point still holds—we've all let personal stuff in at one time or the other. And Garcia was completely crushed when I told him."

"I bet," Nash said. "That kind of mistake haunts a person. I assume you're calling to ask for my help?"

"Yeah," Nikki said. "We want to get the evidence from Mariah Gonzales's case, but Detective Sergeant Johnson is now captain. He'll never let anyone check it out if he knows I'm involved."

"So it's true?" Nash asked. "The story about you coming in and chewing him out in front of officers actually happened?"

Nikki wasn't proud of it. "Mariah's mother had told me how dismissive he was about Mariah's death, because she'd been a prostitute. Any fool with training could see that wasn't a first-time killer."

That still didn't excuse the way she'd gone off on Johnson, especially in front of others. She'd already felt guilty for the way she'd spoken to Mariah at the clinic, and learning about her death had been more crushing than Nikki could have anticipated. Aided by stress and pregnancy hormones, she'd lashed out. "Johnson completely mishandled the case," she told Nash. "But I still went in and apologized after I came back from maternity leave."

"Johnson's old guard, right?" Nash asked. "I'm pulling up the district's website. Oh yeah, he's close to retirement. I bet a woman dressing him down went over real well."

Nikki snickered. "It did not, but I learned a valuable lesson. Respect the local police, period. The vast majority want to do the same thing we do, and that's solve crime."

"Was the case ever entered into ViCAP?" Nash asked.

"No, because it was considered solved."

"You want me to track down the evidence?"

"That would be amazing," Nikki said. "It may have gone back to her mother, but there was so little, I'm worried Metro has already gotten the court's permission to destroy it."

"Was Johnson the primary on the case?" Nash asked.

"Yes, and as captain, he'll be notified of an evidence request. He'll want to know why you're asking."

"I'll tell him we have a cold case older than Mariah's and we want to see if it could be the same person," Nash said. "Hang on, let me check something."

She heard Nash typing, followed by the sound of a text. "I think Johnson's wife knows my mother. I know she has a few contacts in that precinct. I texted her, but she may take a while to get back to me. Either way, I'll get some details on his wife from Mom. She just ruled in Metro's favor on a big case, too." Nash's mother was a federal judge.

"You can still schmooze and bullshit better than anyone I know," Nikki said.

"Thank you," Nash said. "I'll call as soon as I get the information."

"No matter the time of day," Nikki said. "We may have another victim out there."

EIGHTEEN

The Ramsey County medical examiner's office in St. Paul looked like a parking garage with a storage building in front. Hennepin County's medical examiner had been moved to a suburb after years sandwiched between Viking Stadium and the parking garage. Stadium traffic made life even more miserable for the bereft and the employees. But Ramsey County remained in the same brown building it had been in since Nikki returned to Minnesota. Its proximity to Regions Hospital made it hard to convince the county to move it somewhere more easily accessible.

Nikki signed in at the front desk and reception buzzed her through the well-lit, cozy front waiting area to the sterile cross-roads of death. The carpet had given way to tile as soon as the doors closed behind Nikki. Straight ahead, through another set of secured doors were the autopsy suites; to her left the storage cooler, also behind secured doors; and finally to Nikki's right, a third set of doors accessed the medical examiner and death investigator's offices.

The first day her team had gone to meet Dr. Blanchard, the newly appointed medical examiner, Courtney had deemed the hallway the crossroads of death. Nikki pressed the button for the administration hallway, and the doors buzzed open. Blanchard's office was the first one to her left, overlooking the parking lot and interstate overpass.

Nikki knocked on the open door. "You need a badge scanner system like we have," she told Blanchard. "It makes access and tracking who goes in and out a lot easier."

The medical examiner looked up from her notes. "That's a fabulous idea. Perhaps you could pitch it to the city council at the next budget meeting?"

Nikki scowled. "I understand the system, but I have no patience for people trying to save a buck by narrowing down crucial human services. I couldn't play the game."

"Sure you could," Blanchard said. "How many times have you pretended to empathize with a scumbag in order to gain their trust?"

"But that's a strategy," Nikki said. "To push them in the right direction, to get a result that will save future lives. This is just... gross."

Blanchard snickered. "You're not wrong." She motioned for Nikki to sit down.

Nikki settled into a chair, its padding mostly gone. She was glad Blanchard asked to meet in her office and not the autopsy suite. She'd witnessed many autopsies, but Kiania was different; the case felt too personal. Watching the autopsy felt like disrespect to yet another young mother taken too soon.

Unlike the cold autopsy suite, Blanchard's office smelled like the fragrant begonias on her desk. Green plants lined the window in her office, classical music playing on her computer.

"Thanks for coming here," Blanchard said. "I wanted to speak with you in person, and as usual, I'm behind on everything." She opened the file on her desk, her expression serious.

"This poor woman suffered beyond comprehension." The medical examiner's normally steady voice shook. "It will be a while before toxicology reports are back. In addition to the physical trauma she endured, Kiania's left wrist is snapped, possibly from fighting restraints. She had blunt force trauma to the back of her head, and her mandible was dislocated. Repeated trauma to the breasts, until he mutilated them. She was a nursing mother." Blanchard stopped, seemingly steadying herself. "The mutilation took place over different sessions, because there's some healing."

Nikki didn't know much about Blanchard's private life, but she did have children. Breastfeeding was a personal choice and sometimes impossible, but those who were able cherished those quiet moments when the baby nursed. The mutilation took that away from Kiania while she was still alive. How long had she held out hope that she would see her baby again?

"Mariah Gonzales didn't nurse," Nikki said. "He destroyed her uterus instead."

He hated women, specifically those who'd borne children. Nikki wondered again about Mariah and his relationship.

"Kiania's cause of death is asphyxiation. Her hyoid bone snapped."

"Snapped?" Nikki knew hyoid fractures could occur with strangulation, but she'd never heard any medical examiner say anything like that.

"Snapped," Blanchard confirmed. "He shook her to death, likely slamming her head against a hard surface while doing it."

They were looking for killer with no conscience, able to hide the rage he carried until he found his next victim.

"Mariah's cause of death was blunt force trauma," Nikki said. "What about Kiania's stomach contents?"

"A first for me." Blanchard scanned the file. "Artificial protein, caffeine and creatine."

Horror rippled through Nikki. It was exactly what they'd found in Mariah's system. "That's a pretty specific combination, right? How often do you see that much protein and creatine in someone's system?"

"All three? Usually in an athlete or a diabetic," Blanchard said. "Kiania's numbers were similar to a diabetic patient with late stage kidney failure, not a healthy young woman."

"Where do you find those things together? Are they some sort of supplement?"

"Well, creatine monohydrate is used in pre-workout formulas. So is caffeine."

"You're talking about the stuff swimmers take before they swim, for a boost of energy?" Nikki had learned more than she wanted to about competitive swimming during the prior case she'd worked with Brenner.

"Any athlete," Blanchard answered. "Combined with the protein drink, the creatine would definitely provide the user with a burst of energy. How long that lasts depends on weight, dosage, that sort of thing."

Horror rippled through Nikki as it clicked together. This was exactly what they'd found in Mariah's system. "He wants them to have energy to fight back."

NINETEEN

Nikki's desk phone rang with a call from the Bureau's administrative department. They fielded all incoming calls for agents. If her desk phone rang, it was usually important. "Agent Hunt."

"Agent Hunt, I'm sorry to bother you, but a woman has called the main line four times asking for you," Sid Sayers, the head of the administrative department, told her. "She says she has information on a murder victim for a case you're working."

"Which one?" Nikki asked.

"The woman found in Stillwater two days ago."

Sid had worked the phones since before Nikki returned to Minnesota, and she trusted his instincts. She wondered why this woman was contacting her and not the local police—but her name was now associated with it, mentioned in the press release Garcia sent out, and she often forgot that she was so well known from her bigger cases. She was like a celebrity to true crime buffs in the area. "Put her through."

Nikki answered the phone before the first ring ended. "This is Agent Hunt. You have information on an active case?"

A woman cleared her throat. "Not exactly." Her voice trembled. "I don't have any proof, but I saw the news this morning. They said the woman murdered had been missing for three weeks and had a ten-week-old baby."

"I can't discuss those details with you. If you have information that might help, I'm all ears. But if you're just looking for—"

"Please don't hang up! I think my friend might have been taken by the same person."

"I'm listening," Nikki replied quickly. "First, give me your name and number."

"My name is Annie White." She gave Nikki her phone number and address. "My friend Cassandra King works with me at Midwest Plastics in Woodbury."

Nikki sat up straighter. Kiania's mother-in-law lived in Woodbury. "When did she disappear?"

"Four days ago. She went out for a cigarette break at work and I haven't seen her since. The police aren't taking it seriously at all. She hasn't been heard from for four days, and her husband is telling everyone she probably left the state. But Cass would never have left that baby," Annie said confidently.

Nikki turned to a fresh page in her notebook. "How old is the baby?"

"Eight weeks. Cass has two older boys in high school," Annie replied. "They didn't expect this baby. Cass didn't have a choice," she said quietly, almost as an afterthought.

"She and her husband disagreed about having the baby?"

"At first, but she knew she had to warm up to the idea. Her husband, Shane, is an overbearing, ignorant beast of a man." Disgust colored her tone. "Cass stayed with him because of the boys, but she'd been thinking about leaving when she found out she was pregnant."

"What do you think happened?"

The woman hesitated. "I thought he'd lost his temper and finally done something to her, because she'd found things that belonged to other women and planned to confront him."

As in a serial killer's precious collectibles? Probably not, but Nikki wanted to talk to the husband. "What did the Woodbury police say?"

"As little as possible, even though I told them she wouldn't have left that baby. Her card had been used at an ATM, from an account her husband didn't know about, fifty miles away. She's had it forever, saving up for when she got the chance to leave."

That's probably exactly what happened. "Does he have a history of violence against her?"

"Yes." Annie hesitated. "But that's not why I'm calling. I don't think it's him anymore. The news said the killer you're hunting stalked that poor woman he killed, probably for weeks, so he knew exactly when to strike."

"That's one strong possibility." Nikki tried not to confirm anything concrete. "Had Cass noticed someone following her?"

"In the past two weeks, a black Chevy Malibu parked next to Cass twice. I was in the car both times. Neither one of us recognized the driver, but he had a company tag hanging from the mirror, and it's a big building. We don't know everyone. That car hasn't been in the parking lot for the last few nights. It disappeared the same time she did." Annie choked down a sob.

"Do you know if anyone's tag has been misplaced?" If Cass turned out to be another victim, he could have easily stolen someone's parking tag.

"No, but I wouldn't know that. The night supervisor—my boss—might."

The image of the masked man in Appalachia flashed in Nikki's head. "Did you get a look at the guy?"

"He's a white guy. Pale skin. Very blue eyes."

Nikki struggled to hide the excitement in her voice. "Would you mind meeting with me, Annie?"

. . .

Nikki spent her afternoon studying the cases in North Dakota and Detroit, looking for similar stomach contents. Unfortunately, both sets of remains had been too decomposed for organ testing. She also looked for anything they might be able to test for DNA, making notes for Courtney.

She wanted to call Miller and update him out of habit, but he'd made it clear Kiania's murder wasn't his problem. She called Lt. Chen on the way to Midwest Plastics instead.

"Have you seen Kiania's autopsy report?"

"I was just looking at it. Sadistic bastard."

"The victim in Virginia I told you about, Mariah Gonzales, had similar stomach contents. I've confirmed the man found in North Carolina wasn't the guy from the woods. We've found additional possible victims in Detroit and North Dakota. Information about the one in North Dakota's hard to find, but Liam's still looking."

"And they were both postpartum like Kiania Watson?" Chen asked.

"Yes," Nikki answered. "Unfortunately, they were too decomposed to look at stomach contents. We may have another victim, too, from Woodbury. Her friend called today after hearing the information Garcia put on the news. She's coming in during her day off to talk to me. I'm headed to Midwest Plastics now."

"We have a serial killer," Chen said.

"A lust serial killer. In my experience, they have very little humanity left by the time they start killing. But keep the information between us. If the media hears the slightest whisper about a serial killer, they'll be relentless."

"We sure as hell don't need them doing any more," Chen said. "Let me know what you find out about the woman from Woodbury."

. . .

Nikki navigated through the streets around the factory. Her GPS had taken her to the address, but figuring out which driveway actually belonged to Midwest Plastics took some effort.

Nikki had expected a generic building, probably a big rectangle, but Midwest Plastics' massive facility on the border of West St. Paul and Woodbury reminded her of the White House.

A large campus surrounded the massive building, with trees spread throughout the grounds. The massive front lawn was no doubt emerald green in the summer.

Nikki found some open parking spots near the front entrance. She scanned the area for Brenner, who she'd asked to come along for a couple of reasons. She hadn't told Brenner about Mariah so she'd stay objective, and since she'd worked Kiania's disappearance, Nikki hoped Brenner might catch details that Nikki might miss since she wasn't as intimately familiar with the case as Brenner.

She arrived before Brenner, so Nikki called home to check in on Rory and Lacey.

"Are you going to be home for supper, Mom?" Lacey asked.

"I don't think so," Nikki told her. "But keep a plate warm for me, okay?" She asked her to give the phone to Rory. "A woman may be missing in Woodbury. I'm here to talk to her co-workers." She looked at the Jeep's clock. "I'm not sure when I'll be home."

"Be careful," her husband warned. "A wintry mix is supposed to start in the next hour. They're already putting salt down."

"I will." Nikki spotted Brenner's car pulling into the parking lot. "I love you."

"Love you too," he said. "And be careful, please."

Nikki grabbed her bag. "Thanks for coming." She shut the Jeep's door and locked it.

Brenner nodded. "I hope I can actually help. The main thread I'm working on is that Kiania worked nights."

"Kiania always worked nights?" Nikki asked. "I thought she was called in the day she disappeared."

"She was, but her regular shift was three p.m. to midnight, during the week. She had enough seniority to take weekends off but stay on call. That's why she was on call for that time period. He must have actively watched her."

"Have you seen the autopsy report?" Nikki asked.

Brenner looked sick. "I had to google the stuff found in her stomach. Do you think he wants them to have enough energy to struggle? As if a new mother doesn't have enough reason to fight for her life."

Nikki leaned against the Jeep. She hadn't stopped to consider the will of a mother fighting to get back to her baby.

"Mariah disappeared at night."

"Who's Mariah?"

A petite woman with salt-and-pepper hair headed their way, hurrying across the large parking lot. "I'll tell you after we talk to Annie."

"Agent Hunt?" Annie asked.

Nikki offered her hand. "This is Detective Brenner with Minneapolis PD. She's working Kiania Watson's murder."

"Sorry for the calluses," Annie said. "I run one of the machines."

"No problem." After Annie's call, Nikki had checked with the Woodbury police about Cass's disappearance. They had told Annie that Cass was an adult, but they'd check with the family. Her husband said she'd disappeared for a few days before and didn't think it warranted a missing person's report.

"After I spoke to the Woodbury police, I called Stillwater PD," Nikki told Annie. "Cass's husband told the officer he's not concerned about his wife's disappearance."

"I'm not surprised," Annie said. "He's a no-good piece of

shit on his best day. She's supported him for too long. I can't tell you how many times I told her to just leave and take the boys with her."

"But you don't think that's what she's done?" Brenner asked.

Annie looked each of them in the eyes. "Hear me when I say this: absolutely not! She stayed with him because of her kids. There is nothing on earth that would make her willingly leave them, especially a newborn baby." Annie's eyes filled with tears. "I'd stake my life on that."

"You've known Cass a long time?" Nikki tried to rein in Annie's emotions before they got the best of her.

"Six years, since she started here," Annie said. "It wasn't hard to figure out her husband was a louse."

"Is it possible he did something to her?" Brenner asked.

"He never physically abused her, at least not that she told me about. He's just controlling and emotionally abusive." Annie shook her head. "As much as I want to say he did something to her, I don't think her husband would want to be stuck taking care of the kids. He needed her."

Nikki pointed to the long, white building. "Where would Cass have gone to smoke?" Nikki asked.

"I'll show you." Annie led them to the south side of the building. "We aren't supposed to smoke on the property, and Cass had pretty much quit once she found out she was pregnant. But she started smoking more and more after she came back to work."

Nikki noticed a path from the edge of the parking lot to a small grove of evergreen trees. Most of the property's trees were oak and maple, their branches close to bare. Green hedges surrounded the building, the parking area butting up to the pine trees. "Is that the smoking area?"

Annie nodded. "We don't have a camera on that side of the building, so that's why everyone goes over there." She glanced at

Nikki. "They expanded the parking lot a few years ago. Used to be six rows of pine trees, but they all had to go. Company kept that little section for the smokers."

"Did you ever notice the man in the black Chevy Malibu out here smoking with anyone?"

"No, but I don't smoke. I'm not out here much." Annie led them around the building and across the parking lot. Nikki estimated the distance between the door Cass had exited and the grove of trees to be less than three hundred feet.

The pine trees hid the steel bucket that someone had set out for butts and trash, but it was nearly empty. "Who else comes out here when Cass does?"

"Mick Jones, sometimes." Annie rolled her eyes. "He's had a thing for Cass for years. She turned him down more than once. He's got a girlfriend now, though. I'm not sure he's bugged Cass about sleeping with him in a while."

Women were murdered by men they rejected all the time. Regardless of Nikki's serial theory, she wanted to talk to Mick. "Did you tell the police that? Did they speak to him?"

"No," Annie replied. "They barely asked me any questions."

"Is Mick here?"

"He's on the late shift. I'm his supervisor, so I can give you his contact information."

"That would be great," Nikki said. "Where did Cass park?"

"In the west lot, behind the building," Annie answered.

"Did Cass ever mention anything about this strange guy being around her more than just parking? Did she run into him anywhere else?"

Annie shook her head. "No, she didn't."

"I wonder about the trillium," Brenner muttered to Nikki. "Maybe we need to track down areas where it grows to find this guy. I assume you've thought of that?" she asked Nikki.

"The petals are dried," Nikki replied. "He can keep than

anywhere." Nikki liked Brenner, but she wanted to shut down her comments. She shouldn't be talking about the details of the other active cases around a witness. The flowers were kept out of the news.

"Petals?" Annie asked. Nikki and Brenner turned to her in unison. "The night before Cass disappeared, someone left a flower on her windshield."

"Who's Mariah?" Brenner shoved her hands in her pockets.

Nikki unlocked the Jeep as they walked towards it. Her head was still spinning from what Annie had told them. "Get out of the wind."

She turned the seat warmers on. "Mariah was killed in 2014." Nikki started from the beginning, minus her outburst at Mariah that first day. "I let him go in the woods. And I'd do it again to have Lacey." Nikki swallowed the emotion threatening to burst out of her. "Maybe that makes me culpable in all of this."

"I don't think it does." Brenner's normally matter-of-fact tone was gentle. "You faced an impossible choice. Any mother would have done the same thing."

"I know," Nikki said. "I'm going to be kicking myself for not following up after I got back from maternity leave. I just wanted to forget it."

"You have the right to be human every once in a while," Brenner told her. "I see why you turned white when Annie mentioned the petals."

"Kiania lived for more than three weeks after she was taken," Nikki reminded her. "If he took Cass, we have time."

"But very few leads," Brenner said. "I've got uniforms looking for Vernon and Jerry in the hopes they saw something more at the hospital. Ty Watson didn't do this. Kiania's parents are having a hard time accepting that."

"I can imagine." Her touch screen lit up with a call from Elwood.

"This is Agent Hunt." As much as she tried, Nikki could never be completely informal with her old mentor.

"Just wanted to let you know I've retrieved it from my storage unit, and it's safe in the original evidence bag," Elwood said. "I'd marked the area, but the blood isn't visible since it's been so long. Do you want me to have someone look at it under a microscope before your forensic specialist flies all the way out here?"

Courtney had been adamant no one touch the sample, and Nikki wasn't about to risk her wrath. "Keep it in the bag. Courtney doesn't want any chance of cross-contamination."

"I assumed as much," Elwood said.

"Courtney is hoping to get more physical evidence from Mariah's case. And we may have a new missing victim." She told him about the victims being postpartum, along with the commonalities in the autopsy reports. "We're just spinning in circles."

"Not really," Brenner interjected. "We're nearly certain Mariah and Kiania were killed by the same person. You've figured out enough to know Cass is a victim. That gives her a chance."

"He kept Kiania alive for three weeks," Nikki said. "We still have time."

"Text me the flight information, and I'll pick Courtney up," Elwood said. "We'll go to the lab so she can confirm it's worth testing right away."

"What now?" Brenner asked after the call.

"Get on the uniforms to find Jerry and Vernon," Nikki answered. "We need an eyewitness."

TWENTY

1984

Papaw jerked his hand in Fifi's direction. "Where are those nails?"

She grabbed the box and raced to where he crouched on the weird, yellow wood floor of his hunting cabin. She thrust the nails at him. "Why did you yank up the old floor?"

"Because your dumbass brothers decided to skin that thing inside the cabin." Papaw's gray beard trembled with anger. "My great-grandpa built this cabin in 1889. It's stood the test of time until those two nimrods let blood run all over the floor."

Fifi had come from the pond with Nathaniel and Jerod, getting their stories straight. Fifi had simply walked to the mailbox to get the paper when Nathaniel drove by and took her fishing. They'd caught two big catfish, so she figured her sister would get over not being helped with the chores.

They could hear Papaw screaming at the boys from outside. The three of them had sat on the porch listening to Papaw whip the teenagers with the belt. It wasn't until that night when Fifi had finally learned the boys had killed a deer even though they never ate venison. "Why'd they skin it inside?"

"Why do those two do anything?" Papaw seethed. "I'm sure it was Everett's idea."

She touched the bump on the back of her head. Fifi hadn't seen Everett in four days, not since the punishments.

"But there's no blood on this floor." She tapped her foot on the thin wood.

"Because it's just plywood. Sub-floor," Papaw said. "Real wood floor goes on top of the sub floor. Hand me that nail gun and then stand back."

Fifi obeyed. "Papaw, can I ask you a question?" Fifi couldn't stop thinking about the way Papaw had ignored the Clegg boy's hatred toward her in favor of punishing her half-brother for defending her. Did he love her or hate her? He was so cold to her around anyone outside the family. How could he love her and be that way?

"What?" he asked without looking at her, fiddling with the nail gun.

"How come ..." The words caught in her throat. She knew the answer. He was embarrassed her father was some black sharecropper who'd come and gone in one night. He was embarrassed of his family lineage, which they could trace back four generations, was marred by her skin color. Nathaniel's friend Jerod said their family helped bring slaves from Africa, and that's who she'd descended from. Or half of her, anyway.

Papaw sat back on his heels, pushing his cap off his head. He'd sweated through his shirt and smelled sour. "What, girl?" His blue eyes had started to look angry,

Fifi shoved her thoughts down deep. She'd ask another time. "You want some water from the well?"

. . .

Nikki hadn't realized how close Cassandra King lived to Kiania Watson until she'd turned onto Highway 36 driving into Still-water. Her house on the corner of 3rd Street was about a four-minute walk south from Kiania Watson's home in Stillwater. Had he spotted Cassandra King while he'd been stalking Kiania?

Nikki went over what little information she had about Cass's family. Her husband had been a long-haul trucker before an injury landed him on disability. Her two older boys were in high school, and Nikki hoped both would be home from school when she arrived. Since Annie had reported her friend missing instead of her husband, Nikki had decided to surprise him instead of calling ahead.

She called Stillwater PD first.

"Chen."

"Hey, it's Nikki. Did you guys do a welfare check for Cassandra King?"

"Name sounds familiar. Hang on." She could hear Chen typing over the speaker. "Yeah, a friend asked for the check, we spoke to the husband, Shane King. Is that the missing woman you called about earlier?"

"She lives in Stillwater," Nikki said. "What did Shane King say?"

"That she probably took off. He confirmed her car, bag, cell are missing. The cell is one of those cheaper options, so once it's dead or turned off, there's no GPS. My officers did look for cell tower pings. The last one happened near Midwest Plastics, around five thirty p.m."

"How do you know that's the kind of phone she had?" Nikki asked. "Did they check with her husband?"

"Yeah, and he said she went through those like water. In the end, they didn't see enough to call her missing persons. She could have dumped that phone, got another and left." Chen lowered his voice. "Is she postpartum?"

"Eight weeks," Nikki said. "I'm headed to talk to Shane King now as long as you're okay with it."

"Whatever you think is necessary," Chen said. "I'm in court all afternoon, or I'd join you."

"I'll keep you posted," Nikki promised. "Good luck in court," she added before hanging up.

Bits and pieces of information had become a swampy mess in Nikki's head. She had to stay impartial regarding Cassandra King's disappearance.

Despite the similarities to Mariah and Kiania's disappearance, she needed to stay open-minded. Without more evidence she had to consider the people closest to Cass as suspects, assuming she was actually missing and hadn't left on her own accord.

Annie refused to consider that option, but everyone had secrets they didn't tell a soul. Maybe Cass had decided to walk away from her life. Nikki made a mental note to ask about Cass's postpartum experience and whether or not she'd experienced any depression or other issues.

Andrea Yates was a terrible victim of this. She hadn't just decided to drown her children in the bathroom that morning. Yates had endured psychological problems for years and had been advised not to have any more children because her meds, including Haldol, had stabilized her depression and suicidal thoughts. Instead, she got pregnant with her fifth child right away and the children's fates had been sealed.

Her husband deserved empathy for all that he endured, but his lack of attention to his wife's mental state—including having another child—also made him partially culpable in Nikki's mind.

Yates had been a nurse, and her husband a NASA engineer. Healthcare had certainly been available to them, but mental health, especially women's, hadn't been a priority in 2001.

Nikki parked in front of the white house with brown trim

where Cass lived with her family. Like most of the houses in working class Stillwater, the home and grounds were well maintained. As soon as she hopped out of the Jeep, she nearly fell over a wide stump between the street and sidewalk.

Beetles had destroyed a lot of the ash tree population and judging from the amount of ash trees scattered in the area, Nikki guessed the tree had to be cut down in order to keep the bugs from spreading.

Nikki crossed the yard, dead leaves crunching beneath her boots. Many of the houses on the street had decorated for Halloween, making the King family the odd one out.

A gangly teenaged boy answered the door, holding a crying baby wearing only a diaper. He blew his dark, shaggy bangs out of his eyes. "Yeah?"

Nikki showed him her badge. His face lit up. "Thank God. Dad won't do anything, and I know Mom didn't just leave." He motioned her inside, trying to soothe the baby. "Dad, this is Agent Hunt with the FBI."

Shane King eyed her across the table, his bald head shining underneath the kitchen lights as he looked at his phone. "No offense, Agent, but my wife's not missing."

"Her friends at work are worried about her." Nikki tried to sound objective, but the man's ambivalence rubbed her the wrong way. His wife hadn't come home for four straight nights, leaving him with a crying infant that wanted her mother. Yet Shane seemed unbothered.

"When was the last time you spoke to your wife?" Nikki asked.

"Four days ago, before she left for work." He popped a handful of peanuts into his mouth. "She wanted me to find a part-time job so she can cut back on hours at work."

"To be with Emma," Sam added. "I heard her say it."

Shane glared at his son for a beat before turning his attention back to Nikki. "I can't work. I fell in 2018 and my doctor put me on disability." He shook his head in disbelief. "What am I supposed to do, work from home on some shitty call job or something?"

Nikki couldn't believe how callous he sounded. "Is that why you think she decided to take a few days to cool off?"

He shrugged. "She's done it before."

Sam's pinched expression made it clear that wasn't the entire story. "Not for a long time, Dad." He bounced the sleeping baby in his arms. "She wouldn't just leave Emma."

Shane ignored him, stroking his graying goatee. "You should check with Mick Jones. She's probably shacked up with him."

Sam rolled his eyes. Evidently this wasn't a new argument.

Nikki played dumb. "Who's Mick Jones?"

Shane's square jaw set. He looked flat out mean in that moment. "Ex friend of mine. Hauled with him for years. Helped the sonofabitch get a job at Midwest Plastics.

"Cass wanted to give the baby up for adoption when she found out about the baby." Shane glanced at his son, barely masking a smile at the boy's surprise. "I wouldn't allow it. Mick took her side."

"Mom wouldn't leave us." Sam stood up, still cradling his sister. "You're wrong."

Shane snickered as Sam left the room. "I knew when he wanted to play the saxophone he was going to be a sissy."

Nikki struggled to hide her distaste for the man. "Your older son's at football practice?"

Shane sat up straight. "Sure is. He's a tight end and they won't go far in the playoffs without him." He sipped his coffee and then chuckled. "I think that's why Sam wanted to be in a band. Marching band's the only way he's going to be out on the football field."

This man wasn't going to win any award for parent of the year. "Since he's sixteen, I need your permission to speak with him."

"Don't bother him at football practice."

"But stopping by school's okay?" This time, she didn't try to hide her judgment.

"Yep."

"Just so I've covered everything, what did you do that night after Cass left for work?"

"Went to the bar. Had a pool tournament to win." He eyed her. "Why? I told you she's just laying low for a while."

She hated to pacify the man, but Nikki didn't want to spook him. "You know your wife best," she lied. "But since a report's been filed, I have to follow up. We always look at the spouse first. You have any receipts, anything to confirm how long you were there?"

"Paid in cash. Call the bar and ask. They all know me."

"Thanks for your time," Nikki said. "Off topic, but a friend of mine who lives near here just found out she's expecting. She's over forty so it's a little risky. Where's Cass's OBGYN located?"

Shane thought about it for a second. "I don't know the name. Only went once, to find out the sex. It's in Woodbury."

Nikki caught movement out of the corner of her eye. Sam hovered in the adjacent room, only his toes visible, listening. She took a card out of her bag and dropped it on the table. "Call me if you think of anything else, or if you hear from Cass."

Shane grunted and put the card into his shirt pocket. "Sure."

Sam peered around the wall, his dark eyes boring into Nikki's. The kid wanted to tell her something. "You can also call the Minneapolis office and ask for me." She looked past Shane, whose attention had gone back to his phone. Her gaze met Sam's. "Just tell them your name, and they will put you through."

. . .

Third shift started soon, and this time of day and the drive would take at least forty minutes, but Nikki wanted to check a few things on her GPS before choosing her route to Midwest Plastics.

"36 is around the corner," Nikki said to herself, putting in the Kings' address. GPS informed her that the fastest route from Cass's home to her work in Woodbury was 36 West to Interstate 494 and then onto Nikki's personal hell, Interstate 694. Looking at CCTV on the interstate would be futile, and the intersection of 3rd Street and 36W didn't have a camera, but there were several businesses along the road that could have picked up the black Chevy Malibu—if they could narrow down the time frame. Nikki made a note to ask for at least the last few days' CCTV during the times Cass would have driven by.

Following 3rd Street south on Stagecoach Trail past the Oakdale Heights Correctional Facility, eventually taking I-94 would have been Cass's second option, and this time of day, the option with less traffic, at least until I-94. The prison had buildings on either side of the road, with several cameras positioned to view the road. She hoped the prison didn't auto recycle the CCTV footage from the night before.

Hopefully Annie knew the route Cass took home.

Nikki called into the office during the drive to Midwest Plastics to talk to both Liam and Garcia. "Good news first. Elwood has the rock, sealed in an evidence bag. He'll pick Courtney up at the airport tomorrow."

"What's the bad news?" Liam asked.

"Kiania Watson and Cassandra King live within walking distance of each other," she told Liam. "If Cass has been taken, he likely spotted her while spying on Kiania. Cass is also postpartum."

Garcia swore in Spanish.

"Which means there's a decent chance he drove by her house frequently," Liam said. "Or even lives nearby."

"Annie said the stranger drove a black Chevy Malibu," Nikki said. "It's a long shot, but check the DOT and see if there are any cars matching that description between the two houses. I'll text Cass's address."

"Are you headed back now?"

"No, I'm going to stop at Midwest Plastics again and talk to Mick Jones, as well as some of Cass's co-workers. I'll let you know if I turn anything interesting up," Nikki answered. "Can you call Oakdale Heights Correctional and ask them to go through their CCTV? I'm praying they don't recycle it right away." She gave him the other locations with CCTV near Cass's house.

"Don't get your hopes up on the prison," Liam warned her. "Pretty sure they don't keep that exterior footage very long. They focus on the yard and other prisoner areas."

"I know," Nikki said. "Still worth a shot."

"Have you spoken with Chen?" Garcia asked. "We need to make sure he stays in the loop."

"He's aware," Nikki answered. "I haven't told Miller. How did he take your PSA on the news?"

"He said it wasn't his case and hung up." Garcia sounded irritated. "Don't waste your time updating him."

"I haven't heard back from Nash yet, but he asked me to give him until tomorrow," Nikki said.

"What about Cass's husband?" Liam asked. "It's weird he's not worried."

"You wouldn't say that if you'd been there," Nikki told him. "He's not worried about Cass and it's pretty clear he makes the rules, but one of her sons, Sam, knows more than he said, I think. I made sure he knew how to reach me." Her stomach turned at the idea of Cass being at the mercy of a killer. "I'm going to talk to Mick at Midwest Plastics because I want to make sure I can rule him out as being the man in the woods since he used to be a long-haul trucker," Nikki said. "Blanchard put Kiania's time of death at no more than sixteen hours before her body was found," she reminded Liam. "She'd been missing for three weeks. We still have time to find Cass."

"He won't kill her until you find him," Liam agreed. "He took her so you would have no choice but to hunt him down."

TWENTY-ONE

"Thanks for meeting with me." Nikki had been surprised when Mick Jones suggested they speak in a conference room instead of somewhere private where his co-workers couldn't pry on him. Chairs surrounded a round table, a smartboard on the front wall. Generic motivational quotes adorned the walls.

Mick Jones stood as she entered and pulled out a chair. He immediately flushed. "Was that presumptuous? I don't mean to seem like I don't take you seriously."

"Of course not." Nikki took the seat he offered. He wasn't the guy in the woods. Mick was several inches taller, with brown eyes and Mediterranean-toned skin. "Thank you for meeting with me at such short notice."

"I have nothing to hide," he said. "And I'm worried about Cass."

"Her husband thinks she's staying with you."

Mick scowled. "That lazy bastard. He used to be a decent human being, even though he was a blowhard. Then he fell down an internet rabbit hole and turned into a complete loser."

"Does Cass feel the same way?"

"She wouldn't say if she did," Mick said. "That's her man." He folded his arms on the table.

Nikki hadn't missed the disdain in his voice. "He said you supported her wanting to give the baby up for adoption."

"Sure did," Mick said. "I'm not political—least I try not to be—but with Cass being over forty and higher risk, I felt like it should have been her decision." He looked up at Nikki. "My opinion didn't matter; Shane made that real clear."

"He suggested you have feelings for her."

"He's stupid," Mick countered.

Nikki knew in her gut Cass had been kidnapped, but she had to investigate other angles. Shane could have killed her for insurance money and stashed her car. Maybe the petals were a coincidence. "Annie said he was verbally and emotionally abusive, but he never hit her. Do you think he's capable of hurting her?"

Mick's eyes bored into hers. "As much as the selfish side of me wants to say yes," he answered, "I can't see it. He's one of those stocky guys with short man syndrome who bullies people into thinking he's tough. But killing her? Nah. He's got a brand-new baby. You think he's going to take care of her?"

Fair point, Nikki thought. Mick Jones seemed like a standup guy. He could have taken advantage of Cass and as far as Nikki could tell, he hadn't. "So it seems that you and Cass stayed friends even after the fight over keeping the baby."

"I tried to stay away, do the right thing by my so-called friend, but Cass was a smoker, at least until she found out she was pregnant. She knew I'd quit ten years ago; she wanted to know how I managed it. I guess Shane told her she couldn't use nicotine patches or lozenges because of the baby, but that's not true. It's only ingested stuff that's bad for the baby. Dumbass. I told her to try the patches and gum. Pretty sure she hid them from Shane just so she didn't have to hear about it." He checked his watch. "I only have ten more minutes on my break. You gonna ask me if I did it?"

"I was going to ask you where you were that night she disappeared since employee records show you took it off," Nikki said.

"Home." Mick shrugged. "Alone. And I was home with a migraine."

If he was telling the truth, Nikki doubted Mick had left his apartment that day. "House or apartment?" If he rented an apartment, the building likely had security cameras.

"House." He gave her his address. "I live at the dead end. You can talk to my neighbors."

"I will." She'd also see if any nearby CCTV footage caught him coming and going, just to cover all of her bases. "Did she tell you about the guy hanging around here?"

Mick slumped in his seat. "No, I didn't hear about it until this evening when Annie told me. Far as I know it seems like no one else noticed him."

Nikki feared as much. Ten years of experience had taught him how to blend in. "Is there any chance Cass could have left on her own? Shane thinks she wanted to get away for a few days."

"No way in hell," Mick said. "She was afraid of starting over at her age, but Cass loves that baby. Emma's all she's talked about since she came back from maternity leave."

Darkness had descended by the time Nikki left Midwest Plastics. She scanned the parking lot and street for any sign of the black Malibu, relieved not to see it.

A white man in a janitor's uniform could blend in pretty much anywhere. The idea was as brilliant as it was simple. Most people rarely paid close attention to janitors because they were a normal fixture in an industry constantly hiring new people due to job turnover.

How many times had Cass chatted with the night janitor

who likely hadn't even been on the books? He likely made sure no one from management saw him, to be safe.

Nikki's stomach tightened as she thought about the killer's skill. He'd been doing this for at least a decade, and she didn't want to know how many lives he'd taken. He'd had years to master his craft. He'd probably been planning his reveal to Nikki since that day in Appalachia.

She hadn't been completely honest earlier when she'd said that she wouldn't trade herself for Cass. Even if Nikki had to surrender every weapon, she'd still have a better chance at survival. GPS trackers were so tiny now she could put one in her shoe or sock and he'd likely never notice it.

Unless he'd already thought of that. He'd been planning this for years, dozens of steps ahead of her. How could she possibly hope to stop him?

A flash of white just outside of her blind spot caught her gaze. Nikki glared at the white van riding her ass. She slowed down, irritated at the bright lights he was flashing. The van moved into the left lane as though he planned to pass, but instead paced Nikki, managing to keep his license plate out of her vision.

He flashed his lights again. Did he think she was going to pull over? She thought about digging her badge out and plastering it against the window, but the van crossed the white line into her lane, barely missing her bumper.

Nikki jerked the wheel to the right, into the exit lane for the interstate. She double-checked to make sure no one else was behind her and then hit her brakes. The van sped past, her dashcam recording as it sped away. She didn't see a back plate. Hopefully the camera picked up something her eyes hadn't.

TWENTY-TWO

Nikki managed to sleep for a couple of hours before dragging herself out of bed to get breakfast for Lacey. It was harder than usual to be away from her right now. She was picking up Courtney to take her to the airport in an hour, but Nikki hated going days without seeing Lacey, which happened often during big cases. She let Lacey do the talking as they sat. Her chatterbox daughter spun stories the way Nikki's father used to when she was a little girl. They usually contained a few nuggets of truth inside a pile of exaggeration.

"Mom, what's a miscarriage?" Lacey's question came out of nowhere. She'd jumped from the school Halloween party to a question Nikki really didn't want to answer.

Nikki tried to keep her voice steady. "Sometimes, when a woman gets pregnant, the baby can't grow. There's something wrong, and the pregnancy goes away." She chose her words carefully. Lacey already knew how babies were born thanks to a friend's older brother, but Nikki didn't want to go any deeper than that. "Where did you hear that word?"

"One of the third-grade teachers had one," Lacey said. "I

heard the other teachers talking about it. One of them sounded like she was crying."

"It's a very sad thing," Nikki said. "But they're very common, more than we even know. All sorts of things can go wrong during a pregnancy. Every healthy baby is a true miracle." She knew the words were a mistake as soon as they escaped her lips. Lacey never missed an opportunity to ask a follow-up question.

"Have you had one, Mommy?"

"Had what?" Rory entered the kitchen, dressed for work. He kissed Nikki on the cheek and ruffled Lacey's hair.

"A miscarriage."

Rory's eyes widened. "Not at all the kind of answer I expected."

"A teacher at school had one," Nikki explained to her husband. "And the answer is yes, I have, before I got pregnant with you."

"What happened?" Lacey asked.

Rory's strong hand squeezed Nikki's shoulder.

"It wasn't a healthy pregnancy," Nikki said. "A few months later, I was pregnant with you."

"So I should have a brother or sister?" Sadness lingered in her voice.

"Well, no," Nikki said. "It takes a long time to grow a baby so it can be born. If that had happened, you might not be here." She leaned over and squeezed her daughter. "And I don't know what I'd do without you."

"I'm about ready to leave, Bug." Rory spoke before Lacey could ask more questions. "You don't want to be late for school."

Lacey wanted to ask more questions, but she complied and headed for the front door to put her shoes on.

Rory brushed a curl out of Nikki's eyes. "You okay?"

"Oh yeah," she lied. "It was a long time ago."

"Somehow I don't believe you," he said. "To be continued tonight... or the next time I see you."

Nikki had never loved him more than she did in that moment. After he and Lacey left, she took a quick shower, brushed her teeth, found a pair of clean jeans and a red, long-sleeved shirt. She nearly left the house wearing different sneakers.

Even though Brooklyn Center didn't exactly have the best residential neighborhoods, Courtney had managed to find a one-room apartment in Lake Point, a gated community with a pool she never had the time to use. Courtney had lived at Lake Point since she'd followed Nikki from Quantico to work on the Violent Crime Unit eight years ago.

"Hey." She tossed her duffle bag into the back seat and then climbed in next to Nikki. "Thanks for taking me to the airport."

"Thanks for dropping everything and going to Quantico," Nikki answered. "Is Merida okay?"

Courtney had named the pretty calico cat after the head character in Disney's *Brave*. According to Courtney, the six-month-old cat lived up to the name, tearing through the apartment and wreaking havoc. Courtney had moved her potted plants to her bedroom and locked the cat out after she destroyed an orchid Courtney had managed to keep alive for nearly two years.

"I'm gone less than two full days," Courtney said. "Miss Queen has fresh litter and a full feeder that gives her a snack every couple of hours. She'll be fine. I'm not sure about you, though. Have you slept?"

"A couple of hours." Nikki entered the airport into her GPS. "We may have a new victim."

Courtney listened as Nikki told her everything she'd learned since the last time they spoke. "No way that's a coincidence," she said when Nikki told her about the flower left on Cass's windshield.

"I know," Nikki agreed. It was all weighing heavily on her.

"Are you okay?" Courtney asked.

"Yes. This morning, Lacey asked me what a miscarriage is. One of the teachers at school had one. I could have done without that question—it's a pretty heavy subject to cover over breakfast, and I wasn't even supposed to be there this morning."

Courtney nodded sympathetically. "And then she asked if you had one, right?"

"You know her too well." Nikki cursed morning traffic on I-494. "I told her that I did and explained it was because something was wrong. She accepted it, but Rory knows there's more to the story. I promised I'd tell him tonight."

Courtney leaned forward and closed one of the vents in front of her. "You know, you can tell him the details of the miscarriage without telling him about Mariah."

"No," Nikki said. "I want him to know what I did the day we met."

Courtney sighed. "You beat yourself up over that, but I bet she forgot about it, especially after the baby was born."

"Her mother didn't." Nikki's cheeks flushed with shame. "That's why she thought to contact me after Mariah's murder."

"Well, if you believe everything happens for a reason, that's why the two of you encountered each other in the first place."

"Because she was going to be murdered?" Nikki asked. "It's no one's fate to be murdered, Court."

"How do we know?" Courtney said. "Whatever you believe, it's all conjecture. No scientific proof. You have to rely on faith. How is this any different?" She twisted around in the seat to stare at Nikki. "If that one event hadn't happened, there's zero chance her murder would ever have been solved, much less stopping a serial killer."

Nikki glanced at her friend and smiled. "Thanks for having my back."

"And I know you feel guilty for this guy continuing to kill women, but you were the only one who didn't fail Mariah, in my opinion. The D.C. police treated her like she didn't matter, and Garcia was checked out. If anyone should feel responsible, it should be him."

Nikki almost told her that she'd learned Garcia was gay but stopped herself. She couldn't just blab to Courtney because they were friends. It was Garcia's story to tell.

Nikki maneuvered her Jeep into the long drop-off lines at the airport. MSP had multiple lanes for drop-off and pickup and getting through usually felt like a game of Tetris.

"I can't believe Garcia paid for my ticket." Courtney fought back a yawn. "Elwood is picking me up at Dulles?"

Nikki nodded. "The ASAC will take you both to evidence."

She hadn't met the current Assistant Special Agent in Charge at Quantico, but Elwood had assured Nikki getting the evidence wouldn't be an issue. "The earliest return flight is tomorrow afternoon, so I booked a room at the Marriott Stafford, near the FBI campus. Elwood will pick you up and bring you back to Dulles."

"I can just call Uber," Courtney said. "I hate for him to drive into the city again."

"He's staying at the hotel, too," Nikki told her. "We want Elwood with you as much as possible to ensure there are no issues with chain of custody, assuming we get this guy to trial."

"You will." Courtney grabbed her overnight bag from the backseat. She checked her watch. "Flight leaves in about ninety minutes. Just enough time to make it through security."

"Show them your credentials," Nikki said. "And text me once you're at Quantico."

TWENTY-THREE

It had still been dark when Nikki had picked Courtney up, but the rising sun made her eyes water. She yanked down her sun visor. As always, morning traffic moved slowly. At least most of the vacation traffic was gone for the season. As the main artery running north and south, I-35 always swelled during the summer months, when everyone wanted to come to Minnesota and enjoy the lakes.

Excitement raced through her as Nash's call reverberated through the vehicle. "I didn't expect to hear from you this quickly." She hoped that didn't mean Nash had failed to locate the remaining evidence from Mariah's murder.

"Well, when a federal circuit judge asks for a favor, the D.C. police jump." Nash's tone turned serious. "Mom had a clerk of court check to see if the D.C. police had petitioned to destroy the evidence yet." Police kept evidence from solved cases until the court who tried the case allowed them to either destroy it or release to the family.

Nikki's hopes sank. "They did, didn't they?"

"About four years ago," Nash said. "Thankfully, Mariah's mother has contacts in the system and heard about it. Mariah's mother sued for the evidence and won. The court didn't even care that Anita believed the police had the wrong information, because she had a right to the evidence as next of kin. With the case closed and the alleged murderer dead, Mariah's personal items belonged to her mother."

"Were you able to find Anita?" Nikki asked.

"I did," Nash said. "She's got the socks and the bracelet found with Johnny Trent. It was in an evidence bag, with tiny bits of Johnny Trent's decomposed body. The D.C. police never bothered to test it after Trent's body was found."

Nikki nearly rear-ended the car in front of her. "What?"

"Anita told me that the bracelet had some dried black residue on it. Can't tell if it's been swabbed. There's no record of it ever being tested. Anita says she's never taken it out of the evidence bag, because she knew one day it could be tested."

"Out of curiosity, who petitioned to destroy it?" Nikki asked.

"Not the then Detective Sergeant Johnson and now captain, if that's what you're thinking. It was part of a routine sweep of evidence rooms. Anita wanted to know why we were interested in the evidence now, so I told her you'd called me and that you're afraid Johnny Trent wasn't the right guy and are on the case. She started bawling."

Shame rushed through Nikki. "I hate that we had to upset her and give her any hope. I'm sure she's furious with all of us."

"I didn't get that impression," Nash disagreed. "Anita asked if you were the one requesting it. She said she knew you would solve Mariah's murder one day."

Nikki drove down North 7th Street in downtown Minneapolis, a short walk from First Avenue, the dance club made famous by Prince's early performances, searching for a parking spot. The tiny building looked gray and lonely in the morning light, but at night, especially during weekends, local bands still performed. The early hour resulted in several empty parking spots on the street. Nikki pulled the Jeep into the last spot by the intersection of 7th and Hennepin.

She zipped her fall jacket to her chin, wishing she'd worn a heavier one. Nikki normally left her gun locked in the Jeep during witness interviews, but she grabbed her bag, making sure she had her notebook and pen.

The crosswalk signaled it was her turn, and she hurried across the street. She'd been surprised to hear the Starbucks inside the city center allowed the homeless to come in from the cold, but now she realized its central location on the direct route between Hennepin County Healthcare for the homeless and the adult shelter a few blocks northwest made it the most likely refuge given Starbucks's hours.

At least some good remained in the world.

Inside, the smell of coffee and sugary treats made Nikki's mouth water. She waved at Brenner, who sat at a corner table with two men in old Vikings coats. Nikki ordered a caramel macchiato and a slice of warmed banana bread. She joined the others at the table, and Brenner made the introductions.

"Vernon's a Vietnam vet." Brenner nodded to the black man sitting across from Nikki.

"Called up in the last draft in '72." Vernon nudged the younger, white man in a wheelchair next to him. "Jerry went to Afghanistan after 9/11."

Nikki thanked the men for their service. She'd noticed Jerry's left leg had been amputated below the knee, likely from an IED. Jerry appeared to be the quieter of the two men, his haunted eyes matching his demeanor.

This country needed to take better care of their veterans. Nikki didn't know the hard numbers, but she'd met countless vets living on the streets over her career. She asked the two men if they wanted anything more to eat.

"No, ma'am." Vernon patted his stomach. "Detective Brenner made sure our bellies got full."

"Thank you for meeting with us," Nikki told them. "I know talking to the police isn't always easy."

Vernon shrugged. "My philosophy is to work with the police, not against them. They're usually more tolerant." His voice cracked. "I can't believe Miss Kiania is gone. She was a nice lady."

Jerry sniffed and nodded. "Real nice. Never made me feel less-than, no matter how fancy she might be that day."

Brenner explained that Vernon and Jerry liked to spend time in the medical parking garages in the summer for the shade and proximity to the homeless healthcare center.

"I just can't stay in one place," Vernon said. "If I'm living on the street, I might as well travel a little. Plus, parking garages can be ..."—he glanced at Brenner—"profitable."

Nikki guessed he was referring to the accounts of vehicles being robbed during the summer months. "I'm not here to judge any of that," Nikki said. "How frequently did you guys see her?" Nikki asked.

"Over the summer, a fair amount," Vernon asked. "First time, she had a flat tire. Poor thing was getting pretty big and really struggling with the jack. Me and Jerry helped her change it. We wouldn't take anything for it, so after that, she kind of kept an eye out for us. Gave us extra food and even some clothes."

"Before you got here, Vernon was explaining they'd seen her the Sunday she disappeared, talking to her husband."

"What time?"

"After dark," Jerry said. "We saw her car, in a different ramp than she usually parked in. First time we'd seen any sign of her since she left to have the baby. So we hung around a while, hoping to say hi."

"Did you see her?" Nikki asked.

"We didn't talk to her," Jerry said. "Some time around dinner, she came outside with a guy we figured was her husband. So we didn't bother them."

"She went back into the hospital," Vernon said. "But her husband sat in his car a while. Smoking some strong stuff. We 'bout asked for some."

"These guys saw Ty Watson sitting in his vehicle smoking for several minutes," Brenner told Nikki. "That matches with his story. He left the parking garage stoned."

Not exactly the ideal frame of mind for a kidnapper. "Did you notice if he came back that night?"

Both men shook their heads. "We stayed a while after he left. Maybe an hour or two. Never saw him come back."

"Tell her what your friend heard," Brenner encouraged.

"We tried to get Billy to come with us, but he doesn't trust cops," Vernon said. "He's got some addictions."

"What did he hear?" Nikki asked.

"He was hanging around the elevator area, out of the heat, and she came off the elevator, followed by a janitor. He said he looked forward to seeing her after she had the baby. Billy said Kiania looked kind of freaked out, said thanks and hurried to her car."

"Had Billy seen this man around?"

Both men shook their heads. "Didn't recognize him, but he was a janitor. They change all the time."

"Did Billy tell you what he looked like?" Nikki asked.

"Short, stocky, white," Vernon said. "And a skull cap."

"In the heat of the summer?" Nikki clarified.

"That's what Billy said."

Nikki bought the men more coffee and left her card. "If you see him around, call this number. Tell them who you are and ask for me. I'll call you back."

TWENTY-FOUR

Liam had beat her to Garcia's office. He nodded at her, his mouth full of the bear claw he was inhaling.

Garcia paced in front of his office windows. He stopped short when Nikki walked in, silently judging her attire. Garcia prided himself on impeccable suits and flashy ties, and he managed to make a face every time an employee took advantage of the Bureau's more relaxed dress code.

He looked tired this morning instead of tan. He hadn't shaved in a couple of days, and Nikki took a little satisfaction in seeing that his beard hairs had gray mixed through them.

"Are you going to sit or pace?" Nikki asked before she dug into her notes. Garcia had a habit of pacing during meetings, full of nervous energy.

Garcia stopped pacing, hands on his hips. "Just start and I'll figure it out. Kiania Watson's autopsy report came back yesterday, right?"

Nikki found the report in her growing file on the case. "Protein and pre-workout were found in high concentration in her bloodstream and her stomach contents."

"Pre-workout?" Garcia asked. "As in, the stuff that makes you feel supersonic while you work out?"

"The effects would be relatively short-lived, but I think he gave it to her so she would fight him. Protein and bread were barely keeping her alive."

Garcia started pacing. "Did you ask Blanchard to go over Mariah Gonzales's autopsy?"

"I gave her the file I had kept but she had to request the full records from the D.C. medical examiner. They're supposed to get them to her today."

Garcia retrieved the black stone out of his pocket, palming it in his hand. "What about the employees at Midwest Plastics?"

"Mick Jones isn't the guy, but we need to confirm his alibi. No one else saw the man Annie talked about, but if he hung around outside like he did the OBGYNs, he probably could have blended in."

"Agent Wilson, where are you with the OBGYNs?" Garcia asked.

"We're working on calling all of them in the area. So far, no one recognizes the description. We've let them know to be on the lookout in case he's trolling for his next victim."

"Cassandra King's sons texted me last night, wanting to meet this afternoon. I'm hoping they might know something that will lead us to our killer."

"What does Sheriff Miller think?"

"I haven't had a chance to bring him up to date," Nikki said. "I've left messages."

"What's going on with him?" Garcia asked. "I thought you two had a good working relationship. He doesn't think we're on the right track? Or does he not want the help?"

"At this point, I'm not sure," Nikki admitted. "I'll track him down today, fill him in on Cass's disappearance—what Annie saw, the information from Shane and Mick." She didn't mention the argument between Miller and his wife that Rory's parents had mentioned.

"Did Kendall speak with the janitorial company that cleaned the office where Kiania's OB was located?"

Liam glanced at his notes. "Yes, Reece Janitorial. They had a box of gray uniforms without any lettering stolen off the back of a truck four months ago."

"Did they file a report?" Nikki asked. "What about security footage?"

"Wasn't working, and the truck was parked in the alley where there's no CCTV. Easy to grab a box without being seen. They said the description of the man we gave them was too vague."

"I've got one." Nikki told them about her meeting with Jerry and Vernon. "Billy described a white guy, wearing a janitor's uniform, possibly bald or shaved head, very pale skin. That's the description."

"So he wears a janitor uniform and blends right in," Liam said. "People are just going to assume he's supposed to be there."

Garcia looked at Liam. "Make sure you stay in contact with the OBGYNs. He may already have Cass, but he could also be scouting for his next victim. Make sure they know what to look for."

"What about the North Dakota victim?" Nikki asked. Liam had been tracking down information on Audrey Ritter, but ViCAP hadn't listed a specific law enforcement agency assigned to the case, so he'd planned to call the county sheriff.

"The victim was found on the southeast corner of Standing Rock Reservation."

Nikki's head shot up from her notes. "She wasn't native." That's probably why ViCAP hadn't listed an agency. Any crime that occurred on the reservation fell under the jurisdiction of the tribal police. Violent crimes like rape and murder were handled by the Bureau of Indian Affairs, usually in conjunction with the FBI or county police.

"I think the killer screwed up," Liam said flatly. "She was literally ten feet over the reservation's line. He probably thought he'd left her right next to it, because the father of Audrey's baby is a member of the Standing Rock tribe."

"He's stayed off the FBI's radar since 2014," Garcia agreed. "No way he willfully brings in multiple state agencies. He probably wanted to leave her close, so the police would assume it was the boyfriend."

"Banking on racism, but Standing Rock is one of the largest reservations in the country, and they have a really good working relationship with local law enforcement," Liam said. "At least half the county sheriff's deputies are members of the tribe. So Jake Temple, the baby's father, wasn't going to be railroaded that easily."

"Did you get any more details?" Nikki asked.

"I talked with the Bureau of Indian Affairs," Liam answered. "Audrey Ritter worked the second shift at McDonald's in Fort Yates. She got off at midnight and was seen on CCTV getting into her car and leaving work. The last footage of her is at the gas station about a mile away from where her car was found. Everything personal left with the car. They also found fresh blood on the driver's side door as well as fingernail scratches on the dash. She was yanked out of the car, they think."

He handed her a fax from the BIA agent. "Summary of the autopsy report. She's emailed the entire thing on a secure server."

Nikki's mouth went dry. Audrey Ritter looked nothing like Kiania or Mariah, but her baby was only nine weeks old. "He removed her fingernails. Black nylon rope, clove hitch. Crisscross pattern on her legs, along with a wound on her neck consistent with a dog shock collar." She looked at her partner. "Did they have any initial suspects?"

"Not really. Jake was home with the baby and could prove he hadn't left. The parents accused the reservation and police of favoritism. Audrey lived with her boyfriend in an apartment in Fort Yates. When she didn't come home, Jake reported her missing. He didn't have any defensive wounds or blood in his car and his alibi cleared him pretty quickly."

"How long before her body was found?" Nikki asked.

"Four weeks, but it had been there for a few days. Fortunately, it was still early spring, so she was still in good condition when the body was discovered. I'm still waiting on the full autopsy report. The tribal affiliation means more paperwork before it's released. The BIA promised we'd have it by the end of the day."

"What about flowers?" Nikki asked.

"Found clutched in her hands."

TWENTY-FIVE

Nikki met Kiania Watson's brother at the elevator after he'd been given a pass and sent to the fifth floor. His tan suit fit his tall body so well it had likely been tailored, the color enriching his dark skin. Combined with his stoic demeanor, Taji Onyanjo looked more like a distinguished ambassador than a graduate student.

"Mr. Onyanjo, it's nice to meet you," Nikki said. "I'm very sorry about your sister."

"I'm sorry to show up without an appointment." His soft voice had no trace of an accent, but both he and Kiania had grown up in Minnesota.

"That's no problem." Nikki motioned for him to follow her to her office. "Have you spoken with Detective Brenner recently?"

"She told me my sister's case is connected with others you're working." Taji stopped walking and looked down at her. "My parents cannot accept the idea of her being a victim of a serial killer. They refused to see the autopsy report or hear anything about her injuries. They only saw her face." He closed his eyes for a moment. "I talked to the medical examiner yesterday. The violence she endured... that's not something a husband does to his wife." Taji shuddered. "My parents dismiss me, because I'm a psychology student. I want to be a therapist."

"Good for you." Nikki unlocked the door to her office and offered Taji one of the chairs in front of her desk. She handed him a tissue. "Lieutenant Chen and Detective Brenner are working with us," Nikki assured him.

"That's why I'm here." Taji crossed his long legs. "My parents are overwhelmed with grief and not thinking right. They're badgering the sheriff about taking the case and arresting Ty. They're out of their minds."

"Your parents should seek grief counseling," Nikki said. "I can give you a list."

"I intend to make sure they do, but, Agent, I believe they have an agenda." He lowered his tone as though someone might overhear. "They want Ty to go to prison so they can get custody of Willow. That's why they keep calling the sheriff."

"Grief twists people into all sorts of misery," Nikki said. "It's hard to think clearly, and to lose a child... it's unimaginable."

Taji nodded. "They have immense guilt, too. They hadn't spoken to Kiania since before the baby was born, because she told them that if the baby was baptized, it would be in Ty's church, not theirs."

Nikki could only imagine how much harder that made losing Kiania for them. "When was the last time you spoke to Kiania? Were you two close?"

"Reasonably," he said. "We tried to have lunch once or twice a month. The last time I saw her, she was still on maternity leave. She admitted she thought Ty might be selling weed and was going to confront him," Taji said. "My parents have run with that. I don't think she was murdered for some kind of retribution. Drug murders are usually executions, right?"

"Usually," Nikki answered. "Did Kiania ever mention someone watching her, maybe making her uncomfortable?"

Taji retrieved a small flash drive from his suit pocket. "The news said you believe this person might be targeting postpartum women."

"It's one theory," Nikki clarified.

"Kiania emailed this to me a couple of days before she disappeared. She was certain the groundskeeper was the same one she saw at the hospital before going on maternity leave. He told her he would see her after her leave, and she had no idea what he meant at the time." Taji handed her the flash drive. "This is her dashcam footage from that day. She saved it and sent it to me to see if I thought she should say something to the OBGYN's building manager. She didn't tell Ty because she was afraid he would go after the guy." Tears built in his eyes. "I told her she was overreacting, blamed her hormones. If I had listened, she might still be alive."

Nikki returned to Garcia's office, where he and Liam were discussing another case. She held up the flash drive without bothering to knock. "Kiania gave this to her brother, because she thought the grounds guy at her six-week check-up is the janitor who spoke to her when she left for maternity leave. It's dashcam, so I don't know what to expect."

Garcia took the drive and connected it to his USB port. Nikki tried not to expect too much. She held her breath as Garcia opened the file and clicked play. The video didn't have sound, but Nikki recognized the medical complex as Kiania's OBGYN.

Nikki would have missed him if she hadn't known what she was looking for. A man in a gray janitor's suit idled on the sidewalk near the doctor's office, watching the vehicle approach. He turned his head as it neared, revealing a bald head beneath his dark cap. Same pale skin, wearing a generic janitor's uniform, eyes on his phone.

"That's him," Nikki whispered.

TWENTY-SIX

Nikki typed the number Nash had given her into Skype but stopped without hitting "enter." Anita Gonzales wanted to talk to her but that didn't mean she wasn't waiting for her chance to lay into Nikki for forgetting about Mariah. Nikki had no idea if Anita even knew what had happened in Virginia.

Nikki wasn't sure what she was going to say. She clicked the button. Anita had requested Nikki call her at the office during her lunch hour. She'd moved up from analyst to supervising an entire team, and her days were chaotic at best.

Her laptop screen flickered, Anita's face filling the screen. Her naturally tan skin hadn't aged, saved for some wrinkles around eyes. She no longer wore her hair past her shoulders, and the shorter haircut complemented the natural gray streaks in her dark hair.

"Hello, Agent Hunt." Her voice sounded stronger than Nikki remembered, but Anita had still been reeling from Mariah's murder. "I knew I would hear from you one day."

"So Agent Nash said." She filled the beat of awkward silence. "Anita, I'm sorry."

"No." Anita held up her hand. "I know what happened to you that day." Her stoic expression wavered. "I prayed you didn't lose your baby because I'd taken advantage of your guilty conscience. For years, I wondered. And then I heard about the death of your husband—through the Bureau grapevine. Tyler was highly thought of and is missed by many. That's when I learned you had a daughter." Anita rested her hand against her heart. "Praise God."

"Thank you," Nikki said. "Her name is Lacey, and she's nine going on nineteen."

Anita laughed. "So is my Mira. I believe she's only a year or so older than your daughter."

"Mira is a pretty name. It stands out."

Anita smiled. "Mariah named her Miracle, and as much as I agree that she is a miracle, I don't make her go by the name."

"How much does she know about her mother?"

"Not much," Anita said. "She's always known Mama went to God when she was a baby. I've come so close to telling her the truth, but I can't make myself shatter her world like that. Girls have enough to endure in this world."

"I understand. You have to weigh the pros and cons and just hope you made the right decision."

Anita nodded, sadness in her eyes. "I thought I did the right thing with Mariah, and she fell in with the wrong people. I worry so much Mira will do the same."

"I'm sure you do." Nikki wasn't going to lie and say it couldn't happen. "I'm not a psychologist, but I've learned a lot about death and grieving over the course of my career, not to mention how easily a child can be emotionally damaged by a well-meaning parent," she added. "Trust your gut about your child. I've never met a parent who didn't have some inkling something was wrong but talked themselves out of it. The mind can play tricks on us about our significant others and pretty much anyone else in our lives, but it's different when it comes to our children."

"Thank you." Anita inhaled, held her breath for a few seconds, and slowly exhaled. She repeated the process twice.

"I appreciate your patience," Anita finally said. "The four-seven-eight technique is sometimes the only thing that gets me through the day. It's a meditation technique. Anyway, Mariah's killer is still out there, isn't he?"

"I think so," Nikki answered. "I may be wrong about the killer we're currently looking for, but I'm not wrong about Johnny Trent. I didn't know anything about him, and I never asked. I should have."

Anita was silent for a few moments. "Didn't you just say to trust your gut when it comes to our children?" She didn't wait for a response. "That's all you did, Agent Hunt. You took care of your baby. I don't hold that against you. You were the only one who didn't treat Mariah like a prostitute not worth their time."

"Agent Nash told me he wasn't sure if the evidence you now have hadn't been tested."

"When I saw the bracelet, I knew it wasn't rust or tarnished," Anita said. "I've never taken it or her socks out of their individual evidence bags. I knew they would be tested one day, and I hoped you were the one to get it done."

Anita kept the evidence in her safe. They agreed Courtney and Elwood would stop by around six p.m., after she'd had time to get home from work and take a few minutes for herself.

"I was so happy when Agent Nash said you were the one interested in the case." Anita's expression hardened. "If it had been that one who came to tell me Johnny Trent was the killer, I would have refused."

"Why?"

"He was a pompous ass," Anita said. "I didn't understand

how they could be certain it was the man who killed my daughter when they couldn't even tell his race. I asked about having a forensic anthropologist examine the skeletal remains, but his remains had already been cremated by North Carolina, because they didn't have extra storage space in their morgue, and the agent assured them the case had been closed.

"I told him that didn't sound right, that they had to find some kind of biological matter to test." Anita's eyes flashed. "That bastard stood there in my living room, in his fancy suit with his hair perfectly styled like he was getting ready to guest star on some shitty detective show and told me that working as an analyst didn't make me an investigator. He assured me I was thinking with my emotions instead of my head."

Nikki gripped her chair arms so hard her nails dug into the fake leather. "I am so sorry. There's no excuse—"

"It doesn't matter now," Anita said. "But I wanted you to know, in case you ever run into him."

She was going to run into him all right. Nikki thanked Anita for her kindness, and they talked about Lacey and Mira for a few more minutes. Nikki found a photo on her phone of Lacey from this summer, dandelion dust on the tip of her nose, her dark curls wild.

"She looks like you. Beautiful," Anita gushed. "Let me find a picture of Mira. I'm so bad at taking good ones, and she hates having her photo taken."

"Lacey looks a lot like my mom did at that age," Nikki said. "We both get the dark curly hair from her."

"Mira would be jealous." Anita tapped her phone. "She hates her hair. Needless to say, she must look like her father."

She held her phone for Nikki to see the phone of a smiling, red-haired, pale girl with plump lips. Her eyebrows were so light they were hard to see. A small patch of freckles crossed the bridge of her nose. She had the same startling blue eyes as the man Nikki had chased.

Nikki's stomach bottomed out at the same time her hopes bloomed. She no longer doubted the need to ask for a sample of Mira's DNA.

"Her complexion is stunning," Nikki said. "Suits her red hair perfectly." She hesitated, trying to find the right words. "Did you know Mariah told friends the man she left with that night was different? That he had actual conversations with her and treated her like a human being." The irony disgusted Nikki. Anita's eyes watered. Nikki knew she'd considered the same theory. She let the woman take a breath and compose herself before she continued. "I'd like to get a sample of Mira's DNA," Nikki said. "It might help us."

Anita nodded. "What do you need? I'd rather her not know about it."

"Hair with the follicle attached is the best way without swabbing. Courtney can usually find that in a hairbrush." She took a deep breath to control her shaking voice. "I wish I could be there."

Nikki took a few minutes to digest everything Anita had told her. She wanted to march straight into Garcia's office and let him have it, but she couldn't treat her boss like that if she wanted to stay on his good side. No wonder he had such immense guilt.

Thankfully, Liam was on the phone when she came out of her office. She walked down the hall to Garcia's and knocked on his closed door.

"Come in."

Without any idea what she planned to say, Nikki entered his office. She was surprised to see Garcia had loosened his tie and the top buttons of his crisp desk shirt. "You talked to Anita Gonzales, then?"

"I did." Nikki sat down and waited. The two stared at one another, the heavy truth sitting silently between them.

Garcia looked away first. "Agent Hunt, I'm going to share something with you that very few people in the Bureau know. Can I count on your discretion?"

"If it's personal with no relevance to any case, of course."

"As I told you, my marriage had failed, and I was in the middle of a nasty divorce." Garcia took a deep breath. "I cheated. She caught me. With... another man." He chewed his bottom lip, his gaze on Nikki, no doubt looking for any sign of judgment.

"I'm sorry that happened," she said.

"Don't be." Garcia's shoulders inched down. "I got myself into the situation. She was humiliated. She also had a vindictive side I didn't anticipate. She told my strict Catholic family. My mother had cancer at the time, and I was terrified the news would be too much for her. My wife also threatened to tell everyone at work, and even though it's much more accepted, I'm not ready for the Bureau to know about my personal business."

"It's no one's business," Nikki agreed.

"It's not an excuse, but I was drinking every day just to get by. I took the easy way out in Virginia, and when I spoke to Anita..." His voice cracked. "I kept looking at this woman, refusing to accept what I did believe to be the truth, telling me her daughter was more than a prostitute. The love she had for Mariah infuriated me."

"Because your family refused to love you unconditionally," Nikki surmised.

Garcia nodded. "I'm not proud of it, but I also can't change what happened. I've been thinking about telling you this for days—I just need you to know the full story."

"For what it's worth, I never heard anything about you drinking or having issues on the job," Nikki told him.

"I took a leave of absence," he said. "I screwed up the next case so badly that was my only option if I wanted to keep my job. Fortunately, my superiors believed the drinking was about my marriage failing and that's what my family had issue with. During that time, I got sober and started counseling. I vowed to never let my personal life interfere with work again, and I've done that. I was lucky enough to be reassigned when I returned, so I could start over in a new office. It set my career back a few years, but I didn't care. I could control the narrative at the new office."

"And what is that narrative, exactly?" Nikki realized she didn't know much about Garcia, because he never put himself in a situation where personal questions might come up. Living that way had to be exhausting.

"My private life is my private life," he said. "I'm the poster child for why agents need to remain detached, why supervisors shouldn't get close to their agents. That's why they sent me here. They want me to lead by example." He shook his head. "So much for that."

As much as Nikki wanted to be angry, she just felt bad for him. "Sir, you have led by example. Until today, I knew very little about you."

"Thank you," Garcia said. "I think highly of you, Agent Hunt. It's important to me that you know my head wasn't in the right place at the time. It's not an excuse, and I own my decisions, but I wasn't awful to Anita just to be awful. And it's bothered me for years."

Nikki wished he would have told her about speaking with Anita sooner, but she doubted it would have made any difference in how they handled the case. "I believe everything happens for a reason. If you hadn't acted that way, she may not have fought for her daughter's personal items the way she did."

"The bracelet?" Garcia asked.

"She's never touched it, or the socks Mariah wore. If it is biological material, Courtney should be able to get a DNA profile. We can test it in case the rock ends up not having enough biological material."

"We'll still have the same issues as far as trial is concerned in terms of the rock," Garcia said. "But this is probably our best option to catch him before Cassandra King's time runs out."

TWENTY-SEVEN

Nikki called Courtney three times before she picked up. She took the South Saint Paul exit too quickly, accidentally cutting off a school bus. Cass's son Sam had called and asked to meet. He'd suggested a little diner in South Saint Paul that served breakfast all day.

"Is the rock any good?" Nikki asked Courtney. Elwood had taken her to the lab at Quantico so she could look at the rock under the microscope.

"There's definitely blood in the crevices," Courtney said. "I don't know if it's enough for a sample."

"Fingers crossed," Nikki replied. "Nash called me after I dropped you off at the airport. Anita has the bracelet found in the car with Johnny Trent. It's never been tested, and was on the floor behind the passenger seat. Anita said it looks like blood."

"Testing it would only confirm it was Mariah's," Courtney said.

"Unless the killer bled on it," Nikki told her. "She also has the socks."

"That's what I'm talking about," Courtney said. "The M-

Vac loves socks. Anita said it was okay for us to come and get them?"

"Yeah, and there's something else," Nikki said. "Mariah's daughter has the same complexion as the man in the woods."

"This is horrible," Courtney said. "Did you tell Anita?"

"She suspected it," Nikki said.

"You must be tired," Courtney said. "I can use the kid's toothbrush. Any word on Cass?"

"Nothing," Nikki said. "We ruled out the people in her life quickly. How long will the test results take?"

"A few days at least, and that's me putting everything else on the backburner and possibly not sleeping, but I think I can pull it off. If I get anything from the rock, I'll put that profile in CODIS before I test the other stuff, including the daughter's DNA."

"Are you at Quantico right now?" Nikki asked.

"Elwood dropped me off at my hotel. I figured I'd take a nap."

"Good idea." Nikki parked on the street in front of the diner the boys suggested. "Sleep when you can."

"You, too."

Nikki opened the door to the Sunlight Diner just a few blocks from Cass's home. "Holy hell." Six people were crowded in the tiny entryway, wedged in between the counter and wall. "Is everyone here waiting for a table?"

The gray-haired man in front of her smiled and nodded. "It's pretty much always busy. Great food and cheap prices. Hard to beat."

Nikki counted the tables. Two of the fifteen were hastily being cleared, but the rest were full of hungry customers, most without food. Nikki took out her phone to text Sam and ask if they could meet somewhere else and then saw Sam waving at her from the other side of the restaurant. He motioned for her to come join them.

Her cheeks grew hot. Wasn't this cutting? The line started at the front door, and she didn't want to excuse her way through people who'd been waiting longer than she had.

"Go on," the man ahead of her encouraged. "They seat from both entrances. Don't know how they keep track of who's next, but they do."

Relieved, Nikki excused herself, squeezing through the small opening between the line and counter. Sam and Logan sat at a rounded corner table. She took the seat across from the two boys, a flash of pink next to Sam catching her eye. "Is that Emma?"

"Dad doesn't know we're meeting with you," Sam answered. "He went out to look for Mom."

The taller boy next to him pushed his hair out of his eyes. "Yeah right. He went to the bar."

"I know that. I was just telling her what he said he was going to do." Sam glared at his brother. "Agent Hunt, this is my brother, Logan."

"Thanks for talking with me." She retrieved her notepad and pencil from her bag and looked at Logan. "Since you're the adult but not Sam's legal guardian, I have to direct my questions to you. Does your dad have a drinking problem?"

"He doesn't think he has," Logan answered. "But he's usually there more than he's home."

Nikki felt for the two boys. "When was the last time you talked to your mom?"

"Before her shift," Sam answered. "I get home a little bit before she leaves."

Logan looked at the table. "I've got practice right after school," he said. "I barely see her during the season since she works second shift." A muscle in his jaw twitched. "She talked about getting on the day shift, but Emma's in daycare. Second shift pays more."

On cue, Emma's babbling turned into frustration, her little pink socks popping above the table every time she kicked her feet. Sam soothed her with a pacifier.

"Your dad doesn't watch her during the day?"

The boys looked at each other and smirked. "He's not a baby person."

Evidently they'd heard those words from their father more than once. "So the last time you saw her that day, Sam, did she seem like anything was bothering her?"

"No," he answered. "I mean, she complained about Dad being lazy, but she does that every day."

"Your parents have been married a long time," Nikki offered. "Sounds like they know how to push each other's buttons."

Both boys shrugged, Sam's focus on his increasingly fussy sister. Logan met Nikki's gaze. "Dad didn't do anything to Mom."

"I never said he did."

"I know," he said. "But isn't the husband always the first suspect? I'm just telling you so you don't waste precious time finding Mom."

"Fair enough," Nikki answered. "Has your dad ever been violent with your mom?"

"Couple of times," Logan answered. "But that was when we were little. He's too lazy now."

Little Emma squirmed and spit out the pacifier. Sam looked on the verge of tears.

"Do you mind if I hold her?" Nikki asked. "Maybe a female will calm her down."

Sam practically thrust the crying baby at her. Nikki slipped her arms around the baby, making sure to protect her head. Emma wailed and sucked on her fist.

"Bottle."

Nikki adjusted the baby to make her more comfortable and put the bottle to her lips. Emma took the nipple, her cries quieting as she nursed. "There." She smiled at Sam. "She just needed a change of pace. Back to your dad. You said he was lazy. I thought he was on disability because of an injury and can't do everything he used to?"

"He got hurt a few years ago getting out of the semi. Missed the step, fell hard on his back. So yeah, I know he's in pain," Logan said. "He doesn't even try. He used to drive across the country and back and then come home and work on the house. Once he stopped working, he just kind of stopped doing everything else."

That sounded like depression in Nikki's opinion. "I don't know your father, and I'm not here to lecture you guys, but I will say that your dad went through trauma, and that changes people."

"That's what Mom said."

"Do either one of you remember if your dad got home from the bar around his usual time the night your mom went missing?"

"I heard him come in after we went to bed," Logan said. "That's normal. I didn't look at the time."

Nikki had already confirmed with the bar that Shane had told the truth. "Can you think of anyone your mom might have argued with lately?"

Sam leaned forward, his elbows on the table. "On Thursday, before she went into work, she was chewing someone out on the phone. Her face was all red and she told the person she was going to file a complaint and then hung up. I asked her what happened, and she told me that she'd called 911 on the way home at three a.m. Because she thought someone deliberately swerved into her lane after she left," Sam said. "I asked if it was someone she worked with and she said she wasn't sure. She'd just seen him hanging around her car a couple of times."

Logan jumped in. "Sam told me about it that night, so I asked her about it a few days later. It bugged me that she didn't know if he worked at the factory because she knows everyone who works there," he said. "I asked if she thought he was stalking her, and she got all nervous. Then she finally said that the security at work would take care of it."

Sam rolled his eyes. "They're basically glorified mall cops. What are they going to do?"

Nikki thought about the route Cass would have taken from Woodbury to her home in southern Washington County. "Did your mom say where this happened?"

"Umm." Sam tapped his lips. "No, but when she was yelling at the person on the phone, she said it was on the way home from work. He chased her out of nowhere. Who does that?"

TWENTY-EIGHT

Getting from South Saint Paul to Stillwater at rush hour proved to be a miserable lesson in patience. Construction and an accident had slowed I-494 traffic to a crawl. The GPS offered an alternative route, but Nikki couldn't get over to take the exit.

She'd normally take the advantage to think about her current case, but Nikki's thoughts drifted to this morning at home and the conversation she'd soon be having with Rory.

Nikki sometimes still marveled at the sight of the Washington County Government Center's size. When she'd left Stillwater to attend the University of Minnesota, the law enforcement complex housed the sheriff's office, emergency response center and jail. After a massive upgrade in 2007, the five-story government center building was Stillwater's tallest, featuring a dozen new and remodeled courtrooms, a new data center and a modern 911 call center. Nikki had worked several cases from the conference rooms in the massive building.

She greeted the duty sergeant in the lobby. "Hey, Joy." Nikki had only met her a couple of times, as the duty sergeants rotated.

"Oh hi, Agent Hunt. I don't know if the sheriff's here at the moment."

"That's okay," Nikki said. "I'm actually here to talk to the PST supervisor. I'd like to listen to an emergency call from a week or so ago." The sheriff's office oversaw the countywide Emergency Communications Response Center. The ECRC had over fifteen public safety telecommunicators, or PSTs, the name given to dispatch operators so they could operate as first responders.

After making sure the supervisor was available, Joy buzzed Nikki into the ECRC, located across from the sheriff's office's visitor entrance. Instead of the basement, the PSTs worked in a room with plenty of natural light and modern equipment. Each PST manned six different screens. Nikki would never be able to keep all of it straight.

The old center had resembled an office but these desks were much larger, without the cubicle walls to make the room feel even smaller.

Mike Berman, the shift supervisor, greeted Nikki. They made small talk as he led her past the PSTs and into his office. "I have to tell you, I remember coming to the 911 call center during my eighth-grade field trip. It was dark, crowded and loud. I knew I'd never want the job."

"The ECRC is nice," Berman agreed. "We're lucky to have it." He motioned for her to sit.

She tried not to look too uncomfortable in the straight-backed chair. It reminded her of the smaller chairs at Lacey's elementary. "Thank you for seeing me on short notice. Normally I'd make this request via email, but it involves a missing person."

"Happy to help." Berman logged into his computer, his fingers clunking along the keyboard. "Do you have the date and approximate time and location?"

She gave him the information from Cass's sons. The

ECRC handled all traffic, fire and law enforcement needs in the county. Between all the little towns scattered across the area, that included ten police departments and at least a dozen fire departments. "I hope it's not too hard to find the call."

"Normally, an eleven thirty p.m. call takes a minute to find, because that's a busier time," Berman told her. "But during the week, especially Tuesdays and Thursdays, we usually have fewer calls." He looked at her over the top of his glasses. "This is somewhere on 52 south?"

Nikki nodded. "She left Midwest Plastics in Woodbury, headed to Stillwater."

"You have the last four digits to her phone number?"

She gave him the number.

"Here we go."

A male operator answered, sounding bored.

"Yeah." Cass's voice trembled. "I'm headed south on 494, and this asshole is trying to run me down. I accidentally cut him off in construction, and he's been on my ass ever since, flashing his lights."

"Did you cause a collision?" the operator asked. "Does his vehicle have damage?"

"What? No." Cass sounded furious. "I made a mistake, he's a pissed-off white man—"

"Then this isn't an emergency," the operator said. "You made someone mad, they're letting you know. You need to call the non-emergency number."

"For what?" Cass demanded. "How is this not... oh, my God." Fear replaced the anger in her voice. "I think this is the guy hanging around work. White guy, round face, white van. I bet he followed me from work."

"Ma'am, if you feel like you're in danger, you need to go to the nearest police station."

"Now he's coming up on my right side. No license plate in

front. Isn't that illegal?" Cass didn't wait for an answer. "Sono-fabitch made me miss my exit."

The white van had done something similar to Nikki. Was it the same person?

"Is there anything else I can assist you with today?" The PST still sounded bored.

"You didn't do anything in the first place." The call ended.

Berman rubbed his forehead. "I can't say I'm happy with how that was handled."

"Neither am I." At least she had a better idea of who Cass saw and where to pull CCTV. "We need to pull CCTV from that call as well as Woodbury's over the last two weeks."

Nikki left the ECRC, taking the back corridor into the sheriff's office, where a second duty sergeant told her that she could find Miller in his office. The pit in her stomach grew as she approached his office. He wasn't going to like what Nikki had to say.

She knocked on his door and waited for his response. "It's open."

Nikki stayed in the doorway. "Hey, do you have a few minutes?"

"Just a few," Miller answered, without looking up from his computer.

Nikki shut the door behind her. "Taji Onyanjo came to see me this morning."

Miller's dark eyes locked with hers. "He did. I wasn't aware the FBI was officially working the case."

"Brenner and Chen requested it," Nikki said.

"By the way." Miller glared at her. "Why did you let Garcia put that information out in the media?"

"I didn't have a choice," she answered. "And I'm not sure it's a bad strategy. If I'm right, then he knows he has my attention and doesn't need to do anything else."

Miller finally stopping typing. "Are you still on the back from the dead serial killer?"

"He isn't dead. They misidentified him." Nikki told him the short version of that day in 2014 and how she knew Johnny Trent wasn't the man the second she saw his old mugshot.

"Well, that's too damned bad," Miller said. "But it doesn't mean that this is the same guy. He could be dead or in prison. It's been ten years. And flowers aren't enough to connect the dots for me."

"Mariah Gonzales and Kiania had the same stomach contents. Pre-workout ingredients that would give them a burst of strength, along with protein."

"Who's Mariah Gonzales?" he asked.

Nikki couldn't believe how callous he sounded. "The victim from 2014. Blanchard agreed that combination in two victims with other similarities is telling."

"Then I'd trust her opinion."

Nikki tried to ignore his tone. "I do, and I trust my own." She let the words sink in for a few seconds. "Taji told me his parents have been calling you, insisting Ty Watson murdered his wife despite all evidence pointing to someone else. He's worried they're doing it to get custody of the baby."

A muscle in Miller's jaw twitched. "And he's afraid I'm too ignorant to figure that out?"

"No, not at all," Nikki said. "He didn't say anything about you. He gave me a copy of Kiania's dashcam from her last visit to the OBGYN."

"I've seen it," Miller said. "Kiania told him the same guy had been a janitor at the hospital. I told him to take it to Brenner or Chen."

"Well, he brought it to me." Nikki told him what Vernon and Jerry had said. "Last week, Cassandra King made a 911 call describing a similar man following her aggressively after work. I heard the call," Nikki said. "She was scared. It wasn't taken seriously."

"Make sure Berman knows. That's his department."

"Cass's husband isn't taking her disappearance seriously, and you passed things on to the Stillwater police when her friend contacted you." She snapped her fingers. "Oh, and Cass also found trillium on her car. I'm sure that's coincidence, too."

"It sounds like your team's got it covered," he said. "I've got my hands full here."

"So do we," Nikki countered. "So far, we've found two more murders that match the criteria and there's likely more. The signature element is almost a literal signature. His fantasy world started at a young age, fueled by violence. He's been creating and dreaming about this fantasy for years, and the attack isn't about sexual release. It's about acting out the fantasy. That's why each step is part of an elaborate play."

"I know what a signature is." Miller glared at her. "I don't disagree about your serial killer theory anymore. But I don't have time to deal with a case that's not my responsibility."

Nikki had heard enough. "Ask your PST supervisor to listen to the 911 call that Cass made last week." She reached into her bag. "Here." She tossed a sticky note with information about Cass's car. "Please call me if any of your deputies find this vehicle." She headed towards his door. "By the way, if you ever want to talk about what the hell is going on with you, my door's open."

TWENTY-NINE

During the drive home, Nikki tried to focus on the positive instead of her blowout with Miller. Courtney had collected the items from Anita. She wasn't able to find a flight home until tomorrow morning, but if there were no delays, Courtney should be in the lab by the afternoon.

They were going to catch him, Nikki could feel it.

Then she remembered the promise she'd made to Rory that morning. He wouldn't hold her to it, but it was time to tell him everything about that day.

Lacey was already asleep by the time Nikki got home. Part of her hoped Rory would be asleep, too, but he was sitting at the kitchen table, eating cold pizza. She left her bag and keys on the counter and walked over to her husband, sitting on his lap without saying a word.

Rory squeezed her. "You don't have to say anything tonight. You don't even have to tell me."

"No, I want to," Nikki whispered. "Maybe telling you will help me let go of the guilt."

. . .

Tears stung Nikki's eyes as she stumbled out of her OBGYN's office.

She'd prayed the bleeding was normal, but the test had confirmed she no longer had the pregnancy hormone in her body. She'd miscarried.

This is normal, the doctor had assured her. Most women experience at least one miscarriage, even if they don't know it. In a few months, they could try again.

She couldn't go through this again. Even though she'd only been pregnant a couple of weeks, she'd already started getting used to the idea of being a working mom. Tyler worried that her stressful job in the BAU would affect her pregnancy, but Nikki had insisted that every job had its stresses. She'd be more stressed working a job she hated.

Her throat constricted and burned as she'd asked the gray-haired doctor whether or not stress had caused her to lose the baby.

Not likely, she'd assured her. But if her job as an agent was too high stress to manage pregnancy and then a baby, she might have to make a hard choice.

She may not have been as condescending as she sounded, but her judgment had been clouded.

She reached her car, hands shaking as she tried to unlock it. Loud voices a few cars to her left caught her attention.

"If I want to go back to my friends, I will," the heavily pregnant, young girl in the waiting area shouted at her mother. "You can't tell me what to do."

"I will not let my grandchild be born on the street," her mother shot back. "Why are you being like this? I thought you were happy at home."

The woman tossed her wavy, black hair over her shoulder. "I'm not going to be controlled. You're the one who made me have this baby. I'm only eighteen."

Something in Nikki snapped. She stalked over to the

women. "Hey." Nikki looked the young woman in the eyes. "Instead of complaining about a situation you got yourself into, try being grateful. Do you know how many women would do anything to get pregnant? Who've tried for years and years with no results?" Her temple throbbed, the voice in her head begging her to stop. "For every young girl like you, there are a dozen women like me. You should be ashamed."

Motionless, the girl stared at Nikki, her face red.

"Excuse me." The mother grabbed Nikki's arm. "How dare you speak to my daughter that way? You have no idea what her situation is—"

"I'm sorry." Nikki felt like she'd woken up after a blackout. "I just lost..." Her gaze drifted to the older woman's open bag sitting on the hood. She worked for the Bureau. "Please forget what I said." She backed away, beseeching the young girl. "I'm sorry."

Nikki buried her face in Rory's warm neck. "That's why Mariah's mother remembered me when she was killed."

"And why you feel like it's your duty to solve her murder," he said. "You can't put that on yourself, babe."

"I'm trying not to, but it just feels like that's why I encountered her in the first place. I couldn't stop her death, but I can solve her murder."

Rory wrapped both arms around her. "Did Courtney get what you needed?"

"I hope so," Nikki said. "I don't know how we're going to find Cass King alive if she doesn't."

THIRTY

Nikki cut through downtown Stillwater, taking the scenic byway north toward O'Brien State Park. Morning fog rose from the river to her right, so dense the homes along the river disappeared into the gray abyss. So much for a glimpse of the fading fall colors along the river.

She'd already let Liam and Garcia know Cass's car had been found and that she'd come into the office after looking at the car. Miller hadn't said much when he'd called to give her the information, his tone just as gruff as the last time they'd spoken.

North of Marine on St. Croix, O'Brien State Park had some of the best hiking trails in the state. Hikers could enjoy the soil deposited thousands of years ago by glaciers as well as the riverbanks and flood plains. A restored oak savanna, the thick woods and presence of bogs meant the area had something for everyone. It wasn't unusual to see birdwatchers and hikers at all times of the year, but most of the outdoor recreational facilities were closed for the season, including the picnic area where Cass's car had been left.

Mark had taken the entire family camping in the park earlier that summer in his new thirty-two-foot Airstream. Liam and his girlfriend, Caitlin, her son Zach and Courtney had joined them for a barbeque. Liam and Zach would have put up a tent and stayed if the women had allowed, but as tough as both Courtney and Caitlin were, neither had any interest in camping.

A park ranger flagged her down at the entrance. Miller had likely asked him to monitor traffic in and out of the park while they processed the car. Nikki showed her badge, and the ranger told her to follow the road until it forked and take the left fork. She'd see Miller's police SUV in front of the parking area, blocking the entrance just in case someone stopped at the nearby bathrooms and decided to see what the police were doing at the picnic grounds.

She did as directed, sad to see the trees had lost most of the summer foliage. Winter was coming to Stillwater, and Nikki already dreaded the cold and snow, not to mention driving on icy roads. She could work from home if she needed to, as long as she planned to do desk work. She couldn't remember the last time she went into work knowing she'd be sitting behind the desk all day.

Nikki parked the Jeep behind Miller's SUV. She grabbed her phone and keys, leaving her gun locked in the Jeep. Thankfully she'd worn a warm coat, because the icy wind coming from Alice Lake to their west made it feel more like December than the end of October.

The picnic area had only Cass's red car and the sheriff's crime scene investigators preparing to process it. As one of the CSIs approached the Honda, Nikki remembered Courtney's comment that the M-Vac had successfully retrieved DNA from vehicles in cold cases.

"Wait," she shouted, jogging toward the car. "Don't process it yet."

Miller's head shot up from his phone, and Nikki was relieved not to see anger in his dark eyes. "Why?"

"Courtney's going to use the M-Vac to hopefully retrieve DNA from the 2014 murder. It's a wet vacuum designed to pull biological material from tough surfaces, like rock and nylon and a lot of other things. Have you opened the doors yet?"

"Just to pop the trunk." Miller pointed to the car. "Empty, thank God."

"Look, I know you think I'm wrong, and that's fine," Nikki said. "I hope I am, but the only way to know is to test the car."

Miller motioned for Nikki to follow him. "I want to show you something."

They were still a few feet away from the car when Nikki saw the flower tucked between the windshield wipers and windshield. "Pink trillium." Heart racing, she grabbed Miller's arm, all thoughts of their disagreement evaporating. "Even if he used gloves, he may have left DNA on the wipers or glass." She looked up at the sheriff. "Would you be okay if we took the car into evidence so Courtney could use the M-Vac when she gets back?"

He looked surprised and pointed to the flowers. "You were right. There's no way these flowers are a coincidence. Not when this happened so close to Kiania's body being found."

"I know."

"I was a jerk."

"You were," Nikki agreed. "I know cops don't like it when federal agents talk about other cops, but I have worked with plenty of police to know your decision to call me, instead of deciding to take the case over because you didn't want to admit you were wrong, is one that not everyone makes. You put your ego aside, as I knew you would."

Tension seemed to melt off Sheriff Miller. "Thank you."

"You're welcome." She unlocked her phone to call for the evidence team. "I have a lot to catch you up on."

. . .

Nikki grimaced at the sleet hitting Miller's windshield, opening her weather app. "This crap is supposed to stop in an hour or so. Courtney's plane should still be able to land."

Kiania had been kept alive for three weeks, and she hoped Cass had that much time, but she couldn't count on it. With Courtney gone, Arim had answered Nikki's call about picking up Cass's car. Fortunately, the crime scene technicians had managed to cover the car with a tarp before the weather hit. Nikki doubted he'd been careless enough to touch anything in the car with his bare hands, but they still had to test it, including the hood and windshield.

"Run through it one more time for me," Miller said.

"The man in Virginia was fair skinned. I don't know if he had red hair as he was wearing a ball cap, but it's possible given how light his eyebrows were and his freckles. A janitor—or a man dressed as one—who had spoken to Kiania in the parking garage before maternity leave also matches the description of the man on her dashcam at her six-week appointment. Two separate witnesses described a similar person, including height. Cass lives down the street from Kiania. We're checking every possible CCTV on the routes she would have taken to and from work, as well as asking for any security footage neighbors might have." Nikki paused to take a breath. "Anita Gonzales still has Mariah's bracelet and socks, which was in the car with Johnny Trent and still has black material that could be her biological matter. Since no one ever entered his DNA into CODIS, we could use that to confirm he didn't kill Mariah, as long as Courtney can get the profile."

"Ty Watson didn't do it," Miller said. "I assume nothing about Mick Jones or Shane King set off any alarm bells in you?"

"No." Nikki couldn't base an investigation solely on her memory that had been addled by a concussion, especially when a woman's life remained at stake. "Mick Jones has the coloring, I suppose. I didn't notice the freckles, but I don't remember how many freckles the guy I chased had. I was trying to focus on as many different details as possible."

"Have you tried florists?" Miller asked. "He got the flowers from somewhere."

"We've called every florist in Hennepin, Dakota, and Ramsey Counties, including greenhouses, and none of them have them in stock right now, obviously," Nikki answered. "I'm told that white trillium is popular around here. It gets too cold for red, and given the apparent smell, most people don't grow them inside. I couldn't find any that regularly stock it. But they can be grown in a greenhouse. He's got to have his own setup." She looked at her watch. "Time to pick up Courtney."

THIRTY-ONE

Nikki made sure the plastic bin containing the evidence was secured on the floor behind her. Courtney's flight had been delayed for traffic, and Nikki had spent an agonizing hour in the parking lot going over the same information until her eyes seemed to cross.

"We found Cass's car," Nikki said. "Abandoned by a lake. Whoever drove it last was shorter than Cass. I'm having it brought to the lab. I'm hoping you can use the M-Vac on it as well."

"Should be able to," Courtney said. "Whether or not it yields anything is another story. Your text said Miller called you about the car? When we texted last night, he'd blown you off."

"He apologized," Nikki said. "We've moved on." She glanced at Courtney. "How was Anita?"

"Good," Courtney said. "Tough as nails. She showed me pictures of Mira. She's wonderful. I hope she's not his," Courtney said. "But it would definitely help us."

An eager group waited for Courtney when they got to the lab. Courtney stuffed her duffle bag into one of the lockers provided for the fourth-floor lab technicians. Nikki carried the evidence container while Courtney unlocked the M-Vac out of storage and rolled it down to the DNA lab.

"Can you give me the basics on how the M-Vac works?" Miller asked.

"It's essentially a wet vacuum for DNA evidence," Courtney answered. "Anything textured, porous, rough or large is always difficult to extract a sample from and if you can, it's miniscule. The M-Vac is able to pull the biological material out, and it's got a deeper surface extraction than any other tool we have." She held up a bottle. "We spray the surface with collection solution, simultaneously vacuuming the surface. It's kind of a mini-hurricane effect that loosens the DNA material. Everything collected in the collection bottle will later be concentrated into a filter, where we can start extrapolating."

"How long does the process take?" Miller asked.

"It won't take long to collect, but the rest of the process takes time," she said. "Since we have a missing woman, I'm going to stay tonight and work on filtering and getting enough to test." She glanced at Melissa, who could barely contain her excitement over being included. "Arim is teaching a graduate class, but Melissa is able to stay and assist."

"Thank you," Nikki said to the young lab technician. "I know it's not a fun thing to do, especially on the weekend."

"It's no problem," Melissa said. "I am so excited for the opportunity. Working with Doctor Hart is amazing enough, but this is incredible. Everyone I know is jealous I get to help with the collection."

"Just remember there is a victim out there, hopefully still alive," Nikki reminded her. "And we're trying to catch a man who has likely killed multiple new mothers."

Melissa flushed. "I don't mean to make light of it."

"You're young and excited to learn," Nikki said. "I never discourage that. Just please don't talk about anything else with your friends. We don't want the media hearing about the M-Vac."

"Why?" Melissa reacted. "This could be one of the best cases for it to make a difference. Doctor Hart should get credit for it."

"I don't care about that," Courtney said. "Right now, the killer doesn't think he's left any DNA behind, Melissa. If the media hears I went to Quantico and brought a rock to test, he's going to figure out and go underground."

"Exactly," Nikki said. "Let's keep everything in this room from now on." She felt clammy watching Courtney carefully extricate the rock from the evidence bag it had been in for the past ten years.

"I remember it being bigger." The pink quartz was small enough to fit in the palm of Courtney's hand. "That's not good, right?"

"It's less area to test, but the cracks and crevices can be harder to get to." Courtney shooed them all away. "If you want to watch, do it on the other side of the glass. We can't risk contamination."

THIRTY-TWO

The following days felt like an eternity, every second ticking time from Cass. Nikki and Liam had kept busy, most of their time spent going through Canada's national crime database, ViCLAS, looking for additional victims. They'd flagged twenty-eight unsolved murders of women, systematically going over the information in search of matching signature elements or stomach contents. So far, they'd identified four victims for Dr. Blanchard to compare with Kiania and Mariah's autopsies. Nikki hoped the ME had called her to meet because she had good news.

"Thanks for coming by," Blanchard said when Nikki arrived. "I've got more reports than I want to admit still to transcribe."

Nikki took her usual seat. "I appreciate you taking the time to compare the autopsies."

"No problem," Blanchard said. "Fortunately, the D.C. medical examiner did a much better job than the Metro Police. The preliminary copy you had didn't have the final toxicology report, or some of the medical examiner's notes." She looked at

Nikki. "I have crime scene photos and autopsy photos. You're okay with seeing them?"

"I've seen them before," Nikki said.

"Just checking." Blanchard opened the file sitting in front of her, placing three photos side by side: Mariah, Audrey Ritter, and Kiania Watson's mangled bodies still at their individual crime scenes.

Mariah lay on her back in the dumpster, trash surrounding her, her black hair covering the top half of her face. "The wound on her neck has always bothered me. The police acted like it was just another injury."

"The medical examiner didn't," Blanchard answered. "The site was infected, but once the body was cleaned, it was easier to tell they were two indents, side by side, with electrical burns."

"Some kind of shock collar?"

"I think so," Blanchard said. "She had a blood infection from the wound that would have killed her in a few days if he didn't take care of it first. The medical examiner believed the marks on her lower extremities were indicative of being held in some kind of cage."

"Jesus."

"They did take fingernail clippings," Blanchard said. "But the samples were mixed with dirt and trash and weren't tested beyond the initial mineral stage. They didn't keep them."

Nikki dropped her head to her hands. "Are you telling me we had his DNA then?"

"Maybe," Blanchard said. "We'll never know."

"She probably scratched him," Nikki guessed. "He learned to take the fingernails off next time."

"Similar torture wounds on both women, hands and feet bound, sexual abuse and mutilation." Her eyes met Nikki's. "The marks on Kiania's neck were larger, possibly from a bigger collar. And tested positive for topical antibiotics."

He learned from Mariah's infection. "What about the North Dakota victim, Audrey Ritter?" Nikki asked.

"The first thing that stood out is that she was only missing for nine days, while both Mariah and Kiania weren't killed for at least three weeks," Blanchard told her. "The tox report showed traces of caffeine, but nothing else that suggests pre-workout. Stomach contents showed she hadn't eaten in at least twelve hours. Audrey had the marks on her legs, but no sign of the collar. She's smaller than the other two women, so maybe he didn't need it to control her."

"Audrey had postpartum depression." Nikki flipped through her messy notes. "Her boyfriend told police that she had trouble bonding with the baby. Maybe she didn't fight hard enough for him to use the collar and continue to deal with her."

"Her fingernails were removed by the killer," Blanchard confirmed. "No biological evidence was found with her. Since she was found on the reservation, the tribal police were able to utilize resources from the Bureau of Indian Affairs. The autopsy and testing were thorough. Did you find more?"

Nikki gave her the information about the additional autopsies she wanted gone over.

"Getting that information from another country always takes longer," Blanchard warned her. "I heard the police listed Cassandra King as a missing person, despite her husband's protest. Has Courtney been able to get any physical evidence from her car?"

"She's up to her ears in it," Nikki said. "After she gets the profile from the rock's sample, she has to prioritize what to test next. We're running out of time to find Cass alive."

Her phone vibrated with a group text from Courtney.

We've got a hit. Meet at the office in an hour.

THIRTY-THREE

Late afternoon sun streamed into the conference room on the fifth floor, between the Major and Violent Crime Units. While Liam chewed on the boneless wings he'd been planning on eating for the last hour, Nikki nibbled on the peanut butter crackers she'd found in her bag.

"So Mira and our killer are a DNA match?" Liam asked between wings.

"Yes," Nikki answered, sadly.

Garcia sat at the head of the table, pencil in hand, legal pad ready. "Where is Doctor Hart?"

"She said she'd be right up." Nikki set the crackers aside and called the sheriff, but the call went to voicemail. Nikki left a message as Courtney entered, her growing, chin-length hair covered with a Twins cap. She'd spent the last two days processing the additional DNA they'd collected.

Nikki hoped their strategy of focusing on the rock and Mira Gonzales had been the right one.

Courtney dropped a manila folder containing a single piece of paper. "The man who left blood on the rock in 2014 is Miracle Gonzales's father."

Nikki couldn't feel excited about the results. Anita would be faced with the decision to tell Mira the truth. "What about CODIS?"

"When I entered the DNA into CODIS, there was no immediate hit. Meaning your killer's DNA has never been entered into the system."

Nikki felt deflated. "Nothing?"

"I didn't say that." Courtney had a flair for a dramatic reveal. "I did get a partial match. A sibling match, on the mother's side, to the victim of an unsolved murder in 1984."

Nikki leaned forward and grabbed the folder. "Zelphia Badby, aged nine. Found strangled in a dry well in Smythe County, Virginia." Adrenaline rushed through her. "Entered into the system just a couple of months before Mariah's murder, by Smythe County Sheriff Jerod Garner." She stopped reading. "He'd been in office a week or so when I met him. He didn't have an interest in Mariah's murder and thought I was wasting my time. I didn't think he'd last long as sheriff, but he's proved me wrong."

"I wonder what made him enter the DNA after all that time?" Liam asked.

"I don't know, but I'm grateful." Nikki shifted in the chair. "Serial killers often start by hurting siblings. Perhaps our killer is the one who murdered her as well." She looked at Courtney.

"I couldn't find any birth records for Zelphia," Courtney said.

"I'm guessing her being born in Appalachia in 1975 has something to do with it," Liam interjected.

Nikki read the rest of the report, much of it scientific jargon that went above Nikki's head. And then she realized. Zelphia might be linked to Zebulan Wahlert. The man in the cabin. She called Horner in Smyth County.

"Agent Hunt, how's it going?" Horner asked.

"A lot better than the last time we spoke," she answered. "We were able to extract DNA from the rock using an M-Vac."

"That's amazing," Horner said. "We don't have the budget, but Richmond has one. Did you get a CODIS match?"

"We did, to a 1984 unsolved murder of nine-year-old Zelphia Badby in Smythe County. She lived near Zebulan Wahlert's cabin."

"Never heard of her," Horner said.

"The DNA source was a hairbrush," Nikki explained. "Entered by Sheriff Garner just a couple of months before I discovered the cabin."

"Not long after he took office, then," Horner said. "Let me see if he's available. I know very little about the Wahlert family. I'm not sure if there are any left around here." The sound of knocking came through the phone. "Hey, Sheriff Garner, Agent Nikki Hunt got a hit on a 1984 unsolved case. Zelphia Badby. That name ring a bell?"

Nikki strained to understand the muffled conversation between the two men, but "come in and shut the door," was the only thing she managed to decode.

"Agent Hunt, I'm going to put you on speaker for the sheriff," Horner said.

"That's fine." Nikki let him know she also had other agents listening in.

A throat cleared. "Agent Hunt, this is Sheriff Garner." He didn't sound like the cocky man she remembered. "Horner told me about your call the other day. I'm thrilled the M-Vac worked so well. Have you been able to confirm that Johnny Trent wasn't the killer?"

Nikki rolled her eyes. How many times was she going to have to explain herself? "Yes," she said bluntly. "What can you tell me about Zelphia Badby? I know the case is before your time as sheriff, but CODIS shows you were the one to submit the DNA evidence."

"Zelphia was the youngest grandchild of Zeb Wahlert," Garner explained. "We never found her killer."

"The same Zeb Wahlert that owned the cabin?" Nikki asked. "What can you tell me about the family?"

"They're true Appalachian history," Garner said. "Smyth County records show Zeb's ancestor was among the original settlers in the area. By 1984, Zeb's daughter had died, and he was taking care of her kids that were still at home. We don't have records for any of them. But I've had some dealings. There's E.J., Andy, little Zelphia. There was also Andrea and Nathaniel, who were older and living away from home when Zelphia died."

"Do you know if they're all still living?"

"Andrea passed of cancer, but Andy, E.J. and Nathaniel are still around."

Nikki made a note of the names. "Do you remember when Zelphia went missing?"

"I do," he said. "Nathaniel had already moved to North Carolina with his girlfriend. I was in the police academy at the time. My grandfather was sheriff. We'd both come home to visit that week. Zelphia left her grandpa's home around noon, to walk to her friend who lived a couple of miles west."

"Police were able to confirm that?" Liam asked.

"Andy and E.J. were both home, as well as their older sister Andrea. She'd gotten married the summer before, but she still cleaned the house for her grandpa. She was there cleaning. Zelphia told Andrea she was leaving, and she saw her walk past the end of the driveway, towards her friend's."

"What about the boys?" Nikki asked. "How old were they at the time?"

"I think E.J. was maybe thirteen, and Andy was eleven," the sheriff said. "Turns out Zelphia wasn't supposed to walk that far on her own. Racial tensions were high, and she'd been threatened before. She was mixed-race, had a different father to the other kids. The boys were supposed to walk her, but they didn't want to. So she left on her own."

Nikki's stomach churned. "Poor thing. How many days before she was found?"

"Three, and that's because Zeb and the boys rounded up people to search for her. My grandfather said she'd probably wandered off. I don't think he cared that much. He didn't think they were under his jurisdiction living out there. Plus, in 1984, I'm certain he'd have been racist and unapologetic about it. No autopsy was done, of course, because those were reserved for important people. The elected coroner surmised she'd probably thought the well was still working, moved the cover and fell in."

"No sign of any kind of assault?" Liam asked.

"Not that I've ever heard," Sheriff Garner replied. "Most of the people in my generation thought it was a racially motivated crime, and several people protested. Didn't change anything."

"What did her grandfather think?" Nikki asked. "I have to assume his being in the same generation as your own grandfather means he probably wasn't too happy about a mixed grandchild, especially if the family was well-known in the area."

"He never said much in front of me," Garner said. "But I do remember he cried. He cared about her. I'm not saying he wasn't embarrassed or treated her equal. I really don't know. I just know his pain was real. They buried her and life went on."

"Did Zeb tell you who he thought murdered Zelphia?" Nikki asked.

"No," Sheriff Garner hesitated. "I'd only been in office a few weeks, and I was in over my head. My grandfather was still alive at the time and he was livid that I questioned his judgment. He told me that my job involved the living, provided their skin wasn't too dark." He sighed. "But her grandfather, Zebulan Wahlert, brought me her hairbrush and asked that her DNA be put into the system. I meant to follow up with Zeb about that comment, but I let it go and just put the sample into CODIS."

Nikki had lost count of the amount of people who'd failed these victims, including herself. "Do you know if there were crime scene photos taken?"

"I doubt we have copies that old, but I can look. I don't really need to, though. I was there when they found her. Her neck had been broken. I questioned the marks around her neck, but the coroner said that was decomp. I was too green to know any better."

"Do you keep in touch with any of the family?"

"I have Nathaniel's number; we text every once in a while."

Nikki wrote down the number he rattled off. "And the other siblings living at home at the time, E.J. and Andy, what happened to them?"

"I don't know," Garner said. "They graduated high school, and I think Andy went to junior college. But they didn't stay in the county. I'm not sure the last time Nathaniel spoke to them," he continued. "Horner told me how the rock came to be important. I should tell you, even if you saw the killer bleed on it, it won't hold up in court. That was still Wahlert property, and those kids played on every inch of it."

"That's true," Nikki said. "We tested in the hopes of narrowing down suspects, but it's not enough to get this guy put away."

"E.J. and Andy were the only ones in the area, as far as I know, other than Andrea. But those boys adored Zelphia."

"It's possible they didn't touch her. But one of them may have grown up to be our killer," Nikki said. "You don't have any idea where they are now?"

"I'm sorry, I don't. But Nathaniel will be willing to help. Zelphia's death devastated him. He loved her dearly," Garner said. "Almost took her with him to North Carolina, because he thought she'd be safer in a city."

"Would you mind not giving Nathaniel any advance notice I'm calling?"

"No problem," Garner said.

THIRTY-FOUR

"Tax records confirm Nathaniel Badby has worked for the North Carolina Highway Department for thirty years," Liam confirmed. "Kendall found a newspaper article from the Raleigh paper. Nathaniel marked twenty-five years with the department this spring, and they awarded him for tenure and for only missing eight days of work in those entire twenty-five years. Kind of hard to murder women in multiple states over several years without missing a lot of work. He's also the only one with a driver's license. Dark eyes."

"So Nathaniel definitely isn't the brother we're looking for," Nikki said. "That's one down, two to go. Did you find tax records for the others?"

"Kendall is working on it, but we need more information to narrow down the list. Hopefully Nathaniel has contact information for his brothers so we can expedite things."

Nikki looked at the calendar for at least the fiftieth time today. "Cass has been missing for seven days. He kept Kiania three, but I'm not that optimistic. We have to find her in the next few days."

"Courtney's processed all of the car," Liam reminded her.

"She pulled a good sample with the M-Vac on the steering wheel cover. Sweat and oil. If he drove it, hopefully she can get enough biological matter to definitely match his DNA."

"He drove it," Nikki said. "Cass is taller than me, and I'm five foot seven. The seat looked like someone not much taller than Courtney drove it."

CCTV from Cass's routes home hadn't been helpful, including the prior weeks' traffic footage from the correctional facility. Woodbury police had gone door-to-door in the area around Midwest Plastics while Miller's deputies canvassed everyone on Cass's street. Her husband still refused to believed she'd been taken.

"Miller's guys turn up anything?" Liam asked.

Nikki shrugged. "I've left a couple of messages for Miller but the duty sergeant said he was out today on a personal matter. What about social media?"

"Nothing I could find," he said. "No tax records for either one of them. If they're living, they're off the grid."

Nikki waited until after six central time to call Nathaniel Badby, hoping to catch him after dinner. She decided to call from her personal cell phone. Nathaniel might remember her name from ten years ago. She'd almost given up when he answered.

"Hello?"

"I'm calling for Nathaniel Badby." Nikki put the call on speaker and hit record on her laptop. "Is he available?"

"This is he," Nathaniel answered.

Nikki introduced herself, uncertain if he'd remember her name. "I found your grandfather's body all those years ago."

"Right," Nathaniel said. "I remember being grateful you'd come, because we could still have an open casket. Didn't they find the killer in North Carolina somewhere?" Anger crept into his deep voice. "Coroner said Papaw coming home early and seeing what the guy had done killed him. I just hope he didn't suffer."

"That's actually the reason I'm calling," Nikki said. "I have reason to believe that one of your brothers may have killed him." Nathaniel didn't speak right away. Nikki gave him the redacted and summarized version of the case they were working and what the DNA results showed. She didn't mention the paternal match to Mira. She wouldn't do that to Anita without permission.

"Obviously it's an open investigation, so I have to omit a lot of details," Nikki apologized.

"How did you get the DNA?" Nathaniel asked. "Out of a rock?"

"New technology," Nikki said. "It can retrieve organic matter from porous surfaces. Our DNA analyst was able to extract five times more than needed for the test."

"You saw the person bleed on it that day?"

"I did." Nikki gambled on his loyalty being stronger to his murdered grandfather and half-sister. "I'm one hundred percent certain the man who chased me is related to you."

Nathaniel was quiet for so long Nikki thought he'd hung up. "I always thought one of them killed Zelphia. Papaw wouldn't hear of it. The sheriff didn't care because she was half black. How much did Sheriff Garner tell you about my family?"

"Not a lot," she said. "Your younger siblings went to live with your grandfather after your mother passed. Did they all live in that cabin?"

Nathaniel chuckled. "No, they didn't. Our family home is located at the edge of the acreage, or it was. My great-great-great-grandfather built it when he first opened Sugar Grove Iron Mine."

She knew Virginia had dozens of mines that had been prospected and claimed, but many were never mined or didn't produce enough. "That was one of the biggest mines in the state at one time, wasn't it?"

"Yep," he said. "Made my family wealthy for generations. By the time I came along, the mine had dried up, but Papaw had invested the money into a machinery business, Smyth County Machine. He ran the family business, and I was supposed to take over."

"What about your parents?" Nikki hated prying, but everything about the Badbys' childhood was crucial information at this point.

"My mom was an only child, and her mom died in childbirth," he said. "She married my dad against Papaw's wishes, because Dad worked in the mines and it was a hard life. Mom grew up with education and talked about going to college. But Dad changed that." He sighed. "I was barely a teenager when Dad was killed in the mine. That's when it all went to shit. My mother never recovered and started doing drugs. She was too proud to ask Papaw for help and had to sleep with men for money, which is how she got Zelphia. She was less than two years old when Mama died."

"I'm sorry," Nikki said. "I've lost both my parents as well, far too soon. It's never easy, but grief ebbs and flows, doesn't it?" She hoped sharing the information made him feel comfortable enough to continue.

"Sure does," Nathaniel answered. "I stayed because Mom needed help with the baby, and most of the others were still in school. But once Papaw got custody, I left. Too many bad memories."

"I get it," Nikki said. "I had two years to graduate and then I got the hell out of Stillwater. Do you stay in touch with any of your siblings?"

"Lost Andrea to breast cancer," he replied sadly.

"What about E.J. and Andy?"

"I'm almost eight years older than E.J. and ten years older

than Andy, so we were never all that close. E.J. had anger issues since he was little. He bullied Andy a lot because he was younger, smaller and smarter," he answered. "They took Zelphia's death the hardest, because they should have been with her. E.J. beat the hell out of some kid and wound up in juvie for a few months. He came back medicated and like a zombie most of the time. He did okay in school and graduated, so I thought he was on the right track, but he stopped taking his meds at eighteen because he didn't like how they made him feel, and Papaw kicked him out."

"Where did he go?"

"I think to a friend for a while, but he left the state fairly quickly, and that was hard on Andy, even though E.J. treated him like shit most of the time. They were still close. I know Andy really blamed himself, because E.J. is the one who didn't want to take Zelphia that day and wouldn't let Andy. I did hear he went to college, but honestly, we're almost two different generations, you know? I just haven't spoken to either of them in forever."

"Do you know what state either of them lives in?" Nikki asked.

"E.J. worked at the machinery business until Grandpa died. He left the area. I haven't heard from him in years. As for Andy, he's doing something with computers. I talk to him every once in a while, but it's been a few months.

"I'm glad Grandpa has passed." Nathaniel got emotional for the first time. "If I'd known when they found him dead on the property that one of my family members had killed him, you wouldn't be looking for them. I would have taken care of it."

THIRTY-FIVE

Nikki turned on her fog lights. She could drive the familiar route from home to the sheriff's station with her eyes closed, but with the sun yet to rise, the low-hanging mist over McKusick Road disoriented her. Even the nearly naked trees in Brown's Creek Nature Preserve had been eclipsed by the fog.

With Halloween only a few days away, the gloom suited the season and Nikki's mood. She wanted to be encouraged from her conversation with Nathaniel. He'd given her more information than anyone else, but the family dynamics hadn't helped. As an only child, she had no idea what it would be like to have a sibling. At times, she envied Mark and Rory's closeness. Rory had never given up on his big brother, and he and Mark were closer than ever.

Nikki had learned over the course of her career that the Todd brothers were more the exception than the norm. Family secrets, money, lies and affairs had affected nearly every family she'd encountered. Rory constantly reminded her there were good people in the world. She humored him, but Nikki had learned enough about human behavior to know better.

She fought back a yawn, making her eyes water. After her

call with Nathaniel, Nikki had checked in with Garcia and
Liam before trying Sheriff Miller again. She'd lost track of how
many times she'd called and gone to voicemail. Her mind had
raced the rest of the night, flipping through various theories
about the Badby family, trying to figure out the missing piece of
the puzzle. Nikki had dozed off on the couch around one a.m.,
and after a few hours of tossing and turning, she pulled herself
off the cushions. A shower, piece of toast and two cups of strong
coffee later, she was headed into the sheriff's station, hoping to
catch Miller before he started his day.

Thanks to the fog, the ten-minute drive took nearly twenty.
Nikki had arrived early enough to park near the main entrance
to the sheriff's department. She unplugged her phone, made
sure her notes were in her bag, and killed the engine. Her bag
fell onto the passenger side floor, spilling mints, lip balm, some
expired mascara and a bunch of loose change, which settled into
the grooves of the Jeep's floor mats.

"Damn it." Nikki grabbed her bag and shoved what she
could reach back inside. The mascara had rolled under the seat
—not that it would do Nikki's tired, pale face any good. She
caught her reflection in the rearview mirror. She could handle
the dark circles and wrinkles, but the silver streaks at the roots
of her dark hair had to go. Nikki had the same coloring as her
grandmother, whose dark curls eventually became a stunning
silver and pepper color, but Nikki wasn't in a hurry to look
her age.

Nikki ducked her head against the freezing mist. She tested
the concrete; her boots still had decent grip, but another hour or
so and travel was going to become difficult.

A duty sergeant she didn't recognize eyed her from behind
the raised desk. "Sheriff doesn't want to be disturbed."

Nikki showed the sergeant her badge. "I understand, but I
have some important information about an ongoing murder
case. Please tell him I'm here."

The sergeant sighed and made the call, hitting the speaker.

"This better be important." Miller sounded hoarse.

"Agent Hunt is here, says it's important about an active case."

"DNA results, Kent," Nikki said. "I'll be quick, I promise."

Miller sighed. "Yeah, okay. Send her back, Sergeant Sayers."

Nikki walked to Miller's office at the end of the hallway, her feet like lead. He only shut his door for meetings, believing that an open-door policy was the only way to foster trust between himself and his staff. She stared at the gold nameplate on the closed door, trying to figure out how to approach Miller without making things worse. As frustrated as she was with the sheriff, Nikki knew her friend was an excellent cop and a genuinely good person. Something other than police work had to be affecting him.

"I can see the shadow of your shoes, Nikki." Miller's voice held none of the irritation from their last conversation. "It's open."

She took a deep breath and turned the knob. Miller sat behind his desk, normally a meticulously organized and tidy space, staring at a clean notebook page. Case files covered every inch of the dark metal, at least a dozen notes with phone messages stuck to his monitor. Several takeout bags from fast food restaurants took up most of his trash can, giving the room a distinct stale grease odor.

"Looks like you've been holed up in here." Nikki sat down across from him in the stiff office chair reserved for visitors. She chewed the inside of her lip, trying to figure out the best way to approach him with the DNA evidence without coming across as a know-it-all.

Miller finally looked away from his computer. The pain in his eyes pushed every thought about the investigation out of her mind. "Kent, forget everything about work for a minute. What's wrong? Can I help?"

He shook his head. "I wish you could."

Nikki waited, certain that pushing him would result in Miller shutting down. He cleared his throat. "I was supposed to tell you that Lacey left her sweatshirt at our house when she stayed a few weeks ago."

Miller's youngest daughter, Ella, was only a year older than Lacey, and they often had sleepovers. "The pink one?" Nikki hadn't even realized Lacey wasn't wearing her new favorite sweater. Kind of hard to do when Nikki left before Lacey in the morning and came home even later at night.

"Probably. I meant to throw it in my truck, but I kept forgetting it."

"Don't worry about it." Nikki tried to give him a tiny nudge. "I'm pretty sure that isn't what broke your heart."

"Is it that obvious?"

"That sort of thing is hard to hide," she answered. "Do you want to talk about it?"

He dragged his hands over his face. "No, but I owe you an explanation, and an apology."

"You don't owe me anything."

Miller ignored her and continued, his voice growing unsteady. "A few days before Kiania Watson was killed, my wife and I found out she was pregnant."

A dozen different theories had been running through Nikki's head all morning, but this hadn't been one of them. She and Kent had been in the same grade at Stillwater High, and even though Nikki technically wasn't "too old," she couldn't imagine starting over at their age.

"You don't know what to say, I know," Miller said. "I didn't, either." He scowled. "Actually, that's not true. I wasn't happy. Our oldest is a teenager, and Ella will be one before you know it. Hell, Sharice just went back to work a few years ago when Ella started first grade."

Sharice had stayed home after their second daughter came

along, and she'd been excited to go back to work at the bank. She'd recently been promoted from teller to loan officer, which required more hours. "What about Sharice? Is she excited?"

"At first, and then my reaction derailed everything. I'd never force her to do anything she didn't want to, but I made the mistake of reminding her she didn't have to have the baby, that Minnesota had protected certain rights." Miller closed his eyes. "She couldn't believe I would go against God that way, because this baby wasn't a mistake. At this age, it was a true miracle."

Nikki saw both points and couldn't imagine being in the Millers' position. The immense pain in his eyes had begun to make sense, and she suspected his past tense had been intentional.

"Did something go wrong?" Nikki asked.

"Sharice woke up bleeding yesterday morning," he said. "She lost the baby. I was relieved at first, but seeing her so sad... I keep wondering if my lousy attitude didn't cause her to lose the baby." He brushed the moisture out of his eyes. "She was only about eight weeks, so we hadn't told anyone. The girls have no idea." Miller's gaze met hers. "Sharice probably blames me. I brought the stress on her."

Nikki's ears felt hot, her stomach turning faster than a roller coaster. She hadn't counted on baring her soul this morning. "That's not what caused a miscarriage, Kent," Nikki said. "Women deal with stressful pregnancies all the time. Something was wrong with the baby. It couldn't have survived."

He started to disagree, but Nikki forged ahead. "I'm speaking from experience. I lost a baby during the Campus Killer investigation about a year before Lacey was born. I was ten weeks when I started spotting. That was right after the fourth body had been found." He'd killed four college women in the span of three months, and at the time, Nikki and the rest of the BAU weren't close to catching him.

"I wanted to blame myself, work, everything I could think

of," she told Miller. "My OB said stress probably didn't cause it, because it was too early. It's the body's way of taking care of things." She swallowed the knot in her throat. "I know that doesn't make it easier. But I also know it's true."

Miller stared at her, processing her words. Nikki continued. "That's how I met Mariah Gonzales and her mother, Anita." She took a deep breath and launched into the story she'd told Rory a few nights before. "I took all my pain out on her, and I was never able to apologize. Her mother realized I worked for the Bureau and called me after the D.C. police bungled the investigation."

"Jesus," Miller whispered. "I'm sorry, Nikki."

"Please don't be," she told him. "I wouldn't have Lacey without the miscarriage. I'm just sharing my story so you know you're not alone. And that Sharice isn't alone, if she wants to talk."

"Thank you," he said. "I'm sorry for the way I've acted," Miller said. "I took my stress out on the job."

"We've all done it," Nikki said. "And like my boss said, you disagreeing helps keep us honest."

"I suppose," he said. "I did get your messages about the results. I planned on calling this morning."

"I know." Nikki pointed to his empty coffee cup. "You want to fill up before I get started? It's a lot to unpack."

After Miller refilled his coffee, Nikki explained everything Courtney had tested and why, along with the DNA results. "I spoke to Nathaniel Badby last night. He didn't give me a lot more information, but I do feel like we're finally on the right track."

"And at this point, I can't argue that Kiania must be a victim, as well as Cass King," he said. "The flowers, the circumstantial evidence, now the DNA. We have a serial killer."

"I need to tell you everything," Nikki said. "I let him go to save my baby. To save Lacey. He promised he'd come back for me, and he's here. But he couldn't anticipate us having a DNA match, regardless of its use in court. That's why we're going to stop him."

"I believe in you," Miller told her. "Why do you think he targets postpartum mothers?"

"He may have more than one reason, but I think a lot has to do with the fight," Nikki said. "Who gets strength from adrenaline more than a new mother? She's going to do everything possible to get back to her baby. He wants them to fight back and stay strong. That's why he gives them the protein and the pre-workout."

"Diabolical," Miller said.

"The most important part of a signature killer's life is control," Nikki reminded him. "Organized non-socials are usually average intelligence, sometimes higher, although most weren't as smart as Bundy likes to think he was," she said. "Ed Kemper's an exception, because he's highly intelligent and self-aware. He'd kill again and he knows it. These guys are sadistic and indifferent and by the time they start killing people, they've spent a good portion of their lives fantasizing about what they would do to a victim."

"Keppel likened them to acting out a play," Miller said, referencing the well-known police detective who'd helped to catch Ted Bundy.

"They are," Nikki agreed. "That play is the only area of their lives where they've got total control. That element is more important than the murder. They're looking for sexual gratification, but the acts of torture aren't necessarily what supplies the eventual gratification. Control is. Rituals reinforce the control."

"Not all have been life's losers," Miller reminded her. "Plenty have been educated from decent families. I know most have some trauma, but so do most of us."

"Sometimes it's not obvious trauma," Nikki said. "It can be emotional trauma, neglect, sibling issues—I could keep going.

But in this case, I think the mother's choices may have helped channel his anger issues into something tangible he could be angry with.

"In this case, we've ruled Nathaniel out. Both E.J. and Andy's whereabouts are unknown, but Nathaniel thinks one of them killed Zelphia."

"And Mariah's daughter's DNA helps link the past and present."

She told him they'd found several other potential victims in Canada's ViCLAS system and passed them on to Blanchard to go over the autopsies. "Four had a trillium flower left with their bodies, but that doesn't mean there aren't others. The flowers could have been blown away or missed."

"The physical path tracks," Miller said when Nikki showed him the map she'd been using to mark murders in the United States and Canada she believed were connected. "Anything to put one of these brothers in Detroit in 2015?" Miller asked.

Nikki shook her head. "I can't place a Badby brother there, no."

"So E.J. and Andy are the most likely suspects. There's been no sign of Cassandra King," Miller said, more to himself than Nikki. "What about the DNA extracted from the sweat on the steering wheel cover?"

"We're still waiting," Nikki said. "The DNA labs are overwhelmed with cases from all over the country, and Courtney can only spend so much time on our cases." She didn't want anyone other than Courtney to perform the DNA tests. She'd basically been living at the lab since getting back from D.C. Nikki had convinced Courtney to go home and sleep in her own bed for a few hours as she needed a break from the confines of the lab and the pressure of Garcia asking for an update every half an hour. Melissa had volunteered her extra time to help Courtney with whatever she needed. Her enthusiasm could be overwhelming, but the lab tech worked hard and had boundless energy. Nikki was excited to see her come into her own.

"You think he killed the little sister?"

"He wouldn't be the first serial killer to start that way. Zelphia's grandpa didn't think she fell down the well, but he waited for decades to give the Smyth County sheriff the DNA sample for CODIS." She drummed her fingers against her notebook. "Interestingly, Zeb Wahlert gave that DNA to the sheriff not long before he was killed. All of the siblings would have known that cabin, and according to Nathaniel, while they didn't stay in touch with each other, they frequently checked in on their grandfather. I asked the sheriff if he remembers any of the brothers being around before I showed up, and he doesn't remember. But it's not hard to hide in that area of Virginia. Appalachia is stunningly beautiful, rugged and dense. People can easily get lost—or lose themselves."

"You think he knew his time was short?" Miller asked. "Zelphia's being mixed and born out of wedlock might have been enough for him to stay quiet if he did suspect one of his grandsons. Surely he suspected them all along if he'd kept the hairbrush."

"Or that's one of the few personal things Zelphia had, so kept it to remember her. He wouldn't have thought to keep it for scientific evidence in 1984. And we didn't have CODIS or ViCAP at the time."

Miller nodded. "So, in 2014, E.J. or Andy showed up and somehow Wahlert figured out his suspicions were true. By that time, he would have learned about hair follicles and DNA and manages to get the hairbrush to the sheriff before the grandson killed him."

"To be clear, it appeared Zeb Wahlert had died in the house of natural causes," Nikki told him. "They didn't do an autopsy, but I wouldn't be surprised if he were poisoned."

"The Smyth County police didn't put the murders on Wahlert?" Miller asked.

"He'd lost a foot to diabetes," Nikki said. "He had a prosthetic and still got around well enough, but between his advanced age and health, we never considered him a suspect. The blood in the room that was eventually confirmed to be Mariah's seemed to be a lot fresher than Wahlert's body."

Nikki's ringtone startled both of them. Liam never called this early unless he had news. "It's Liam," she told Miller before putting the call on speaker. "Tell me something—"

"Get to the lab right now." Terror laced his voice. "Melissa's dead, and Courtney's missing."

THIRTY-SIX

Nikki let Miller drive so they could turn on lights and sirens. Her hands weren't steady enough to drive. Liam's words played on repeat in her head.

Melissa's dead, and Courtney's missing, Melissa's dead, and Courtney's missing, Melissa's dead, and Courtney's missing.

What if Courtney is dead, too?

"What else did Liam say?"

The record stopped and Nikki's training took over, her instincts stomping down the fear that threatened to choke her. "He's getting the SWAT team prepped, with the hostage rescue team on standby. We have to find her first." She couldn't say Courtney's name.

How had this happened?

Stupid question, Nikki screamed at herself. *You put her in the line of fire. She's the DNA expert. He took her to silence her. But she's not the only DNA expert in the world. He took her for another reason.* "Me."

"What?" Miller asked.

She struggled to speak over the weight of terror sitting on her chest. "He's always known my name since I showed him my

ID that day in Appalachia. He's obviously kept track of me. Maybe even stalked me." She looked at Miller. "He took her to get to me. I guess we were taking too long to find him."

"Or this has always been his plan," Miller disagreed. "They've checked Courtney's building?"

"Liam had Arim go over with the spare keys she gave him," Nikki said. "She's not there, her big purple bag isn't there."

"That's significant?"

"Courtney's basically been living at the lab since getting back from D.C. She's had that stupid purple bag since we moved to Minnesota. The entire campus is on lockdown and they're searching every single room, even the locked ones."

"How would they get into a locked room?" Miller asked.

"How did he get into the building in the first place?" Nikki countered. "Even if he somehow bypassed our initial security protocols and made it onto the elevator, he couldn't have entered any room on the lab floor without a badge."

"Someone let him in?" Miller guessed.

"My guess is Melissa, for whatever reason." Every warning signal in her brain seemed to fire at once. "Melissa was so excited about the DNA testing. I wouldn't be surprised if she told someone."

"So he uses her to get into the main lab, kills her and then takes Courtney."

"Courtney's badge will open every single lab," Nikki said. "Only hers and superiors' can do that."

"But Liam didn't see any sign someone tried to mess with results or damage the lab?"

"No," Nikki said.

An unbearable silence swelled between them. Nikki's brain swarmed with terrible possibilities. Was Courtney still alive?

"I didn't realize she came with you from Quantico," Miller said.

It took Nikki a few seconds to realize she'd told him that minutes earlier.

"I asked her to come back to Minnesota with me," Nikki said. "She'd been with the Bureau for a year or so—she was recruited out of graduate school. She earned her master's and doctorate at the U of M, and Mayo recruited her for an internship, too, but Courtney chose Quantico because she wanted a break from Minnesota." Nikki pushed down her swelling emotions. "She didn't like Virginia. Too much humidity, too expensive. I knew she wanted to move back, so when Hernandez initially contacted me about starting our unit here, I offered her the job." Nikki paused until her voice felt steadier. "I don't think I would have come back here without her."

Miller pushed his dashboard computer so he could see Nikki better. "She's alive. Everything you've told me says he wouldn't kill her. She's bait."

"I know." Nikki wasn't going to make the mistake of letting the bastard get away alive this time.

Garcia had closed the fourth floor to everyone but essential investigators, directing the employees who'd arrived after Melissa's body had been discovered to one of the conference rooms on the second floor of the building.

"Seven employees were on the lab floor when Melissa was found dead, so Liam spoke with them immediately," Nikki told Miller during the elevator ride. "None of them had access to the DNA labs but Arim, and he arrived less than ten minutes before they discovered the murder."

The doors opened, a security guard blocking access to the fourth floor. He relaxed when he saw Nikki's badge and allowed them to pass through. Garcia stood in front of the lab window, arms folded across his chest, watching the Evidence Response Team process the DNA lab.

The reality nearly choked her, but she found control of her voice. "Have they found anything?"

"Not yet." Garcia sounded hoarse. "At least, not in the DNA lab. Another employee found Melissa dead, stuffed into an empty locker." Every floor in the building had an employee locker room for personal items, but the employees had to provide the lock. Nikki followed her boss down the hall, with Miller on her heels. They followed Garcia's lead and grabbed booties and latex gloves from the box someone had left by the locker room door. Another security guard stood ready to stop anyone who tried to go into the locker room while Blanchard examined the body.

"The body is still in rigor," Garcia told Nikki as they entered. "Blanchard puts cause of death between ten p.m. and eleven p.m. last night."

"Why was Melissa here that late?"

"Before she left yesterday, Courtney told me Melissa had offered to come in last night and work on some of the cases they backburned during this investigation."

Employees could only enter the complex by scanning the same ID badge they used inside the buildings. A single security guard manned the gate during the day, mostly to vet visitors and keep the media from sneaking into the building. At night, employees with the right clearance were required to do a biometric scan along with the badge.

"Courtney asked me to give Melissa temporary access last night." Guilt crept into Garcia's voice. "She's been a model employee, Courtney trusted her. The lab is behind on other cases—"

"Hernandez would have done the same thing," Nikki interrupted to assure him. "Melissa was alone when she drove through the gate?"

He nodded. "At 22:21. There doesn't appear to be anyone in the car with her, but she's got tinted windows. It's nearly impossible to tell if anyone is in the backseat. She entered the building alone through the employee entrance at 22:27," Garcia said. "Ten minutes later, she opened that same door for a man wearing a janitor's uniform and a hoodie. His face is mostly obscured, but height and overall stature matches the other eyewitness accounts."

"He must have been in the car with her?" Miller asked.

"That's the only option," Garcia said. "All of our perimeter cameras confirm no one else got onto the property. She's giggling when she lets him in, shushes him. Liam and the video technicians are trying to get a better look at the small bit of his face that was visible."

Nikki's stomach turned when she rounded the corner and saw the open locker. Blanchard crouched in front of the body taking photos, but Nikki could see Melissa's silky, dark hair. She'd been alive and excited about test results just hours ago.

"How did she die?" Nikki hoped her family had the support they were going to need.

"Broken neck," Blanchard answered without turning around. "Likely quick and painless."

She shifted left so they could see. Melissa's head hung awkwardly to her right, against the inside of the locker, her stiff muscles bulging. Her knees were tucked underneath her chin, her thin arms wrapped around her.

"Did he dislocate her shoulders?" Miller asked.

"At least the left one." Blanchard pointed to Melissa's small, stiff hands frozen around her calves. Red trillium had been tucked between her fingers.

Nikki's fingernails dug into the palms of her hands. Rage burned through her sadness. Melissa had her whole life ahead of her, just as all the others before her had. She would not let him take Courtney's. "What do we know about Melissa?"

"She's got a boyfriend," Garcia said. "I'm guessing he's the one she snuck inside."

"She probably fed him information," Nikki said. "Whether she knew it or not, she helped him. He's probably spooked by the DNA results."

"Why?" Miller asked. "He wanted your attention. If he hadn't put that flower with Kiania, you'd still think they got the right guy in 2014."

"He didn't know about the blood on the rock," Nikki said. "That gave us the Badby family name, and there's no way he anticipated that." Her heart hammered in her chest. "Melissa knew about Mira, too."

Garcia's worried eyes met hers. "He knows there's a DNA connection that could bring him down."

"Not if the two women working on the case can't testify in court," Miller said.

"He didn't take Courtney for that reason," Nikki said. "She's great, but she isn't the only DNA analyst. The evidence is catalogued and preserved." She looked at Garcia in alarm. "Right? The samples that are left?"

"They're fine," Garcia said. "But Courtney's access card would have gotten him into evidence. If he'd taken it, then I'd lean toward Miller's theory. The results might have spooked him, but he wasn't here for them."

Nikki and the others left Blanchard in the locker room with her assistant. She didn't want to see them forcibly remove Melissa's body from the locker.

She stood with Miller and Garcia, looking into Courtney's office at the opposite end of the hall.

"Arim knew something was wrong when he found Courtney's door unlocked," Garcia told them.

Nikki's chest tightened as she watched the techs process the room. Courtney's cell phone rested on the wireless charger, her backpack still sitting on the desk where she'd set it down.

"He waited for her." Nikki pointed to the single cup coffee maker. "Courtney's predictable. She always puts her bag on the

desk and starts making coffee before she even takes her coat off."
Nikki scanned the room for Courtney's blue, plaid wool coat.
"She didn't even have time to start coffee." She swallowed the
knot in her throat. Courtney didn't have time for Nikki to
lose it.

Garcia nodded. "It took us a while to figure how he got her
out of the building. After the initial sweep, Liam and I looked
at all the security footage from each exit and didn't see her, so
we checked the ground floor and lower level. He took her
down through mechanical and out the service exit." He
handed Nikki his phone, a dark, grainy CCTV still already
cued. "Swipe left. The lights were out in the mechanical room,
so the quality sucks. Only decent quality is from the exterior
camera."

Nikki clicked on the video on Garcia's phone. The exterior
security camera was mounted directly over the door, which
meant the person walked out of frame within a few seconds.
Nikki held her breath as the door opened. A man in a gray janitor's uniform exited first, the hood of the sweatshirt beneath his
uniform covering his face. Black gloves covered his hands, and
he moved with confidence, pulling Courtney out by her left
hand, his grip tight.

"Courtney's five foot two," Nikki said. "He's not much taller
than me, just like the man in Virginia. I can't see anything else
identifiable." She internally screamed at Courtney as she
watched her friend being led away. She restarted the video
twice, searching for anything that might give them a lead.

Miller peered over her shoulder. "Is her hand moving?"

"I hadn't noticed," Garcia answered.

Nikki enlarged the video and zoomed in as far as possible
without losing quality. Courtney's right arm barely moved as
she walked, her body stiff with tension. "Her right hand is
moving." She squinted as though the details would be magically
magnified. "I can't tell if she's just moving them or—" The

words caught in Nikki's throat, her heart galloping. "Where's Liam?"

"Down on the second floor, with the tech guys, going through security footage."

Garcia's phone in hand, Nikki raced to the nearby stairwell instead of waiting for the elevator. She ran down the stairs as fast as she dared, nearly tripping multiple times.

"Her right hand."

Liam's eyebrows knitted together as he watched the clip. "She's signing."

Courtney's cousin had lost her hearing as a child, and the entire family had learned sign language. "Can you tell what she's saying?"

Liam had taken a few signing classes in college, and Courtney would give him the occasional lesson, laughing at how badly he signed. "Okay, okay. How many letters..." he muttered to himself. "Four, I think. Four different signs." He looked at Nikki. "What could she possibly tell us in four signs?"

"A name." Nikki didn't say anything more so Liam could figure it out on his own. She didn't want to suggest something that turned out to be wrong and influence his reading.

"The first two are hard to tell," he said. "They just look like she's making fists." He watched the video again. "D-Y." Hope flashed in Liam's eyes.

"Andy," Nikki said. "She recognized him from the test results."

Hang on, Courtney. We're coming.

THIRTY-SEVEN

Liam flipped the sheriff's emergency lights on as they sped toward Melissa's apartment. She lived in a decent area of North Minneapolis, a twenty-minute drive on a good day. Courtney didn't have time for construction or traffic slowdowns, so they'd taken Miller's SUV.

Nikki tightened her seat belt. Liam was a good driver, but the control freak in her wanted to be the one slicing through traffic. Garcia and Miller remained at the office; while Garcia oversaw the investigation, Miller would coordinate with adjoining counties. Minneapolis Police had been sent to secure Melissa's apartment while others knocked on doors, asking if anyone had seen Melissa with a man matching Andy Badby's description. If they were able to narrow down a search location, the police would launch drones for an aerial search. Garcia had acted quickly, contacting the local police for aid as well as the state police.

"He won't kill her." Nikki finally spoke. Hearing the words out loud must make it so.

"Killing her is a mercy compared to what he's done to the

others." Liam's jaw set hard. "We have to save her, Nikki. She's never going to be the same as it is, and if he gets the chance—"

"He won't," Nikki assured herself as much as Liam. "That's not why he took her." They were in a race against time. He could decide Courtney was no longer useful anytime.

He snorted. "You really think a serial killer—a damned sadist—isn't going to do stuff to her just for the fun of it? Or maybe to pass the time while he waits for you to show up?" Liam white knuckled the steering wheel.

"Garcia says Melissa told another technician hired at the same time that she didn't have time for a boyfriend." Nikki read the text she'd just received out loud. "As far as they know, that hadn't changed."

"How did Badby sucker a smart, pretty woman like Melissa?"

"Andy went to college," Nikki reminded him.

"Denny?" Liam echoed. "How the hell did he come up with that as an alias?"

North Minneapolis usually lived up to its dangerous reputation, but there were pockets of good neighborhoods like Willard-Hay. Most of the older homes were well-maintained, with several converted into multiplexes. Halloween decorations flashed by as Nikki tried to look for house signs.

"Oh, there it is." Melissa's upper-level duplex on Oliver Avenue was easy to spot thanks to the police presence.

Liam parked on the street behind the police cars, and Nikki practically ran up the sidewalk to the officer standing in front of the duplex's entrance. "Thanks for clearing the apartment for us. No sign of anyone?"

"No," the officer answered. "Per your ASAC's insistence, we made sure not to touch anything."

Nikki ignored the tone and headed upstairs. "What was that about?"

"Garcia said he made it clear we were the only ones to investigate," Liam answered. "Guess he hurt their feelings."

"I don't care." Nikki reached the second floor, where another Minneapolis police officer waited. Before going inside, Nikki and Liam slipped on the booties and gloves they'd brought from the office.

"No sign of any sort of struggle?" Nikki asked.

"Nothing," the female officer answered. "It's a tiny apartment, and she had a fair amount of stuff, but everything seems to be organized."

"Thanks." Eight hundred feet never looked so small. A handful of shoes lined the left wall, next to the carpet mat placed in front of the door. Furniture and books covered most of the hardwood floor in the main room. A photo of a smiling Melissa and an older couple, likely her parents, sat on the glass end table between the loveseat and trendy, orange chair, along with a romance novel.

They checked between the cushions, searching for anything that might lead them to Badby, but found only crumbs. The kitchen was too small for a table, and small appliances covered half the L-shaped counter.

"She liked coffee, huh?"

"Specifically cappuccinos." Nikki checked the drawers while Liam went through the handful of cabinets. All they learned was that Melissa liked sugary cereal and ate a lot of packaged meals.

Melissa's double bed had been left unmade. Her closet was jammed with jeans and sweaters, and her drawers were also filled to the brim. Nikki shifted through T-shirts and socks, uncertain of what she hoped to find. They already had his DNA.

"No journal?" Nikki asked. "What about a laptop or tablet?"

"Nope." Liam knelt to check under the bed. "Wrapping paper and more shoes." He cursed as he started to stand, then froze. "Nik, look." He crawled over to the heavy wood nightstand and wiggled his hand behind it.

Nikki's heart leapt. "Is that what I think it is?"

Liam clutched the Apple Watch as though it were gold. "It was charging. I bet it fell off and she forgot it." He turned the device in his hand. "As long as she wore this, it tracked her." He jumped to his feet. "It syncs to her phone."

Nikki yanked her own from her pocket and called Garcia. "We need Melissa's phone."

"They're having a little trouble getting her out of the locker because of rigor," Garcia said. "We're pretty certain her bag is inside, stuck between the body and the locker. We've searched everywhere else."

"Call it." Nikki put the phone on speaker and waited while Garcia had someone look up Melissa's contact information and call.

"God yeah, it's vibrating against the locker. Or maybe her." Garcia sounded ready to crack. "Did you find anything at her apartment?"

"Her Apple Watch."

"You need her phone," Garcia said. "Get back to the lab with it. We'll get her phone."

"Don't let Blanchard take the body," Liam said. "An iPhone requires facial recognition. That's the fastest way to access the information. That's Courtney's best chance."

Nikki finally gathered her wits. "In the meantime, see if you can fast-track a subpoena in case we have to get the information from Apple."

THIRTY-EIGHT

Nikki paced the fifth-floor conference room while Liam downloaded the information from Melissa's cell phone. Since Melissa had left her watch behind, they needed to sync the phone and watch to access the GPS information.

"How hard was it to get the phone unlocked?" Nikki asked Miller and Garcia. Blanchard had taken Melissa's body to the morgue by the time they returned.

Miller looked at the floor. Garcia shook his head, looking pale. "Blanchard took care of it. We acted as witnesses."

"Did you have trouble?" Nikki asked.

"I don't want to talk about it," he answered. "All that matters is the phone's unlocked."

"Here we go." Liam had barely spoken before the others crowded around him to look over his shoulder. "Looks like she wore the watch home yesterday, so there's nothing tracking her whereabouts last night, but she wore it regularly before that. The last couple of weeks have been longer hours at work, so there's a lot of back and forth between here and her place, but she went to southern Washington County three nights this past week and twice last week. Same place every time. She stayed between two and three hours each time."

"Could be a part-time job," Nikki said. "I'm sure she's got college debt."

Liam opened a new tab on his laptop and typed the GPS coordinates into the search bar. "Bright's Farm." He looked up at the others. "Anyone heard of it?"

"It's a pumpkin patch," Nikki and Miller answered at the same time. "We were going to go a couple of weeks ago, but they didn't open this year. Who owns it?"

"Denny Bright retired last fall," Miller said. "They sold the place. Melissa told co-workers her boyfriend was named Denny."

"I hope they sold willingly," Garcia said.

"They did," Miller answered. "Moved to Florida. When did the place sell?"

"According to property records, Z.W. Holdings, LLC purchased the house and thirty acres in July."

"Zeb Wahlert," Nikki said. "When I spoke to Nathaniel again he told me Andy had been their grandfather's executor. There was no issue with dispersing things, but Andy could have retained the LLC."

THIRTY-NINE

Courtney drew her knees to her chest and wrapped her wool cardigan around her body, but she couldn't stop shivering. She stared into the pitch black trying to figure out where he'd taken her. Damp earth caked her fingers, but she wasn't outside, because she could feel walls on either side of her. One corner meant three more corners, and that meant a room.

The cabin Nikki found in Appalachia... is long gone, Courtney told herself. But maybe she'd been knocked out longer than she realized, and he'd taken her to Virginia.

Don't be stupid. He didn't knock you out. He put you in that thing.

They'd driven away in Melissa's car, his gun pressed into Courtney's side. Not that anyone could see through the tinted windows. He'd taken her right through the gate and across the interstate, where he'd parked next to a white van sitting in the parking lot of an abandoned factory.

Her heartbeat raced at the memory of Andy ordering her into a van at gunpoint. It looked like every other large-sized van, except for the big, wired dog crate sitting in the middle.

"Go," Andy whispered in her ear.

"No. I'd rather die, Andy."

He didn't seem to care that she knew his name. "You're not my type, so as long as you do what I tell you, you'll get through this."

"Nikki will find you," she hissed.

"I'm counting on it."

Courtney fought against the images of Mariah and Kiania's bodies. Andy's pasty, freckled face had been the last one they saw. Had they spent their last days in this crate?

How in the hell did Melissa get involved with him? Melissa was smart; she had everything in life going right for her.

"Andy must be a snake charmer," she muttered to the darkness.

But why kill Melissa when he clearly wanted Nikki to find him? He could have left her alive in the locker and given her a chance.

Courtney's empty stomach soured. She'd had a good sleep at home, clocked in and gone to her office and stupidly left her cell phone and glasses on her desk. She always carried a change of clothes and toiletries, because she inevitably wound up spending at least one night a month at the lab to catch up on work.

She'd thought the locker room was empty. Then she heard Melissa's voice on the other side of the wall.

"Doctor Hart, would you mind helping me with something?"

The hairs on the back of Courtney's neck stood up. Something about the voice wasn't right. She'd never been one to run away from danger, and no one could get past the FBI's security measures.

"Yeah, what's up?"

Courtney almost threw up on the dirt floor remembering Melissa in the bottom locker, her neck broken.. Andy had his gun in her back before Courtney could do any more than gasp.

She couldn't see the gun, but the barrel pressed against her spine. She thought about screaming, but he had at least six bullets—fifteen if the gun was a nine-millimeter. She hadn't seen anyone else in the office to hear her screams anyway.

"Just a recording, I'm afraid," the man whispered.

"I'll go with you and make it look normal." Courtney's voice shook. "Just please don't hurt anyone."

"Thatta girl. Follow my lead."

Her mind had raced as they left the locker room and took the stairwell. "All the way to the basement."

He was taking her out the service entrance because there were fewer cameras. Fear nearly choked her as they neared the first floor. She had to get a message to Nikki and Liam, and she only had a few minutes to do it.

Courtney knew her friends would watch the video countless times. They'd see her hand moving.

Please let Liam remember what I taught him.

FORTY

"We should not have waited until nightfall." Liam leaned against Miller's SUV, scowling at the SWAT team suiting up across the road. As part of the critical incident response group, the FBI SWAT team would lead the raid. In most situations, the sheriff's SWAT team was more than sufficient, but with an FBI employee's life on the line, the critical response team outranked everyone else. FBI SWAT members were among the best in the world, many coming from elite military teams like the Navy Seals and Army Rangers.

Sleet slid down Nikki's nose. She adjusted her ball cap to protect her face, but the icy mix was coming in sideways.

"What the hell is taking so long?" Liam seethed.

Nikki checked her weapon and extra clip again and made sure her boots were laced tight. She flexed her fingers against the cold. Fingerless gloves didn't exactly provide warmth. Apple orchards surrounded Bright's Farm in southern Washington County. A single entrance off Highway 76 led into an overgrown field once used as parking for the old attraction.

Nikki had been living in Virginia during Bright's Farm's

heyday, so everything about the area felt unfamiliar and unsettling. The new owner hadn't maintained Bright's website, but they were able to find a map of last year's Halloween attraction. In the drone footage taken earlier today, the structures on the property appeared to be in the same area as last year.

"Christ, finally."

Garcia and Miller shook hands with Townsend, the SWAT leader, and headed toward them, their faces grim. Nikki had been in similar situations with Miller before, but she didn't know what to expect from Garcia. He hadn't been in the field in a few years. Nikki hoped he didn't hesitate if needed to act.

"The goal is taking him alive." Garcia blew on his hands as he and Miller rejoined them. "Getting Courtney and Cassandra King out alive are number one, but we know there are more victims out there. He's the only one who can give their families any sense of closure."

Miller unrolled the aerial photo they'd brought. "Bright's is in between four cornfields, which helps our cover. Xcel Energy says there's no electric or gas turned on in the house. Z.W. Holdings, LLC is paying for the water. USPS hasn't delivered mail here since the Brights moved."

"The field bordering Highway 76 was used as parking," Garcia said. "Miller and Liam will approach with SWAT from there, while Nikki and I will head west. There's a drainage ditch on the border of the apple farm and Bright's." He looked at Nikki. "We've got to clear at least four attractions, so once our team crosses the ditch, you and SWAT's Rodriguez will come in through the trees here and clear the trailer sitting on the north end of the property—it was a zombie attraction last year."

"We've had the drone up in the last hour, and there are no heat signatures in the maze, so SWAT will run through it to make sure, and then our group will meet at the salvage area."

"Salvage?" Nikki asked.

Miller nodded. "Sam's Savage Salvage... bunch of old creepy cars, including a hearse. We've got to clear all of those."

"Agent Wilson, you and the sheriff have the tougher assignment," Garcia said. "The first attraction is the house—it was a funeral home last year. The barn is a gravedigger's hangout or something. It's two levels."

"What if they're not here?" Liam said. "We could be walking into a trap."

"I don't think so," Nikki said. "He couldn't know we have the GPS."

"Unless that's what he's counting on," Liam said. "If Melissa came to this area to hang out with him, then he knows everything about her. Even if he didn't see the watch, he knows her phone was left behind. It's only a matter of time before we get into it."

"SWAT did the recon," Garcia said. "They're ready to go."

Liam shook his head. "I don't like it."

"You were raring to go a few minutes ago," Nikki said. "I don't think he's interested in an ambush, anyway. I wish you'd agree to my going in alone to negotiate—"

"No." All three men spoke at once.

"That's what he's counting on," Miller said. "We go in five minutes."

Liam walked over to the truck and grabbed more ammunition. Nikki followed him. "Don't take unnecessary risks."

He stood. "You don't take stupid risks," he countered. "I don't like your being with Garcia. He hasn't been in the field in a while."

"Rodriguez is leading," she reminded him. "I'll be fine. Now let's go get Courtney."

They crept out of the orchard, stepping on rotten apples. Intel had been correct—it was a ditch and not too steep, but she wasn't sure about the drainage part. The pile of debris five feet to their left looked impenetrable.

Their group reached the top of the hill; Nikki and Garcia dropped to a crouch, following Rodriguez's lead. They walked through the thicket of trees used as a haunted forest, fake headstones still in the ground.

"Amazing how scary the dark can make something like this seem," Garcia muttered.

"You don't like haunted attractions?" Nikki stepped over a busted garden statue that had probably looked scary at some point.

"No," Garcia. "But I get dragged to one every year."

Nikki wanted to ask if his significant other was the reason, but Rodriguez had stopped and dropped to his right knee. The two SWAT members who'd been walking at the back hurried forward, preparing to go through a yellowed trailer used for the zombie attraction.

"It's not big and could be tight quarters if it wasn't dismantled last year," Rodriguez said. "Evans, Moore and I will clear the inside while you two watch the perimeter."

Rodriguez didn't leave time for argument, so they pushed forward. They'd taken a risk not bringing in the battering ram, and Nikki breathed a sigh of relief when Rodriguez's bolt cutters took care of the padlock.

Nikki took cover behind the trailer and listened to them making sure it was clear. The fog provided enough cover that she couldn't see the other team on the other side of the property. Rodriguez's group returned and they moved toward the salvage yard attraction.

Sam's Savage Salvage was larger than Nikki had realized, with twenty or more feet between the various vehicles: a hearse, an old Dodge Pinto, a couple of lawn mowers, along with an old white Chevy that looked as though it had been pulled from the water.

"I think the Brights put their old shit out here and some kids in costume and called it an attraction," Garcia said.

Rodriguez checked the little building labeled "office." "Just a prop."

Evans wrenched the hearse's back door open. "Clear."

"No one's getting in that Pinto," Moore said.

"Let's check the other vehicles and then we approach the barn from the back end, to meet up with the others."

The sleet came down harder, making the fog even more dense. Nikki could see the top of the barn, but she had no idea if Liam and Miller had made it. The quiet was starting to unnerve her.

What if they were in the wrong place? What if she'd missed something?

Garcia and Moore headed toward a box truck with no wheels. Nikki walked toward an SUV with a flat tire, Rodriguez behind her. She shined her light on the ground around the SUV but didn't see any footprints. "Hell's Gate Ambulance Company." Nikki rolled her eyes at the name and went to check behind the SUV.

Nikki stopped, shining her light on the SUV's rear doors. What SUV had two rear doors? Maybe it had been an ambulance at some point.

Or was it a white van? Her heart pounded. A white van had chased her after she left Midwest Plastics. Could this be the same one? Nikki shined her light behind the van, looking for tire tracks, but the sleet was coming down like knives.

"Shit." Nikki jumped to her feet and jogged to the front of the vehicle. The words "Hell's Gate Ambulance Company" weren't covered in grime like everything else. She tried to find the others through the fog and sleet, but the weather was growing worse by the minute. Nikki double-checked her safety was off and tried the driver's door. Locked. She walked to the back again and checked the back doors.

The right handle lifted easily. Nikki aimed her gun directly into the van and slowly opened the door.

Andy was sitting at the back, his hoodie pulled up around his face. He held up his right hand, revealing a remote trigger. "Not one word, Agent Hunt, or I'll blow them all up."

FORTY-ONE

Nikki climbed into the van and closed the door. Her heart lodged in her throat while her eyes took a minute to adjust. Despite the cold, sweat beaded across her forehead. He might be bluffing, but she couldn't risk all of those lives.

"Take the magazine out of the gun," Andy said as she shut the door.

He turned on a small camping light, the black clothes and skull cap making him look like a specter. He sat on the long wooden box behind the seats, with padlocks on each end. "Don't worry, no one's in here." He patted the spot next to him. She sat down, and he snatched the gun out of her hand. "Now the coat and Kevlar so I can see what you've got hidden."

"I don't have anything but extra ammo." Nikki shed the vest and her coat. She put her hands up and turned around. "See?"

The small pistol strapped to her leg felt heavy as she sat down, praying Andy wouldn't think to check. The scent of damp earth clung to him, his shoes caked with drying mud. How long had he been waiting for her in here?

Nikki's radio crackled to life. "Agent Hunt, where's your location?"

"Rodriguez won't stop until I answer," Nikki said.

Andy nodded. "I trust you."

She pressed the button. "Just double-checking the vehicles." Nikki clicked the mic off without breaking eye contact.

"10-4, what's your ETA? Whatever the hell the barn was last year is still up, and there's no lights, so we're going in cautious, but I really don't think anyone is here."

Andy smiled.

"Probably not," Nikki answered. "But Courtney's out there, and I know she's alive. Please keep looking." She clicked the radio off.

Andy silently clapped, still holding her gun. "Good job. And she is alive, by the way."

"I know she is."

"How do you know that?"

Her confidence bottomed out for a moment; this man had been killing women across Canada and the United States for at least ten years. He stalked his victims until he knew their routine and the right moment to attack. He'd obviously been stalking her before he took Kiania and Nikki had no clue. But she was in it now, so she forged ahead. "I'm not going to act like I know how you think," she said. "But everything I've learned the past couple of weeks, I believe you have a set of rules."

"I'm a serial killer with a conscience?" He smirked.

"No," Nikki said. "There's no such thing. The rules are to keep you from getting caught."

"That they are," he said.

"Can I ask you a question?"

Andy spread his arms wide. "I'm an open book."

"Why do all of this to get my attention? You may never have been caught."

He shrugged. "I needed the challenge, Agent Hunt. Do you know what it's like growing up a genius in a family like mine?

And not just my family, but you saw where I grew up. Not the best place for someone like me."

Nikki doubted the genius moniker. His brother hadn't mentioned anything other than Andy going to college. "No, but I imagine you felt like a black sheep."

"A trapped one," he said. "My grandpa was smart enough to get out of the mining business before it was too late, and he ran one of the biggest machine shops in the county. But he was still a bumpkin and wanted all of us to be, too."

"You went to college," Nikki said.

"To help run the family business," Andy said. "In my family, you only received attention for bad shit. Papaw spent so much time dealing with E.J.'s issues and then Zelphia came along." He looked at her with ice in his blue eyes. "One of the wealthiest families in the area and we still lived like paupers. My mother blew through money after Dad died. Then she had to whore herself out and wound up with that damned kid."

Liam and the others would realize she hadn't shown up and find her. She just had to keep him talking. "What happened to her?"

"She didn't want to play with me anymore, so I broke her neck and threw her down that well."

Nikki assumed he meant sexual abuse. "Did you know Papaw kept her things?"

His nostrils flared. "I didn't until I came to visit that summer, and by then he'd already given it to the sheriff."

"Is that why you killed the man who took care of you after your mother died?"

Andy flinched as though she'd smacked him. "I didn't kill Papaw. He was supposed to be visiting my sister for a few weeks when Mariah and I used the cabin. He interrupted me and had a heart attack right there on the spot." His eyes bored into hers. "He ticked me off about a lot of things, but I wouldn't have done him like that."

"Papaw suspected you," Nikki said.

Andy snorted. "Papaw suspected E.J. because he's a dummy with a temper. He thought the sun rose and set on me."

"Why do you target postpartum women?" She had to know.

"Because it's fun," he said.

"I know part of it's because you want them to fight. That gets you off. But there's a psychological element too."

"Is there? Do share."

"Your mother failed you," Nikki said. "She got into drugs and had a baby that embarrassed your family."

"So?"

"Why did you let me go?" she demanded. "Because I was pregnant or FBI?"

"Both," he admitted. "I'm not interested in ending a life that hasn't had a chance to thrive," Andy said. "But there's not a mother in this world who didn't screw up her kid, so I figure I'm doing the kids a favor."

Her radio crackled to life again, followed by Liam's voice. "Did you find the flowers, Nik? You were supposed to look for them."

She fought to hide the relief melting through her. "I ran into them," she said. "Any sign of Courtney or Cass?"

"No," he said. "Where are you?"

Nikki's mind raced. She couldn't risk Andy pushing the trigger. "I thought I heard something in the maze."

Andy reached over and tore the mic off her shoulder. He tossed it out of Nikki's reach and then smiled, holding the trigger so she could see. "Jump in the passenger seat, but get on the floor."

Nikki obeyed, trying to get a better look at the trigger. Was it a prop? "What's your plan here, Andy? The van has a flat tire, and it's a long way to the road."

He dropped her gun on the other side of his seat, out of her reach. "Don't worry, it's up to the challenge."

Her heart dropped to her feet. If he managed to get off the property with her, she'd never make it out alive.

"You shouldn't have let me go that day, Agent Hunt," Andy said. "But you did. Once I got to safety and settled in, I started learning everything I could about you, Nicole."

"It was an impossible choice," she said. "But I'd do it again to save my daughter."

"Would you?" His voice rose. "Because I know what's happened to that little girl, Agent. Her daddy was murdered, and she was kidnapped because of you. How's she doing with all that, Mom?"

Nikki managed to contain the urge to slap his round face. "She's doing really well."

"But damaged, right? Damaged because of your choices." Andy's eyes narrowed. "I thought you might retire, and yet you continue, leaving others to raise Lacey."

"Do not say her name," Nikki said through clenched teeth.

"Why not?" he demanded. "You've ensured she's scarred for life. That's the truth."

"That's why you're here." Nikki choked back her fear. "I'm no longer worthy of not being one of your victims."

Andy grinned. "Now you're getting it." He put the key in the van's ignition.

"You didn't have to kill Melissa," Nikki said. "You could have incapacitated her."

He shrugged. "Easier to just get rid of her. Are you ready to see Doctor Hart?"

Nikki nodded. "Me for her."

"I suppose. The other one's about used up."

Cass is still alive.

He started the engine and hit the gas. They lurched forward, and Nikki smacked her head on the driver's seat. Andy barreled toward the front drive, the van sliding over the slick ground. She caught a glimpse of Liam's shocked face as they careened past the barn, the van headlights barely cutting through the fog.

Nikki stayed doubled over, pretending to be dazed from hitting her head. She leaned her forehead on the dash and used her left arm to block Andy's view. He tossed the trigger onto the dash, well out of Nikki's reach, and grabbed the steering wheel with both hands.

They were almost to the road. The county sheriffs had every route blocked and would throw the spikes. Without warning, Andy wrenched the van to the left and drove parallel to the road. Her stomach turned as they crested the hill. Nikki had no idea where the field would come out. She didn't have any more time.

She took the safety off and sat up, pointing the gun at Andy. "Stop or I'll shoot."

He reached for the trigger, and she fired a warning shot through his driver's side window. Andy turned red and reached for her, wrenching the wheel to the right towards the deep ditch. Two sheriff's deputies tore through the field towards them. Andy hit the brakes and the van slid, the tires unable to find grip on the sleet-covered ground. Nikki braced between the seat and dash, keeping her gun on him.

"You will die tonight, bitch." Andy jerked the wheel hard. The van's left tires started to lift, and Nikki barely managed to wrap her arm around the headrest. The trigger slid toward her. Nikki shot forward and grabbed the wheel with her free hand, yanking as hard as she could. The van rolled down an embankment, throwing Andy towards her. His stubby hands reached for the trigger, a maniacal gleam in his eye.

"Now everyone dies," he screamed.

She held onto the seat with her left hand, gun on Andy, until the van finally came to rest on its roof. Andy scrambled for the trigger.

"Don't," Nikki warned. "I will shoot."

"But you might kill me, Agent. And you don't know where Doctor Hart is. She'll starve to death."

Nikki smiled. "I know where she is."

Andy lurched for the bomb's remote. Nikki closed her eyes and pulled the trigger.

FORTY-TWO

Courtney needed water. She didn't know how long she'd been here, but it had been long enough to feel dehydrated.

"Cass, you okay?" Courtney asked the darkness. Cass had woken up at some point after Courtney arrived.

"No." Cass sounded weaker than she had just a little while ago. "I'm not sure how much longer I can make it."

"Just hang on a little longer," Courtney said. "Then you can see Emma and the boys. I know they're taking good care of her." She told her about Nikki's visit with the kids in the diner.

"I wonder how much she's grown since I saw her," Cass whispered.

"You're going to find out soon, I promise."

Cass coughed for several seconds, moaning in pain. "My ribs are broken."

"It's going to be okay."

"Stop saying that," Cass hissed. "This son of a bitch told me he's done this for more than ten years. They're not going to find us. I'm going to die and you're next. You better just start accepting it."

The hell she would.

A noise broke through the darkness, the sound of metal on metal and something moving. Cass started sobbing. For the first time, Courtney considered she might not make it. She wouldn't fight like the others had. She'd go limp and let him kill her. She wouldn't give him the satisfaction.

She realized they were in something metal as boots stepped into the structure. Light suddenly came through the darkness, the glow preventing her from seeing the person carrying it. She tried to take in as much as possible before he came for her. A long piece of wood seemed to separate her prison from Cass's. What the hell were they inside?

She shifted against the back of the crate as the person rushed toward her.

"Courtney!"

Nikki knelt in front of the crate, bolt cutters in hand. "Are you okay?"

Courtney nodded. "Cass is here, too. She's in bad shape. You're bleeding."

Blood trickled down the side of Nikki's face.

"Why the hell aren't you wearing your vest and coat?" She saw the blood on Nikki's fingers. "Is he still alive?"

Nikki finally snapped the padlock. "He'll probably lose his hand." She cut the barbed wire he'd wrapped across the crate's door, and Courtney scrambled out of the crate. Nikki threw her arms around her and hugged her tight.

"Everyone's okay?" Courtney asked.

"I think so," Nikki said. "Emergency responders are on the way." She broke the hug and wiped tears from her eyes. "Cass, my name is Agent Hunt with the FBI. Can you hear me?"

"Please get me out of here."

The plywood partition split the pod down the middle, so Nikki had to shimmy around the edge to get to her. Andy had put the storage unit in the low, wide part of the ditch they'd crossed earlier and covered it with the debris from the trees and fields he'd cleared to access the ditch. Lousy weather mired most of their aerial footage, so they hadn't seen the bulldozed path Andy had cleared. He'd spent a lot of time making the pod secure, including propping it up on five feet worth of cinder blocks. Shattered glass surrounded the container like a moat.

"Stay there." Nikki looked at Courtney's feet, shocked to see she still had her shoes on. Maybe Andy really hadn't meant for Courtney to be a victim. "It's about five feet down, and you have to use the blocks to climb up. We need to wait for Liam."

Courtney ignored Nikki and slipped around the edge of the container. They both hurried toward Cass. She sobbed quietly, thanking God for saving her.

Nikki handed Courtney the flashlight. "Keep the beam low so it doesn't hurt her eyes." Cass probably hadn't seen light in weeks. Nikki cut through the padlock and opened the door. Cass stared at her like a wild animal.

"Where is he?" Even her whisper sounded weak.

"He's with our SWAT team," she said. "A couple have medical training."

"What happened?" Cass asked. "Is he dead? He told me all their names, but I don't remember every one. If he's dead—"

"He's alive," Nikki soothed her. "I just put a hole in his hand." She held her own out to Cass. "Do you need help getting out of the crate? My partner and boss are bringing the paramedics back here as soon as they arrive," Nikki said.

"I don't think I can stand," she whispered. "I'm so weak."

"That's okay," Nikki said. "They'll take care of you."

Liam shouted from somewhere in the fog. "Courtney? Are you okay?" His flashlight finally broke through the fog.

"Hey, Big Red! Come get me down from this thing."

EPILOGUE
THREE DAYS LATER

"And together through the gateway that led back into the real world." Nikki closed the book. "The end."

"Finally." Lacey threw herself back on her pillow. "It's really hard to wait for you to read sometimes, Mom."

Nikki ruffled her hair. "I know," she said. "If you want Rory to read it that's okay."

"No." Lacey shook her head against the pillows, tangling her curls. "Reading is a you and me thing."

"Sounds good to me." Nikki leaned over and wrapped her arms around Lacey.

This was why she never regretted her decision in the woods that day.

"You're choking me," Lacey gasped dramatically.

"Sorry." She checked her watch. It was almost time. "You've got school in the morning, so no sneaking around and playing."

Lacey grinned. "I won't."

Nikki left the door open a couple of inches and limped down the hall to her and Rory's bedroom. She had tweaked her knee climbing out of the wrecked van and three days of rest had only made it bearable. Rory lounged on the bed, eating popcorn and watching hockey. "Wish me luck."

Rory grinned and then blew her a kiss. "You don't need it. It's going to be fine."

"I'm going to shut the door so the hockey game doesn't get too loud," she told him. "And by that, I mean you."

"Why can't the Wilds be good one year?" he asked. "One year. That's all I ask."

"Pretty sure they've had winning seasons," Nikki said.

"By good I mean going deep into the playoffs." His smile faded. "How's Courtney today?"

"*Fine.*" Nikki made sure to mimic Courtney's tone. They'd forced her to spend the night in the hospital and be treated for dehydration. Courtney had insisted on speaking with Melissa's family, despite Garcia's insistence that the Bureau would take issue with her speaking to the victim's family before Courtney could give her own statement.

Courtney suggested the Bureau kiss her ass and ended the video chat they'd been attending to debrief the case. Arim had offered to step in for Courtney so she could rest, but she refused. "She's still running on adrenaline, I think." Courtney didn't have any physical injuries, and she'd insisted that she didn't have any emotional injuries. "Her mom arrives today." Courtney's parents had been on vacation out of state when Nikki had called to let them know their daughter had been taken and subsequently rescued. "I have a feeling that's when the dam will break."

"She can't hold it in forever," Rory agreed. "How long are they making her take off work?"

"A minimum six weeks of counseling at a therapist of her choice," Nikki answered. "If the psychologist agrees she's ready to go back to work, the FBI will send their own therapist to assess her. They make the final decision."

"Complicated."

"It's the federal government. What else would you expect?" Nikki's smile faded. "I'm worried about her."

"She'll be okay," Rory said. "She's got a great support system and plenty of resources. She just needs to process and rest."

"That's the problem. Courtney's never been good at that."

"I know," Rory agreed. "But her job—her career and reputation—have never depended on it. She knows that she has to be in the right head space in order to get back to work."

Nikki wanted to explain that Courtney would have no problem fooling everyone in order to work, something she'd done in graduate school, but she had one more call to make.

She kissed the top of Rory's head and went across the hall to her office, still worrying about Courtney. In college, her body had nearly broken down from the stress of school and taking on every possible internship or project her advisors offered to pad her résumé. Forensic sciences were ruthless across the board. Mediocrity rarely flourished, despite the need to fulfill workplace demand. Only the best got the best jobs, and Courtney had been so determined to be the best it had nearly killed her. She'd promised Nikki at the hospital this would be different, but Nikki would believe it when it happened.

Nikki planned to give Courtney time with her family for a few days before pushing her about anything. Time with her mother would probably do wonders for Courtney. And Rory was right—Courtney did have a strong support system. They just had to make her utilize them.

Nikki woke up her laptop and opened Skype. Nikki fluffed her wavy, dark hair and smoothed her shirt. She'd even put on mascara and lip gloss, even though she didn't need to impress Anita or her granddaughter.

The call flashed onto her screen. Nikki took a deep breath and accepted the video call. Anita Gonzales waved at Nikki.

"How was the ballet?" Nikki asked.

Anita had decided Nikki should meet Mira, and tonight

after the Washington Ballet seemed as good a time as any. Mira wanted to know more about the man who'd taken her mother's life, and after talking with Nikki as well as her granddaughter's therapist, Anita had agreed it was time.

"Incredible." Anita looked radiant in a simple black dress and pearls. "I cried it was so moving."

"I always meant to go," Nikki said.

"You must make time one day." Anita leaned over to look past the camera. "Before I call Mira in, have you spoken to any of the man's family?"

Nikki nodded. "I spoke with Nathaniel for a long time yesterday. He feels like he should have done something. According to Nathaniel, everyone else in the family treated Andy like he was the Second Coming. Andy never threw fits to get his way, he just got it. Andy was quiet and well-mannered and never got in trouble. Their middle brother, E.J., had a bad stutter and temper issues, and Andy knew how to quietly wind him up and get his brother in trouble, but not himself. Nathaniel was the only person who saw how manipulative and sneaky Andy was, but their grandfather wouldn't hear it. He believed E.J. was the problem because Andy provoked him. Nathaniel said he was born with a chip, and it got worse when Zelphia came along, because she embarrassed the family."

Nathaniel had fought with his grandfather over his suspicions about Andy, and their disagreement eventually made him move to North Carolina. He was supposed to run the family business, but he didn't want to, so the daughter and E.J. ran it. "Turns out, E.J. just needed someone to give a damn. He's autistic with ADHD, and now he's on meds and in therapy thanks to his wife."

Nikki had fumed when Nathaniel initially admitted lying about E.J.'s whereabouts, but he felt like he had to protect him. People wanted to accuse him of killing his grandfather and Zelphia because he was different, and if he hadn't been working on a job site under the scrutiny of a demanding manager, E.J. probably would have gone down for Papaw's murder.

"Did you tell them about Mira?" Anita asked.

Nathaniel had been silent for so long Nikki wondered if they'd disconnected. Then she'd realized he'd started weeping— from joy, he'd assured her. He understood Nikki couldn't give him very many details about his niece. He just wanted to do what he could to make the child's life better, and the rest would be up to her.

"I told him there was a child but gave no details," Nikki answered. "But they would like to speak with you—or at least your attorney. Andy's already given Nathaniel power of attorney over his estate." Andy had been the executor of their grandfather's estate and sold the business after his death. All four siblings wound up wealthy, because Andy had been smart enough not to screw his siblings and get on someone's radar. Andy invested some of his money in a pods franchise under Z.W. Holdings, LLC. The LLC should have been vacated after Zeb Wahlert's death, but Andy had kept it in secret as part of his efforts to hide his whereabouts. He told everyone he worked for an oil company when he lived in Canada, but they didn't know if it was true. He knew how to live off the land and had enough money he likely never had to work again. That's why he'd been able to travel and do what he wanted the last few years.

"I don't understand," Anita said.

"Nathaniel and E.J. want Mariah's daughter to have his inheritance," Nikki said.

Anita shook her head, her eyes welling with tears. "Blood money. My baby's blood money!"

"But is that how Mariah would see it?" Nikki asked. "What would the Mariah you knew say in this moment?"

"She'd want her daughter to have it." Anita reached for a tissue. "I don't know if I can do it, Agent Hunt."

"I can't imagine the decision." As an FBI data analyst lead, Anita likely made over six figures, but that didn't go nearly as far as it sounded in D.C., especially with a child to raise. "It's seven figures, Anita. Double digits. She would be set to do whatever she wanted in life."

"Who are you talking to, Gran?"

Anita looked at Nikki.

"You decide what she hears," Nikki assured her. "I'll tell her as much as she wants to know."

Anita made the sign of the cross. "Mira, come sit with me. There's someone I want you to meet."

A LETTER FROM STACY

I want to say a huge thank you for choosing to read *Stolen Mothers*. If you did enjoy it, and want to keep up to date with all my latest releases, just sign up at the following link. Your email address will never be shared and you can unsubscribe at any time.

www.bookouture.com/stacy-green

I hope you loved *Stolen Mothers* and if you did I would be very grateful if you could write a review. I'd love to hear what you think, and it makes such a difference helping new readers to discover one of my books for the first time.

I love hearing from my readers—you can get in touch on social media or my website.

Thanks,

Stacy

www.stacygreenauthor.com

f facebook.com/StacyGreenAuthor

X x.com/StacyGreen26

instagram.com/authorstacygreen

ACKNOWLEDGMENTS

While the information in this book is fictional, I want to acknowledge the groundbreaking work on serial killers since the 1970s. FBI Agents Ressler, Douglas, Hazelwood and many others opened the door to understanding serial killers. Detective Bob Keppel with the King County Sheriff's Office chased Ted Bundy as a young detective and later conducted the now famous interviews with Bundy. Both the FBI and sheriff worked to finally stop Gary Ridgway, the Green River Killer. The dedication of these men and countless other men and women has not only helped to curb serial murders, but opened the door to psychological advances, all while sacrificing their own peace of mind and at times, physical health. They are the reason people like me can write about serial killers with some degree of accuracy. Thank you to John Douglas for his guidance, as well as Stillwater Police Chief Brian Mueller. Thanks to Commander Andrew Ellickson of the Washington County Sheriff Office's special services division for his help with the county emergency response system.

Special thanks to John Kelly for helping me find the right locations. Thanks to Kristine and Jan for their support and encouragement.

Tessa Russ and her team are awesome and make my life much easier. To my editors at Bookouture, thank you for believing in me and for your patience.

Finally, to my readers, your support means more than I can

ever say. I hope you continue to enjoy the Nikki Hunt series and can't wait for you to read the next installment!

PUBLISHING TEAM

Turning a manuscript into a book requires the efforts of many people. The publishing team at Bookouture would like to acknowledge everyone who contributed to this publication.

Audio
Sinead O'Connor
Alba Proko
Melissa Tran

Commercial
Lauren Morrissette
Hannah Richmond
Imogen Allport

Cover design
Blacksheep

Data and analysis
Mark Alder
Mohamed Bussuri

Editorial
Jennifer Hunt
Sinead O'Connor

Copyeditor
Jane Eastgate

Proofreader
Becca Allen

Marketing
Alex Crow
Melanie Price
Occy Carr
Cíara Rosney
Martyna Młynarska

Operations and distribution
Marina Valles
Stephanie Straub

Production
Hannah Snetsinger
Mandy Kullar
Jen Shannon

Publicity
Kim Nash
Noelle Holten
Jess Readett
Sarah Hardy

Rights and contracts
Peta Nightingale
Richard King
Saidah Graham

Made in the USA
Monee, IL
10 July 2024

61596408R00163